The Minstrel and Her Knight

Minstrel Knights
Book 1

Cara Hogarth

ARE YOU SIGNED UP FOR DRAGONBLADE'S BLOG?

You'll get the latest news and information on exclusive giveaways, exclusive excerpts, coming releases, sales, free books, cover reveals and more.

Check out our complete list of authors, too!

No spam, no junk. That's a promise!

Sign Up Here

www.dragonbladepublishing.com

Dearest Reader;

Thank you for your support of a small press. At Dragonblade Publishing, we strive to bring you the highest quality Historical Romance from some of the best authors in the business. Without your support, there is no 'us', so we sincerely hope you adore these stories and find some new favorite authors along the way.

Happy Reading!

CEO, Dragonblade Publishing

Chapter One

Yorkshire, 1367

AZALAIS DE KELDY pressed her face against the Lady Chapel peephole. Not that it was designed as a peephole, of course, and doubtless she was crushing her carefully starched coif to ruination by employing it so, but the little pane of broken glass in the nunnery's pride and joy, the window depicting Our Lady, was her one chance to gauge her future. Or whether she had one at all.

That particular hope was sinking faster than a scuttled ship.

What in God's name was her brother thinking? He'd agreed to help her, if only after considerable negotiation. And now look what his idea of help entailed!

On her arrival at Wykeham Priory, Benedict had listened patiently to her plan. He had then dissected it in fine scholastic style, thereby proving beyond doubt that what Azalais intended was hideously dangerous. Not that she'd needed to be convinced. She knew it was idiocy, but the alternative was simply unthinkable.

She shuddered—and immediately suppressed it. Any movement against the glass might be noticed. The Lady Chapel was cold, and the glass against her face colder, but the future crept on her like a midwinter frost.

She had declared to her brother that she had a duty to free her father—as did he to support her in the attempt. Benedict was a monk—he couldn't go. And their elder brother … well, that was the very root of the problem. He *wouldn't* go. So, it was her and her harebrained plan, or abandon their father forever. Even so, it took hours, no days, of heated discussions before Benedict had been persuaded. But he had put his priestly sandal down on one point—she must not travel alone.

Azalais had pointed out the obvious problem—who could possibly be trusted? Whoever Benedict enlisted would have to be told her purpose and thus know she carried, if not a king's ransom, then at least a minor lord's. A companion would only increase her danger.

But Benedict said he had a solution, and two days later, here the solution was.

It was no solution at all. The man outside was quite horribly attractive.

Azalais's brow wrinkled against the glass. She drew a deep breath and tried to be reasonable. She would break the problem down to its elements, just as Benedict taught her. The problem was this: when Azalais de Keldy looked at the man in the graveyard below, she was washed with equal parts panic and fascination. Why? The fellow was no paragon of knighthood in any mold she knew.

The first element of this knightly problem: straightish dark hair just long enough to tickle his shoulders. Not so unusual in itself—many men had dark hair. No, it was the way the stuff continually flopped over one eye and must be brushed back with a careless hand that was the issue. Each time the man ruffled it back, it settled into a new and artlessly charming disarray. It didn't *look* like he was doing it on purpose, but something within Azalais told her he knew full well what he did. And its effect.

Element-the-second: beneath that wayward hair smiled two distinctly dangerous eyes. *Smiled?* Her brother had explained how serious the situation was. She had heard him just a moment ago.

The fellow had no business smiling about it. But what *was* it about those eyes? They were dark to match his dark hair, dark-lashed and of perfectly normal dimensions, in no way unusual—until one took in their expression. Azalais shifted minutely against the glass to better examine her subject. Yes, it was their expression that was the problem; the fellow sported a pair of sleepy-lidded eyes arched over by wicked, curved brows, and the whole seemed to brim with lurking mischief. It turned her very innards to aspic.

And the rest? The remaining offenders were chiefly a defined jaw that might have been clean-shaven two days ago but was now rakishly unkempt in contrast with his evidently expensive clothes. One doublet, well-tailored to fit a trim torso, and a pair of hose adhering to rather nicely shaped legs.

And then there were his hands.

Dear God, why must his hands be so beautiful? Of course, Azalais had examined his hands with more than usual attention. But even if she hadn't, she could hardly have missed them. He wore no gloves—the spring weather was warm enough now—and when he spoke, his hands did, too. They were elegant yet evidently strong, and they practically sang, he used them so expressively.

They were musician's hands. Of course, she would his hands a source of endless allure. But why must they be accompanied by all these other, entirely unnecessary attractions?

Azalais shook her head slightly, polishing the glass in the process. Then, face to the broken pane, she tried once again. What *was* it about this fellow in the graveyard that was so wrong? Her brother trusted him. Why shouldn't she?

She tried to think logically, without prior experience coloring her judgment. The fellow was quite different in air and appearance from her elder brother's men-at-arms and assorted cronies. So far, so good. With them, what one saw was what one got, and none of it particularly good. Here, the danger lay in a different department.

The man's every action seemed studied, calculated. This specimen of offensive manhood knew his power. He moved in his own little aura of self-conscious attraction. And all this was glaringly evident *when he was only talking to her brother,* her monkish, unassuming brother who had known this knight since they were boys in cathedral school together. Oh, it was too much. She would not trust this fop with the beautiful hands to escort her across a cloister, let alone through half of France.

Azalais de Keldy turned her face away. She could not pain her eyes with the disintegration of her plan any longer.

So, she put her ear to the peephole instead.

"When you visited me two weeks ago, you spoke of reaching a crossroads in your life, Will."

That was Benedict speaking. Her brother, her *real* brother, and her only ally in this current crisis.

"Indeed. And you declined to guide my way then." It was a voice like melting honey that replied, deep and smooth, but doubtless concealing a nasty sting. "One man cannot tell another how to live, you declared. I must find my own path. Well, have you consulted your astrolabe since, Sir Monk?"

"You might say an astrolabe consulted me, Will. It sought me out. And it has suggested a direction of sorts for you—a temporary direction that may help clear your view."

"Ah. You plan a little activity for me, I see. A *temporary* activity. What on God's good earth might a monk want from this sorry piece of humanity, I wonder?"

Azalais heard the laughter beneath the velvety tones. Oh, he had a voice, this vain one. It sang to her. It matched the music of his hands.

"Yes, Will, I offer you a task," answered her brother. "You will be paid, of course. You bemoaned your lack of funds at our last meeting—"

"Oh, *money*! The infernal tyranny of coin! I want little, my friend, yet I want so much. Without money, I am not my own master—my father steers my future by threatening my very patrimony, what little that amounts to—and yet the direction my heart tugs me in requires so little money. Ah! What is a poor nobleman to do?"

Azalais tried to sift through the mixture of sincerity, mockery, and affectation in that speech to some kernel of truth. It was hopeless. And in her attempt at dissection, she had missed whatever her brother replied in return.

"Let us cut to the chase, Sir Monk," continued the velvety voice. "You say this little task—this well-funded task of yours—is both dangerous and of high importance. Whatever makes you think that I—who has shirked his duty to ravage the French with such determination that his father turns to blackmail—could possibly perform it? Or would have the faintest desire to perform it, for that matter?"

"Because, Sir William," answered her brother, "I ask you to discard your knighthood for a season and become a wandering minstrel."

Azalais expected the knight to laugh. Such a response seemed in keeping with his flippancy, his infernal airs. But when no such reply reached her ears—not a word or the hint of a chuckle—she could not help but turn to look at him again.

The fellow had seated himself on one of the low, green mounds that hummocked the graveyard. Graves. He had evidently been taking his ease upon the deceased, gesturing in that eloquent way of his. But now he sat as still as the weathered wooden cross at his couch's head. He was looking up at her brother, and there was no smile in his eyes.

Was he offended? Had her brother pushed his acquaintance with this un-knightly knight too far? Azalais found she was holding her breath. Why? What did she care if this strange apparition dismissed her brother's suggestion out of hand? She had dismissed him already. He was too...too...well, altogether *too much.* She wouldn't trust him an instant. She couldn't divine anything he thought, beyond that he thought quite highly of himself. And yet still she had trouble convincing herself to breathe. Too much rested on his reply.

"I think you had better expand on this notion of yours, Ben." The knight spoke with no discernible expression upon his face, save perhaps for watchfulness.

Her brother expanded: "I ask you to don the guise of a minstrel and accompany a young man of my acquaintance—also posing as a wandering player—upon a task that young man must undertake."

The knight's watchful expression transformed into a frown. The drooping dark hair was flipped back from his forehead. Azalais forced herself to breathe.

"Can he play?"

"I have heard him play, Will. And sing, too. It is my opinion he does both well."

A soft snort. The smile was back in the dark eyes. They crinkled at the corners as they looked at her brother.

"And since when has your opinion in matters of music been worth a hen's tooth? I recall the vicars choral banned you from choir. Your growling had them convinced a dog was loose in the church." He grinned. "And not a tuneful dog at that."

Benedict stuck out a monkish sandal and kicked his lounging companion. Azalais blinked. Her brother? It wasn't a hard kick, admittedly, but still...

"Which is to say," the knight went on. "I would hear this youth's performance first."

"But you haven't asked why or where or what else is required," her brother protested. "I warned you this is no straightforward task. It involves considerable danger. It would send you back to France, and the French have no love for Englishmen these days."

"And who can blame them? Christ knows, I have no love of Englishmen when I recall certain experiences ..." Then his voice lightened. "Oh, we're an unmannerly lot, Ben. We burn their barns and trample their corn, never mind skewering their sons. And their daughters...oh, never let an Englishman near a French damsel, Sir Monk. I will spare your celibacy the details. Suffice to say, I would not let *my* sister loose in France these days. A Frenchman might conceive the score requires a little evening."

Azalais's nails dug into her palms—at least, the nails on her right hand did. Those of her left hand were too short to inflict damage. Her right-hand nails, however, were long and carefully shaped. They threatened to draw blood. She stared at her brother, willing him to hold to their agreement, tentative as it was.

Benedict was looking decidedly thoughtful. His mouth opened, then closed again.

"Well, what do you dally for, Sir Monk? Produce me this youth, your minstrel-in-the-pip. But have a care you tune him up first." The knight on the gravemound craned about him in exaggerated fashion, peering first under a yew tree, then at a quietly cropping sheep. "He does not appear to be hovering in the vicinity. I trust you have him stowed nearby?"

⇛⇚

"FOR GOD'S SAKE, find someone else, Benedict!" she hissed. "Or find me nobody at all. I can't go with that …that … He is far too… No, it is out of the question. He is utterly unsuitable."

All spoken in the barest whisper, just in case a nun happened by to trim the candles or murmur an *Ave*.

Benedict knelt beside her in the Lady Chapel. The casual observer would assume they were praying, a novice taking spiritual guidance from the nunnery's prior.

Not arguing.

"There is no other, Azalais. Not at such short notice. And you cannot go on your own. I will not let you. I would sooner tell Robert. Didn't you hear what Will said about French damsels? No, it must be him."

"I don't trust him!"

"But I do. Trust *me*, Azalais. I have known him for years. We were students together at York. Remember?"

"But that was years ago! You were children. He has probably changed since then. *You* have taken holy orders, and he is some kind of knight. Or so he said. Besides, was he such a ... a poseur back then?"

Benedict surprised her by uttering a soft laugh. "Poseur. Yes, I suppose he is. Rest assured it *is* a pose, Azalais. I do not trust him with the care of my only sister lightly."

"And that of your father," she hissed.

"Yes, and my father." Benedict gazed at her, his brown eyes soft with concern. "But it is you I worry about. Father got himself into this mess, and it is Robert's duty to extricate him. *You* should not have to, and especially not in this manner."

She grabbed his hand. "I must! You agreed! You cannot back out now."

He gently freed himself from her grasp. She had forgotten— no woman can touch a monk. Not even his sister.

"Then give him a chance, Azalais. I believe he can and will aid you in this. It may even be God's will, for my friend, too, is in need of ..."

"Of what? Money?"

"No," murmured Benedict. "Well, yes—always, but money is not truly the problem. It is something more intangible, unfortunately. But it is not my place to tell you what he seeks. Doubtless, he will tell you himself in time—if he sees fit."

Benedict genuflected to the altar and rose.

"Come, Azalais. Ready yourself. Give God's will a chance."

SIR WILLIAM CONTINUED to take his ease upon the gravemound in his friend's absence. It was, he reflected, a fresh height in dissipation even for him—loitering in the nuns' graveyard upon a sunny spring day and contemplating tossing knighthood away for a life on the road. Ah, how his father would grind his few remaining teeth.

Benedict seemed gone for an inordinate length of time. Will twitched a primrose from its bed on the sheep-cropped turf and twirled it idly. Was his friend entertaining second thoughts—or perhaps his protegee was? Will began to pluck the primrose. It occurred to him, whatever this youth's musical ability, Will was strongly inclined to accept the task. He shredded the primrose, dropped it, and looked about for another one. Perhaps he should inquire into the non-musical aspects of this monkly mission.

Movement around the corner of the church. For a moment, Will wondered whether a bevy of outraged nuns was coming to evict him, but no—it was only their monk returning, and with a shadow in tow. Slowly, Will lifted his gaze from primroses to observe his future.

A young man trailed Benedict between the gravemounds. He possessed medium height, a slight build, and a loosely fitting tunic and hose in nondescript shades of brown. A hood shadowed his downturned face, but Will could make out no sign of facial hair upon the youth's tight jaw. Will observed the mouth, too, was rather set. Quite a shapely mouth for a man if it relaxed a little. He had hopes of its singing ability yet.

So, the fellow was nervous, was he? That did not bode well for his impending performance. For amid all the nondescript details of the approaching youth, one aspect did stand out—he held an instrument and quite a fine one at that. Will's gaze narrowed upon the polished wood cradled under the fellow's arm. A lute, its body like a plum cut in half, rounded at the back, flat in the front. Quite a large and valuable instrument for one slight youth to own. Will was intrigued—and a little jealous.

"So. You reappear, Sir Monk. I thought the good sisters had hauled you away to confessional and even now you were hearing of innumerable sins of cloistered lust."

Benedict sighed, but Will's attention was drawn by the young man's reaction. He seemed to hesitate and draw back. Will cocked a brow. Bashful, eh? Well, a minstrel must deal daily with innuendo. Play the game, lad, or give it up.

The monk drew his shadow forward. "Sir William de Fauconberg, I give you Alain de Keldy."

The pair stood before him now. Will tilted his head to offer the newcomer a half-smile. He supposed he ought to rise, but he had no wish to concede that advantage.

"Keldy? The same Keldy Castle from which you hail, Brother Benedict?"

"Yes, the same Castle Keldy," the youth answered with a touch of defiance. "I am a by-blow, Sir William. Born outside of marriage. Benedict and I share the same father."

Will's mouth quirked. He considered the speaker. An unusual voice for a lad. This Alain's voice had not broken, it seemed, but nor did it not possess the piping pitch of a boy. There was a pleasant mellowness to it, a hint of delightful husk. Ah, but it was too soon to judge.

"You are direct, Alain de Keldy," Will returned. "Ben never mentioned any paternal indiscretions before. How many half-siblings have you got strewn about Yorkshire, my monk? Perhaps I can discern a likeness between you…"

The youth seemed to shrink back into his hood under Will's gaze. "I mention my birth only that you understand why I must undertake this journey, Sir William."

"Indeed. So now we come to whys." Will turned to Benedict. "Your father is held prisoner in France and has been for years, I have heard. I suspect that I am enlisted in a plot to free him, a strangely secretive plot that involves a younger son and his bastard and even younger brother. How so? Surely it is the eldest legitimate son's duty to ransom his father?"

The youth rounded on his brother. "Benedict!" One hand flew up. The other remained tucked about his lute. Will observed the hand's unroughened delicacy with some interest. "I told you …"

Will cocked an eyebrow at the monk. "Yes?"

His friend positively dithered. He reached a hand out to his bastard brother, then let it drop. His lips opened. Closed. Then he sighed and turned to Will.

"Yes, William, you are correct. It is the eldest son's duty to ransom his father. But my brother Robert is…well, he…"

"Oh, just say it, Benedict," the youth interrupted. "Our brother is happy to let his father rot in France for the rest of his life. Heaven forbid he be required to dig into his precious inheritance in order to free the man who gave it to him. And gave him life."

Then the fellow narrowed his eyes upon Will and continued.

"Yes, I am tarred by an ignoble birth, Sir Knight, but *I* will not let my father molder in a French dungeon, and nor will his *true* son." At which the youth flung a hand toward Benedict, very nearly whacking the monk in the process.

The lad's hood slipped back from his brow. That delicate hand flew up to twitch it back into place, and Alain seemed to recall himself. He looked about him, noted an upended block of masonry some paces away, and moved to settle himself upon it, lute on lap.

Then he advised his brother to do likewise. "Sit down, Benedict," Alain said more restrainedly. "You wish me to talk to this knight. Let us do so in comfort."

Will's lip twitched as he watched Ben eye gravemounds and sheep turds. Eventually, he settled upon a cleanish patch of grass.

"You chose a strange location for this assignation, friend monk," Will murmured. "I understand you could not meet me in the cloister itself, but surely the nunnery provides you rooms in which you may entertain male visitors?"

"A nunnery is strictly sealed off from the world of men, Sir William," the monk began. Then paused.

"Yes. Including you, no doubt? And yet you are a man, or you were when we were students together." Will grinned. "In fact, I recall it distinctly. What boys do not compare weapons? And do you remember when—"

"I share quarters with other men," Benedict interrupted. "We may have been overheard. And, as you say, there is a need for secrecy in this discussion."

Yet Will noted the odd look the monk threw toward the youth. Alain was not welcome in the men's quarters, perhaps?

"Pray elaborate upon this need for secrecy, friend monk," Will prompted. "I take it your brother Robert is not only unwilling to part with the necessary himself, but that he would oppose your efforts to free your father, too. How very strange."

Benedict gave a sharp nod but offered no explanation.

Will looked from one brother to the other. "Well, I have met Robert but once, Sir Monk, and I conceived no great liking for him then. A swaggering sword swinger barely able to read, as I recall. I have no qualms about keeping secrets from him. But what I *do* have qualms about—" Will straightened upon his grassy bed and looked direct at Alain, the bastard of Keldy, "—is traveling in the guise of a minstrel with one who cannot play the role."

The chin beneath the hood lifted. "You doubt my skill?"

"Of course."

A sharp intake of breath and a narrowing of overshadowed eyes.

"What, do you wish to be serenaded in a graveyard, Sir Knight?"

Will gave Alain a slow smile. "Oh no, I insist. I am sure the good nuns—" he waved a hand at the landscape of mounds, "—will not object, so long as your subject is not too bawdy. And who knows? Maybe they'd enjoy that, too."

Will watched as the youth stretched his legs before him and settled the lute upon his lap. The hood bent to the soundbox as Alain plucked each string softly, checking its pitch.

Plucked?

"You do not use a plectrum, boy?" Will said sharply.

Alain paused and looked up at him. Then he raised his right hand.

"Why limit myself to one plectrum when I can use four?" He wiggled fingers and thumb. Each was tipped with a smooth nail.

A good point. Nevertheless. "It is unorthodox."

"What matters is the quality of the tone, not its orthodoxy, surely, Sir William? Perhaps you should listen before you judge."

And without waiting for a reply, Alain bent to his instrument and began plucking the strings in earnest.

Notes rippled out like water in a brook. Will blinked, then sat forward. Such a strange technique. He frowned at the instrument, at the pale fingers flickering over the sound hole. Alain was using his thumb as most lutenists used a plectrum—to strum the four courses of strings—but his fingers interspersed the chords with a bird's twitter of single notes, a melody to interweave the harmony. It was as if the instrument sang to its own accompaniment.

Then Will ceased to scrutinize. He leaned back on the mound and closed his eyes, letting the notes dominate his senses. He felt his muscles relaxing—he had been unaware they were tensed— his lips softening as if they wished to shape words about the lute's warm tone. Ah, the bastard could play. He played oddly, it was true, but the very oddity was like a new spice upon his tongue. Why, Will could practically taste it. The tune was familiar, but its manner of playing was decidedly not.

"Do I send you to sleep, Sir Knight?"

The music stopped.

Will opened his eyes. He offered Alain a half-smile. "But you do not sing."

"I do."

"Pray demonstrate then."

The hood angled down. "My…my throat is scratchy. I have caught a chill." Alain followed the pronouncement with a sniff.

Will permitted his smile to grow. "Indeed?"

"But he plays well, does he not?" Benedict inserted hurriedly.

"Yes, my tone-deaf monk. Your bastard brother plays passing-ly well."

A sharp intake of breath above the lute.

"Well?" the purportedly scratchy voice demanded.

Will chose to take the query in the direction that suited him best.

"Well, I suppose I may be prevailed upon to endure your company in a little minstrel jaunt through France, O minstrel boy. Where did you say your father was incarcerated, Ben?"

The monk's face lit up.

"The Chateau de Bruniquel, on the Aveyron in central France. You will take a ship to Bordeaux, then travel east to—"

But Alain sprang to his feet, his lute discarded on the grass.

"No!"

Chapter Two

"No?" Azalais could feel the knight's eyes on her, but she kept her face angled toward her brother.

"No," she repeated. "You two have decided my fate between you. Just because I am a by-blow, an illegitimate accident. But this is *my* mission, my plan. And mine is the greatest risk." She swung upon Sir William. "This is just a minstrel jaunt for you, a pleasant little diversion from your knightly life."

"It is too dangerous to go alone, Alain," her brother broke in. "You have never been to France or traveled through a foreign land alone. You need protection. After all, you are just a—"

"A youth?" she interrupted, holding her brother's gaze. "A youth who speaks French as well as any native and who will slip unnoticed through France, playing at village and inn for his food. What protection does such a youth need?"

"France is a land at war," Benedict replied. "And soldiers are a savage breed."

As she had reason to know. Benedict did not need to say it. The knowledge hovered between them.

"And most of those soldiers have now crossed the Pyrenees to exercise that savagery upon the Spanish," Azalais retorted. "Which is precisely why I thought this mission was possible in the first place."

"But the dregs will remain, not to mention an impoverished and hard-used peasantry. You carry a valuable instrument, Alain," the knight murmured. "Should that be stolen or damaged, what then? Your guise as minstrel is gone. And then there is the matter of the ransom."

"What? Who would ransom me?"

"I refer to your father's ransom, good youth," the knight returned, and Azalais could have slapped herself. Of course, *Alain* had no value.

"I assume you will carry the money with you," the velvety voice continued. "Given your brother Robert's unwillingness to pay, I doubt whoever holds your father will consent to release him on the strength of a mere promise."

Azalais looked at her feet. Indeed, it was a little startling to see them so clearly, encased in plain leather at the base of a drab pair of hose. She would not confirm or deny his too-shrewd assertions.

"No matter. You, Sir Knight, have declared I play *passingly well*—"

"Ah, have I stung your self-regard, my whelp?" her audience murmured.

"—but you have yet to convince *me*. Can you play your part, Sir Minstrel? Can you pass as a jongleur in the land in which music was born?"

The dark eyes smiled up at her. Was he laughing at her? Or had he seen straight through her?

He spread his palms, cupping empty air. "I regret I left my instrument at home. Nor do I customarily play the lute."

"Sing, then!"

The lounging fellow glanced at Benedict. Her brother inclined his head. And the knight shrugged—and stood.

Azalais immediately wished he had not. Sprawled upon a gravemound, he had exerted little presence. Now he stood before her, filling his lungs with air, humming a little under his breath, and the spring world about him shrank to nothingness. Even before he sang a word, she knew it—this man was a performer. He knew how to command his audience. It seemed even the birds fell silent. Azalais was no better than a spellbound sparrow.

Then he began to sing:

I love to see the lark hurl himself
Into the air, against the falling sunbeams,
And until he alights
On leaves trembling in the wind.

She knew the song, and William sang it as it should be sung—in the language of southern France, the *langue d'oc*. It was centuries old, a troubadour's tune from the Golden Age of minstrels. All this she registered on some distant, logical level. But his voice, seized hold of her senses. It wrapped a fist about her very heart and sent a shivering tingle through every fingertip—a voice as velvety as his speaking tone, only richer and fuller. It slid over the notes effortlessly, sounding the words with soft precision and weighing them with meaning only for her.

He looked at her as he sang. Those dark eyes flickered with secrets and his mouth … ah, his mouth was too fascinating to linger upon. It shaped the words of love and longing so intimately. So, she fastened her gaze upon his hands instead, hands that moved in mute echo of his song.

Christ in Heaven, it was a relief when he finished. And yet…not. Her fingers flexed. Could she accompany him, enter that intimate musical dance? She had never played to any voice but her own, let alone with such a performer.

And he was still watching her.

So, she turned to her brother. Benedict did not open his mouth, but his eyes spoke entire manuscripts. The message writ clear. If she didn't accept this knight-minstrel's dubious protection, her younger brother would inform their elder brother, and she would be hauled out of the nunnery and into the too-loving arms of the man Robert had selected as his future brother-in-law.

And her father could die in France for all Robert cared. Benedict did not wish to betray her, but he was far too concerned for her safety.

Perhaps Benedict had a point. Just a small one. France was a war-torn land, impoverished and hardened by decades of invasion. Such conditions bred desperate men and women, and it was England who had rendered it so. She could wield a lute, but she wasn't so confident with a blade. A knight had his uses.

So, Alain of Keldy looked at Sir William. The bastard minstrel-boy summoned up a smile. It wasn't a very convincing one.

"It seems you can sing, sir. And my brother here will not rest on his priory pallet at night if I attempt this by myself." She drew a deep breath. Her stomach seemed filled with small fluttering birds. She looked into a pair of brilliant black eyes and let the fateful words escape.

"I suppose I may be prevailed upon to endure your company in my little minstrel jaunt through France, Sir William."

"A WORD, WILL."

They had agreed on a fee for his services—half now, half upon de Keldy's release—and had arranged to depart the nunnery in two days' time. Certainly, Will was in dire need of the money and would employ it to settle some sadly outstanding debts, but the fee paled into insignificance in the blinding light of the prize offered him.

Praise the Almighty for Brother Benedict and that Will had filled the monk's ears with his litany of woes and wishes a mere fortnight past. Will had thought himself a drowning man grasping at straws to ride all the way from York to this wild, North Yorkshire nunnery just to seek advice of an old friend. And what advice had Brother Benedict bestowed upon him? None at all. But now Ben offered him a solution. A temporary solution, true, but one that lit the way like a burning brand out of the gloom that was his life.

Their business concluded for now, the three had risen to leave the dead nuns in peace.

"As you wish, Sir Celibate," Will replied.

The monk's bastard brother hesitated, lute in hand. Will noted the fine mouth tighten beneath an overhanging hood.

"Go your way, Alain," Benedict murmured. "William is an old friend. I would speak to him in private."

The youth shot him a narrow look but left, nonetheless.

"He is not happy with our arrangement," Will observed, but his words seemed distant to his own ears. Unhappy? At this moment? The birds were caroling, the sun was shining, primroses speckled the gravemounds like tiny yellow stars, and he was going a-minstreling in southern France. It was a ballad come to very life.

"Alain has had some harsh experiences with men, William. He is wary and not inclined to trust. He wanted to travel alone."

"Christ, well if it's more harsh experiences he's after, then France *sans compagnie* is how he'd find it. Why'd you think I avoid soldiering like the very plague?"

"Which brings me to my point, Will. I chose you in part because you can use a sword, but also because I trust you—"

"And not for my superlative singing voice? Oh, Ben, you wound me."

The monk smiled. "What would a tone-deaf monk know? But listen, I worry about Alain."

"What, in my company?" Will presented his best unemployed-soldier leer.

And was startled when the monk replied, "Yes."

He hadn't thought he leered so persuasively.

"God above, Ben, I'm not going to rob the fellow and abandon him in France. You said you trusted me. Christ, I'll swear it if you like."

"Only if you swear in earnest, Will." Benedict tried a small smile.

"Oh, *mea culpa*, my monk. I shall attempt henceforth not to take the Lord's name in vain. But what—" Will broke off, examining his friend's face. "Are you serious? You wish me to swear? To protect this by-blow?"

"He is my brother, Will, and he has been hard-used. I would have your word that you will protect him to the very best of your ability. Protect his body and spirit both. Safeguard his chastity—"

"Christ, Ben, has he had *that* sort of trouble? No wonder he hides his pretty features beneath a hood. But rest assured, I have no fancy for a manly arse, no matter how—"

"Sir William de Fauconberg, I ask you to swear."

Will cocked a brow at his friend. Then he tried a smile on him. There was no alteration in the monk's stern expression.

So, Sir William reached out his hand. He placed it on Benedict's and lifted it to the cross hanging from the monk's scapular. Then he wrapped both their palms about the small wooden crucifix.

"Benedict de Keldy, Prior of Wykeham, I swear on the Holy Cross that I will protect your brother Alain with my very life. I will safeguard his body from harm and his valuables from pilfering." Then, because Benedict looked so unrelievedly glum, Will couldn't help but add, "And rest assured I will protect his posterior from plundering."

AZALAIS DID NOT utter a word all the way to Scarborough.

Admittedly, it was not a long ride—a mere seven miles from Wykeham Priory—and the lumbering company of the priory's layman was further incentive for her to seal her mouth. The layman led the way through lanes speckled with spring flowers and squelching with spring mud. More rain fell as they rode, which was propitious from Azalais's point of view—of course,

Alain needed to keep his hood about his ears when the sky was spitting like a displeased cat.

It was only when they began the descent into Scarborough, its clifftop castle glowering from the headland above that Azalais dared to lift her head and scan her surroundings.

She had been to Scarborough before, of course. It was the nearest harbor to Keldy. But it was not to admire its stretch of golden sand or the cluster of post-and-plaster houses nestling beneath the castle that she looked around her. Azalais searched for ships.

Scarborough was not a major port. If you wanted a bustling harbor full of boats heading to Bremen, Bergen, and Bilbao, you'd be better heading to Hull. So, the know-it-all knight had declared. But Scarborough was close—and the sooner she put a significant stretch of sea between herself and her elder brother, the better she would sleep at night. True, the nuns conceived that a thinly stuffed straw pallet and a single scratchy blanket were salutary for the soul, but Azalais's rest at the nunnery had suffered more from visions of brother Robert and his foul friend. Wykeham Priory was certainly not the last place Robert would think to look for her.

So, she ignored the castle and buildings and sand and scrutinized every watercraft that might possibly be termed a ship.

It did not take long—there were only two.

"So—have you a preference, my minstrel?"

Azalais startled. It was just as well the nunnery's mule was a docile thing, for a horse with any fizz would have taken umbrage at her jolt. The mule merely flicked its ears.

"Whichever boat is going to Bordeaux," she snapped. She did not turn to look at her questioner.

"I doubt either of those tubs will take us so far."

She could practically hear the smile in the knight's voice.

"Well then, what does it matter which I prefer?"

"With luck, one is heading south and will take us to a larger port." Such as Hull, he *didn't* say. "Then we may swap our transport for something more direct." A pause. She could feel him looking at her. She wouldn't turn. He would have no direct view of her face. "It is possible that both are heading south—in which case, your preference is worth considering."

How kind.

"In either case, I require a cabin out of the wind and water," Azalais declared.

She had not been on a boat of any size before, but she had heard men speak of them. She knew that ships were horribly dangerous things, prone to sinking without trace, and—even when they continued to float—liable to soak their passengers with seawater and blast them with icy gales. Both wind and wet could easily reveal her to be no man.

She had wrapped her breasts as flat as was feasible with a length of linen before leaving the convent. Apart from disguising her gender, it had produced a surprisingly practical side-effect— the few times they had managed a trot on their way from Wykeham, her breasts had *not* jolted every which way with bruising inelegance as was usually the case. But, binding or no binding, one soaking wave aboard ship would reveal a distinctly unmanly shape to her torso—or at least suggest some strange bandaging.

Likewise, she would prefer to keep her head well-covered until they were far from Yorkshire. A strong wind on deck would likely unhood her, and her features would be exposed in the cold light of day. She had prevailed upon a nun to shear her hair boyish-short at the convent—after all, if she was successful in her bid to take the veil, her hair would be cut short anyway. But still, she had no faith that something in her features would not shout femininity even beneath the short hair. And growing a beard was entirely beyond her.

It might be that her minstrel-knight would discover she was no man before their journey's end—she would cross that wobbling bridge when she came to it—but if he discovered it too close to home, Sir William would likely call the whole thing off.

He would drag her back to Wykeham, or even to Keldy. Accompanying a bastard youth across France was risky enough, but an unmarried heiress?

She heard the layman snort. She had forgotten about him. What did the fellow make of their odd conversation? Might he put two and two together somehow and report on her to Robert? A faint possibility maybe, but the sooner she got on that ship…

Sir William clarified the snort-worthy aspect of her demand.

"I fear your tastes may exceed what these noble craft can supply, my minstrel. They are cargo cogs merely. Passengers must fit where they may."

"Why did you ask, then?"

She flung him a glare, and then wished she hadn't. She had forgotten the glinting devilry in his eyes. He saw too much.

"This is your enterprise, good youth. But I propose you leave the ship haggling to me. I have, unfortunately, sailed to France a number of times before. I have some idea how to negotiate with the unmannerly breed that calls itself sailor. I merely thought to discover your requirements before I left you to mind the horses and baggage."

They were among the buildings now, clopping along a street that boasted some semblance of paving. There were people about—wives at the well, peddlers eyeing prospective purses, a beggar slumped against a church wall. So Azalais swallowed a pungent retort and settled instead for a curt nod.

It was only when they reined up by the fish-littered, gull-haunted shore and swung down from their mounts that she hissed at him.

"It is not me or *my tastes* that require shelter from the elements, sir." She indicated her lute, slung in a leather case across her back for safekeeping. "Find me a ship with shelter for the sake of my lute."

THE SHIP WAS headed to London. It was currently only half-laden with cargo and was trundling down the coast in a leisurely manner, hauling in at harbors along the way to pick up more merchandise. It was no sleek galley, all oarsmen heaving for Bordeaux, but it was the best he could do, Sir William had informed her. And it had room in the hold amongst the wool bales in which Alain could recline in dark and stuffy ease.

The knight had paid—Benedict had provided him coin for traveling costs. It would look too strange for the elder of the pair to be always applying to the younger for funds. No need to stir unnecessary suspicion. And now the ship was at sea, sailing southward under a stiff breeze, and Alain was in the hold, wondering where precisely she ought to regurgitate her breakfast.

She had boated on rivers before, but never the sea. It felt like every lurch and judder the craft made would be its last before succumbing to the wild North Sea. At least death by drowning would be a respite from this stomach-roiling, limb-weakening nausea.

A hatch in the roof opened, admitting a blast of daylight and salt air, and a pair of rather nicely shaped legs. They descended the ladder, then paused as their owner stopped to seal the hatch above.

"Christ, now I know how Jonah felt. It's as dark as a whale's gut in here and smells about as sweet, too." She observed the silhouette peer about. "Where are you, Alain?"

She attempted to say, "Here," but it emerged as more of a groan.

The shape picked its way in her direction, holding onto bales and beams for balance as the ship lurched like a drunkard about to collapse.

"Will the ship sink?" She said it as much to indicate her location as out of genuine interest. If she was going to die, she didn't want to be trodden on by some lumbering knight first.

"Sink? Not unless a choir of sirens lure us onto some rocks, and believe me, no naked fishy female in her right mind would dally about the North Sea. That water's enough to cause my fingers to freeze off. It was come down here for a spell or risk losing an extremity—and what use is a fingerless minstrel?"

He had found her. He took hold of her shoulder, probably just to assure himself he was addressing a person and not a sack. She flinched away.

He sat down nearby.

He was looking at her, but she couldn't make out his expression. She just hoped he was laboring under the same difficulty.

"I thought we might make some music together to pass the time—once I can feel my fingers again, that is. I still haven't heard you sing, Alain. Yet I suspect your lungs require a dose of fresh air before they attempt any tunes."

Sing? She could barely groan.

She shook her head and produced one such noise.

"Come." The shape held out a hand. "Let me take you on deck. Come see what some fresh air can do. Or at least reassure yourself of the absence of sirens."

Him, take her hand? Support her up the steps and steady her arm across a heaving deck so she would be revealed in two heartbeats as a weak female creature who must be carted home immediately?

"No," she snapped, panic restoring her voice. She batted his hand away.

"Suit yourself, but I do not believe the captain will be amused if you decorate his cargo. Or his deck, for that matter. You will find yourself on cleaning duty, paying passenger or not. I advise the gunwale as the retching place of choice."

"Very well," she growled—or groaned. "But you stay here." She hauled herself up by means of a bale. "Someone has to keep an eye on my lute."

If it wasn't destined for the bottom of the sea.

And Azalais made a staggering procession across the hold toward fresh air and the gunwale. Whatever that was.

WILLIAM WATCHED THE youth haul himself up the steps and inch open the heavy hatch. Light flooded in, bathing Alain's head and shoulders. Will blinked and narrowed his eyes. The hold wasn't entirely lightless—chinks in the woodwork let in occasional spears of daylight—but the sudden glare was too great a contrast. And yet … Will frowned at the form outlined by the light, but evidently, the air had already had a reviving effect, for Alain exited the hatch in a flurry. The hatch thudded back down.

Will shrugged in the gloom and reached where he was fairly certain he'd stowed his bag. After some concerted fumbling, he located what he was after, extracted the requisite items, and proceeded to tune up. Every now and again, he stopped to rub his hands. At one point, he even inserted his left fingers into the opposite armpit. Christ, he was half frozen. It was just as well that he did not intend Alain to play. There was distinctly less of the lad than there was of Will—although quite how much less was hard to tell, what with his loose clothing. He would freeze all the sooner. Well, Alain could exercise his voice instead—once he could open his mouth with no hazard of regurgitation.

Will was onto his third *canzo* by the time the hatch reopened, and his fingers were almost up to speed. He glanced up in time to see Alain turn to twitch the hatch back in place, one hand securing his hood against the gust that followed him in.

Very keen on his hood, was his companion. Was he bashful about protruding ears, perhaps? Or a rash of youthful pimples? Will's mouth twitched. It wasn't a smile. His own youth was not so far away that he had forgotten that constant sensation of being judged—and found inevitably insufficient.

He played on, in part so that Alain would know where to stagger—but also as a not-so-subtle hint.

It is time to show what you can do with your voice, my minstrel. Pretty tunes on a lute alone do not make a traveling jongleur.

Not that Will was singing. Instead, his vielle's mournful strains made a weird accompaniment to the surrounding creak and splosh of the ship. Will's bow moved nearly in time with the sway of the boat. It was as if he and the vessel played together, making wild, unearthly sea music.

"You play the fiddle?"

Alain's voice sounded stronger now. And nearer.

"Vielle," Will corrected with some asperity.

"What's the difference? It's a small lute that you hold against your neck and draw a bow across, is it not? Fiddle. Vielle."

Alain was evidently feeling well enough to argue.

"A vielle is the proper instrument of a troubadour, my rustic. A fiddle is...well it's what peasants saw upon at their weddings."

He kept playing, so demonstrating that his strains were a world away from fiddled dance tunes.

Alain made some kind of mutter in reply. It got drowned in the general racket of the hold, but Will was fairly sure it wasn't an assent.

Will finished his *canzo* and laid the instrument on his lap. It seemed odd to play while sitting down, but he wasn't going to break his vielle by falling on it in these exuberant seas just for the sake of a better stance. He looked at Alain.

The youth had settled nearby and had been watching him intently. At least, that was what his posture suggested. It was hard to gauge expression in this low light.

"Did the fresh air do the trick?" Will inquired.

"Hmph. It chilled me to the marrow and nearly blew me over your gunwale—but yes, I feel better."

"Well enough to sing?"

⊰⊱

AZALAIS FROZE. AND she was just beginning to defrost in the shelter of the hold, too.

It was all very well for her to play the lute before this man with musician's ears, but to sing? Her voice was nearly as high-pitched as a choirboy's, but she knew full well there was something about its tone that was not quite boyish. Yet what could she do? Plead a sore throat again? Her evident freedom from coughs and sniffles would only make him suspicious. In fact, her hesitation right now would be making him curious.

The ship groaned. Waves battered the hull. She could hear the cries of sailors overhead. They were not shouts of imminent danger, she realized now. The sailors had seemed calm enough when she was on deck, and the waves—once she had dared to look over the gunwale—rolled like heaving green hills but did not threaten to crash over the ship. Why, Sir William would barely hear her voice above this ocean racket. If she had to sing, then perhaps now was not such a bad time after all.

"You will have to conquer these performance nerves if we are to pass as minstrels, Alain."

"I have never sung with another," she snapped. "I have always accompanied myself."

"Never?" the knight in the shadows said mildly. "I assume someone taught you, at least at the outset. Did you never make music together?"

"That was years ago, and no minstrels have come to Keldy since my father left. Robert is no patron of the courtly arts." She paused, then her voice softened. "But yes, I have sung with another…so long ago it seems like a dream."

The knight lifted his vielle to his shoulder. He picked up his bow. "Well then, my minstrel. It is time to start dreaming again."

There was an odd tone to his reply, self-mocking perhaps. But there was no time to analyze, for Sir William drew the bow across the vielle's strings. His fingers flickered on the instrument's neck, and a moment later, she recognized the song. She had played it on her lute for him just a few days previously. He had even cast it in the same pitch as she had performed it then.

Azalais clenched her cold fingers and drew a deep breath. It was time to face her fears. Her stomach did not feel so steady anymore. It would just serve him right if she threw up on his feet.

Chapter Three

WILL PLAYED THE song in its entirety. No voice joined him. So, he began again. Still nothing. He was just beginning to think he played for his own amusement—and he wasn't feeling particularly amused—when he realized the words that he thought echoed only in his head were being voiced aloud:

> *With the sweetness of the new season*
> *When forest leaves grow and the birds*
> *Sing, each in his own way*
> *And in a new key, it is then*
> *That men draw near*
> *To what they most desire.*

Alain was singing so softly that his words were nearly swallowed by the ship's ceaseless complaints.

Will played on.

With the second stanza, the youth's voice grew stronger. Still, he did not sing with anything like the power Will sensed he might exercise. Will strained to hear him. Christ, he could practically feel his ears elongating in his direction, but he could discern little in this infernal din beyond an evident accuracy in pitch and familiarity with the words.

They continued—Sir William, Alain, and the percussion of

sea and ship—and when the last stanza had been sung—or whispered—they stopped. At least, Will and his companion did. The ship groaned on.

The shape opposite him emanated a kind of concentrated stillness. Quite an achievement on board this sea-tossed tub. Will smiled. He was fairly certain the youth would not see, not least because his face was angled toward his toes. Awaiting judgment.

"Now you have sung with another," Will murmured. "It is not so hard, is it? Your voice seemed to meld with my music well enough."

No answer, but the shape appeared slightly less stiff.

"I say *seemed*," Will continued, "for it is cursed difficult to judge anything in this racket. And—" He paused and noted the shoulders opposite tense. He decided to be diplomatic. "You need to work on your volume, my minstrel. An audience is an ignorant beast. It chatters and clatters, and its attention is apt to drift. It is our part to seize its senses. We must seduce the beast, set it to swooning, and suck the very coins from its hard-clutched purse. We cannot do that if it does not hear you."

"It is only a disguise, Sir Knight. It will serve our purposes to go unnoticed."

That kicked him where it hurt.

"*Your* purposes maybe, O bastard of Keldy. But not mine. You think I agreed to this fool's quest simply because I was desperate for coin? If we are minstrels, we will do this properly."

So much for diplomacy. Will did not usually reveal himself so, but this Alain was not his father, nor a fellow knight, or even a creature of the court. And this journey was his chance—perhaps his only chance—to grasp at a dream.

"It matters to you—this music, this life we embark on," the figure in the dark murmured.

"It does," Will said curtly.

"Why?"

The bastard of Keldy asks *why*? What, would he have Will strip before him in this dark hold and reveal his naked, beating heart? They had known each other a day. A year would be too short an acquaintance for what he asked. A lifetime, for some.

"That is not your concern," Will snapped. "But know this—if you want my cooperation on this minstrel escapade, you will play your part, my bastard. We will make music together, and we will do it well. No, more than well. You have a good ear, Alain, and your technique with the lute intrigues me. But I demand more. By God, I require your very soul to tremble on the strings of your lute. I want honey dripping from your lips. *Audible* honey, note you. Together, we will make music that will cause angels to weep. We shall be true minstrels upon this trip, or we will not make it at all."

Alain stood abruptly. His silhouette swayed precariously before Will.

"I find my stomach is not so steady after all, Sir Knight. I need fresh air," he said. And left.

⫸✕⫷

IT WASN'T ENTIRELY a lie. Her innards were still not accustomed to the surface beneath her heaving like an ill-trained horse. And the air of the hold wasn't helping matters.

She staggered her way from mast to gunwale, clutched the edge of the boat, and dared a look over. Great rolling waves of an unfathomable black-green pitched beneath her. It seemed incomprehensible they were still afloat in them, but the ship surged on, slicing through the green surface and kicking up curls of white foam. The wind flung her hood back. She did not care. *He* was still below deck, and the sailors would only see a boy. Hopefully. Azalais looked up, beyond the waves. To the west there were hills. The coast of Yorkshire. Her home slipping away.

She stood staring at them, feeling the wind stream through her strangely short hair, and trying to untangle her feelings. They were like a ball of wool that had fallen foul of a cat. Or a basket full of kittens.

That beautiful, mournful music. She had seldom heard the vielle played before, and never like that. As if the instrument itself wept stately tears. And the way she entered into it, lifting and soaring with his bow strokes, voicing a melody in harmony with another human being. She had struggled to rein herself back, and he knew it. He knew her voice was capable of more, and he would not stand for half measures.

And then there was the way his form had moved with the bow strokes. Thank heaven she had not seen his expression as he did so. She did not want to see that darkly beautiful face, so attuned to the song, so intensely *present*. It was too much.

Of course, she could only guess how he would look. Those dark eyes, no longer laughing or mocking but gazing straight into her soul. She could discern no more than the shape of him down in the hold. But she *felt* it, and, by God, it was pure madness.

She was a man, a minstrel by-blow, and she must remain as such in his eyes—and those of the rest of the world.

Yet, if she sang as he desired, if she put her all into her performance, how could he not see what she truly was? Oh, if she could only sever her breasts and sprout a beard. And then acquire those items of which men seemed so inordinately proud—and keen to exercise.

She shuddered.

She'd rather be a eunuch. They were said to have pleasant voices.

Which made her smile, even if that smile wavered. It was an answer of sorts. She must eviscerate her gender, sever herself from all which marked her as female and required her to perform a prescribed part in the world. Yes, the end goal of this whole enterprise was to remove herself from that world and its filthy demands. Complete this quest as she wished, and she would have her father's permission to seal herself up in a nunnery for the rest of her life. And make music.

But in order to achieve that goal, she must play the role Sir

William demanded of her. To pour herself into his music. She must both act a role and be more fully herself than she had ever yet dared to be. And sing troubadour songs steeped in longing and thwarted desire. She could tell he favored such melodies already—they were the choice of a noble musician, one who played the vielle and never the mere fiddle. It was not possible to hide one's soul and sing as he demanded of her. She just hoped he wouldn't identify it as a female soul.

Azalais clutched the rail and stared at Yorkshire—this promise, this *threat* uttered by her knight protector called to her with a siren's voice. It crooned that she might make music with him, join utterly and unrestrainedly with him as his bow sang. As his voice dipped and curved about hers. It practically disjointed her knees to think of it.

The unthinkable danger. It was not only that she would be discovered and returned.

It hit her, then, what a raving idiot she was to have thought she could pull this venture off. She was sailing to a land crawling with soldiers, in order to escape just one debauched creature of war. Benedict at least had seen the danger. But his solution? To make her do so in the company of another such knight. All it would take was one discovery. *O God, the enormity of it.*

Now the gunwale was holding her up. The sea lurched beneath her. The wind howled in her ears.

"Have you fed the fish yet, or are you recovered enough to join me below?" a voice inquired from just behind her shoulder.

Christ! Now she had no joints left in her legs at all. Nevertheless, Azalais dragged her hood up and secured it one-handedly under her chin.

She took a deep breath.

"I was just about to return, Sir William. With all this wind in my lungs, I think perhaps I am ready to try another song."

So, she did, that day and the next. And the one after that. Each day saw him urge her to project her voice more boldly, and she did so—by tiny increments. And in every silence that ensued after the last stanza was sung, she waited for him to cry *woman!* and haul her into the daylight to confirm features too delicate and cheeks that never would sprout hair. She waited with nails dug into palms and a quiver within that had nothing to do with the sea. It never happened—or it hadn't yet.

Azalais blessed the racket of creaking and sloshing that was their constant musical accompaniment and her cover.

In the meantime, the ship bobbed its way down the east coast of England, calling in at an interminable number of ports, large and small. The hold filled a little more at each docking, and their rehearsal room shrank. Wool bales and grain sacks piled up around them and soaked up the sound of vielle and lute, not to mention her voice.

And she and William made music—for there was little else to do. He did not seem inclined to talk about himself, and she certainly wasn't going to spin a web of lies that would only trip her up. She could not sing all day, so she played, too—or listened to him play. And sometimes he sang to her lute's accompaniment. And when their fingers ached and their throats were rough, they talked of music instead—of lyrics, instruments, and performance.

It was exquisite torture. She had never made so much music in her life before nor been so encouraged and urged on. He listened to her, praised her voice's range, her fingers' skill, and then prompted her to consider yet more, to dare more. And beneath it all, shivered the ever-present fear of discovery. He listened so intently to her, leaning toward her in the gloom, cocking his head in concentration, sometimes even reaching out to touch her fingers on the strings.

He *must* discover her eventually. She did not want this melding of notes and minds to end, but end it must, and then what? Thank God, he could not see her, or see him. The increasing cargo blocked up the chinks of light until there were just a few arrows of gold falling from directly above.

They were creatures of sound alone, and it was so much

better that way.

⇉⟫⟪⇇

THE THUMP OF the hatch flung back, followed by a swirl of air and glare of light, all of which was then blocked by Sir William's descending legs, thighs, and torso. Azalais flicked her gaze away. The light must not fall on her face.

"We reach London before dark, Alain," the knight announced.

"Close the hatch," Alain called back. "If the cargo is wetted and it's a landlubber's fault, then that landlubber learns to swim post haste. Wasn't that the gist of our captain's advice?"

"What, never tell me you can't swim, my minstrel?"

"Can you?" Azalais retorted.

"A little." Sir William's voice was nearer now. "I learned in France, in summer when the water won't make a man sing in soprano. Not that you'd know any different, my minstrel. It's quite pleasant, you know. Bobbing about in the water, naked as Adam. That is, until a fish nibbles your nether parts. By Christ, I knew how Our Lord walked on water in at that moment."

He chuckled, and the sound was far too close. Nor did she wish to picture him imitating Adam before the Fall.

"No, I can't swim, and I have no desire to begin by being tossed overboard. So, close the wretched hatch!"

She heard him sit down. She did *not* hear the hatch close.

Instead, "The sun is shining, the Thames is flat, and the only moisture that will descend down that opening is our dear captain's spittle, my landlubber. It is time to pack up your kit. I thought a little light from above would assist. Heaven forbid you leave with a side of ham instead of your lute."

"Hmph." She turned to gather her things. Not that there was much to assemble, but it was preferable to looking at Sir William in the light.

"Have you seen London before, Alain?"

There was rustling nearby. The knight was evidently following his own advice.

"No," she muttered.

"Well then, my rustic, you had better shuffle your shanks on deck forthwith and observe the approach of the finest city in all England. Well, the largest, anyway."

"Does it have a bath?"

Sir William laughed outright at that. "Oh, the bathhouses of London are famous, good youth. *And* the women who frequent them. I'm just not sure your brother Benedict would approve of your availing yourself of their…services."

Azalais kept her face resolutely fixed on her saddlebag. Her ears burned. But at least he evidently still believed she was a man.

"I am sticky with days stuffed in a cargo hold, Sir Knight. I must wash this ship's fleas off me before I board another ship for France. You said we must spend at least one night at an inn?"

Oh, for an inn, with real beds, fresh-roasted food, and ale that did not slop to a ship's irregular rhythm. Not to mention a bath.

She had slept onboard the ship all the slow way down the coast, refusing to disembark, even at those towns where the knight had wandered ashore. He had slept at a number of dockside hostelries along the way, swapping a few hours of minstrelsy in the taproom for bed and board, or so he told her. She had refused his suggestion to do the same. She might be recognized. *He* might recognize her for what she was. She had told him she was not ready to perform in public yet.

"France is not so far away," he had warned. "You must play to other ears than mine there."

But he did not push her. So, she remained in the hold and gradually felt herself to be taking on the odor of the bilgewater below.

And now she had no choice. She must leave this ship and its safe, stuffy darkness, for it would take them no further south. They would seek out a ship to Bordeaux in London. She slung her lute over her back, bundled up her bag, and fled up the steps before the knight had done more than locate his vielle. She would find herself a secure nook on deck from which she could view this London safe from his prying eyes.

How she would evade the scrutiny of those same eyes once on dry land, she did not wish to consider.

WILL FELT A bump as the ship nudged up against one of the innumerable jetties east of London Bridge. The jolt communicated itself up through the deck and the gunwale and into his very sinews, transforming as it did into a quiver. Of what? Excitement that he was finally doing this, living his dream, yes, but also something more complex. What that might be, he had no chance to guess, for the docking was immediately followed by a flurry of action and shouts. Will was required to duck out of the way of a sailor wielding a heavy hemp rope that would, it was averred, be flung ashore whether or not Will got in its way.

So rather than take a rope-assisted flight, Will wove his way to the aftcastle, where he thought he'd glimpsed his traveling companion.

"Aye, go cuddle up to your bum-boy," the hemp-wielding sailor cried in his wake. "And get out of my cursed way."

That sent a different kind of jolt through Will.

He pivoted and strode a couple of quick paces back toward the lout.

"Do not project your foul fantasies on me, sea scum," Will snapped. "I have not so much as touched my companion."

Nor will I have his honor or mine defiled, was what he managed to not to utter. The sailor thought he addressed a minstrel, not a knight. Will had left all his knightly accoutrements behind with Benedict—except for a simple sword and a dagger or two. He would be a fool not to travel with those. No mere sailor would so abuse a knight, at least not one who wished to remain whole. But a minstrel? They were wanderers, creatures of suspect morals and strange habits. They were fair game for insult.

Will knew this, but this was the first time it had slapped him in the face, so to speak. Or worse, besmirched his companion.

Before he could decide whether to turn and leave or exercise his musician's hands upon the fellow, the rope-wielding sailor added a rejoinder.

"Not touched, my arse," he said with a grin, and tied the rope off. Then wiped his own hands with rather more suggestion than necessary on his own posterior. "We've heard you two crooning down there, day after day. Love songs, eh? And you've kept him well tucked away, pretty piece that he is. Want him all to yourself, eh?"

Will found his hands were deciding for themselves what their next action should be. He drew a deep breath and unclenched them. It would not aid his purpose to damage his hands on this piece of nothing. He only hoped Alain had not overheard.

"Your suppositions are beneath contempt," Will replied, and turned away with a fine hauteur. A minstrel fought with words, not with his fists. Or so he tried to tell himself.

It was more than time to leave the ship.

"Ready to go?"

He addressed the Alain-shaped shadow in the shelter of the aftcastle.

"I am, Sir Knight."

The voice did not sound particularly certain of that fact, and Will found himself snapping, "For the purposes of this trip, I am not *Sir*, nor am I a *knight*. You would do well to remember that, my minstrel."

"What am I to call you then?" The shape picked up its bag and materialized out of the shadows.

Will sighed. Alain had possibly just heard himself declared a bum-boy, and what does his supposed buggerer do but bite his head off?

He softened his tone. "Just call me—"

He hesitated. *William* denominated Englishness, but this particular William spoke fluent Gascon-French and sang in the *langue d'oc*. He was to sing his way through French lands, held admittedly in part by the English. But he wished to divest himself of his English Williamness in the weeks to come. That was the whole point. To try on a new skin.

Yet a William had been the first of the troubadours, as the histories told it. William of Aquitaine. No—Guilhem de Aquitaine.

"Guilhem," he murmured, trying it on for size.

"Really?" He could hear the smile in the youth's voice. Indeed, he could see it on his face now that his companion had emerged into the evening light. "William with a French accent? *Par Dieu*, I suppose I could remember that."

William—Guilhem—blinked. He had spent so long holed up in a dark hold with this youth that he'd forgotten what Alain looked like. Not that he'd ever truly seen him, come to think of it. What with the ever-present hood, which was of course still drooping over his brow. But he'd forgotten what a sweetly tender mouth his companion had, especially when it smiled. Christ! Had the sailor's filth infected his mind?

"Remember it, then," Will said shortly. He turned. "Come. We require ale and a bed for the night."

"And a bath," followed behind him.

Will's lips quirked. Perhaps he should find this beardless youth a bathhouse use that offered the full range of services. Feminine services. Benedict need never know. And perhaps a certain knight ought to avail himself of those services, too.

Chapter Four

THEY DIDN'T NEED to look far for the ale and bed. Sir William—no, Guilhem—was negotiating the latter now with a ferocious-looking man garbed in a leather apron. She wasn't sure why two pallets for the night required any extended discussion, but what was she to know? She'd never ventured beyond Yorkshire in her life.

The handful of alleys she'd seen of London so far had made her almost glad of Guilhem's enforced presence. The place seemed to be heaving with unsavory types from all over the world. The narrow alleys that crawled up from the jetties had been full of sailors—and those who aimed to profit from their presence. Innkeepers were only the most respectable of those profiteers. But how did one select between sleeping establishments? Each looked as disreputable as the next. Azalais was content to let her companion take the lead, while she sank into the blessed shadows of the taproom that filled the arched undercroft.

She watched him now as he gestured about the dim room for some reason, then flick back his hair in the gesture she'd become so accustomed. It was not an affectation, she'd come to realize. Or if it had once been one, it was so no longer. It was a completely unconscious motion that seemed to satisfy his hands' need to be constantly moving. Those restless fingers only seemed satisfied when they were coaxing sweet, haunting strains from a vielle—or caressing the air as he sang. That much she had seen clearly in the dim hold.

"Done," her companion declared, and his hand was enveloped by the host's larger, much less shapely one. "I take it our boudoir is up those stairs, mine host? *Merci, mon ami.* My companion and I will return to transform this Hades into a very Elysium of song this evening. *Adieu.*"

"WHATEVER YOU HAVE arranged, you can just *un*arrange it. I am *not* going to sing for my supper below, Sir—"

"Guilhem," he supplied. "Not 'sir' anything, remember? Just Guilhem."

"I will call you something far less acceptable if you do not go down immediately and inform our host that only one of his customers will be playing for his bed and board tonight."

All spoken in a furious whisper.

They were seated on pallets in what passed for sleeping quarters above the tavern, sleeping quarters that Azalais had *thought* her companion had just paid for. It turned out he hadn't. A minstrel didn't pay when he could play, so Guilhem said.

"I assume you intend to play when we reach France, Alain. Why not now? God knows, this innkeeper would extract a king's ransom for putting us up in these palatial quarters otherwise." A languid wave about the long, low-ceilinged dormitory. A few sailors were already snoring midway down. One of them had acquired a companion on his meager pallet. "And doubtless he serves a seven-course banquet, replete with lampreys and stuffed wrens to his guests in recompense."

"I will pay," Azalais snapped. "Benedict provided us coin enough."

"Which we may well have need of before our journey is done. I repeat—why pay when you can play, O Alain?"

She shook her head with force. The action came close to dislodging her hood.

She could feel him observing her.

"You need have no fear, you know. Your voice is pure, and you project it with greater volume and confidence now. Follow my vielle's lead, Alain. I will not let you stumble and fall."

Oh, that velvety voice. Pitched for her ears alone, it caressed and it coaxed. It dared her to open her mouth and agree, to let his music bear her up, buoyant as a leaf in a stream.

She did not.

He was still looking at her.

"You will have to throw back your hood when you perform, my minstrel. Dare I say it, you might leave it off altogether."

"No! I will sing in France, but not yet."

"Why, Alain?"

He did not sound angry or accusatory, reactions she'd come to expect from most men to any defiance from her, a mere woman.

Which only proved he did not see her as one. Praise heaven.

Instead, his voice sounded soft, concerned even. It was so much harder to resist than bluster and threats. But, of course, he was only attempting to manipulate her in his own way. In the manner of the courtly charmer.

Then his hand covered hers. *O, God.* She managed not to wrench it away, but there was no concealing that first jolt.

"You are afraid, Alain," murmured her interrogator. "Why? Is there something to this quest of yours you are concealing from me? It may be that I can help."

She slipped her hand out from under his. She wrapped her arms about herself, only in part to secure them from him.

She had made him suspicious. It seemed she must reveal a morsel more.

"I go in fear of my brother," she whispered.

It was the truth, but only part of the reason.

"Robert?"

She nodded.

"But he is hundreds of miles away, surely?"

"I must not be seen—by him or any of his friends. I cannot take the chance."

She dared a glance up. Those expressive dark brows had drawn together beneath the ever-drooping lock of hair. She dropped her gaze quickly.

Not quickly enough.

He reached out a hand. Fingers touched her chin and lifted it up to face him.

"Why would he look for you? Why would he care?" He scrutinized her face. "Have you taken something from him, Alain?"

"I am not a thief!"

"I did not accuse you of theft."

Sweet heaven, he saw too much.

She brushed his hand away. "I swear to you, my intention is entirely honorable. My brother Robert will not ransom my father, but someone must do it. With Benedict's aid—and yours, good minstrel—I will gain entry to where my father is held, offer up sufficient ransom, and free him."

She took a deep breath. This much he already knew. Clearly, it was not enough; he required more.

"Robert does not wish for our father to be freed, Guilhem. He is too used to being lord of Keldy. My father has been absent for over two years now. Robert finds it convenient to say that he cannot raise the ransom. He is believed, for everyone knows how costly ransoms can be, but it is not the truth. Nor would he wish me, a bastard half-brother, to do what he does not and reveal him for a dishonorable pinch-purse. He would prefer his father die a captive."

She injected those last words with a suitable chagrin. She was ashamed of her eldest brother and had wished to hide his low nature. *Look no further, Sir Minstrel. This is as much truth as I will serve you.*

But she could feel him looking. There was more light in this hostelry than had entered their ship's hold. Not bright daylight, to be sure, but more illumination than was comfortable. Sir William didn't speak—he just looked.

She had spoken the truth, except for the bit about being a bastard half-brother, but she knew there were holes in her story still. And this too-astute knight observed and considered her, while all she could do was stare at the straw poking through her pallet.

She felt it creep over her then—the insidious, idiotic notion that she should just trust him and tell him everything. *After all, he suspects something. He will not be satisfied until he has found you out. You are far enough from Yorkshire now. Even if he refuses to continue this charade, he may leave you to carry on alone. That is what you wanted—remember?*

If she told him, William would probably abandon her. Well, where was the problem with that? True, he had given her a taste of what it could be like to make music with another, to mingle mind and spirit with another on a level far beyond words or touch. But perhaps she would find a similar experience with the nuns. They made music, of a sort. And she would be safe with them.

Or worse, William *wouldn't* abandon her. Instead, he would treat her as Robert and his men treated women. As Lord Leonard would treat her. She wrapped her arms tighter about herself and tried to hold the shudder in. Yes, everything in his manner suggested Sir William knew his way around women, and far too thoroughly.

And still, he watched her.

Finally, Azalais could bear it no longer.

"Sweet heaven, have done! All right, I will join you in the taproom this evening. But *I* will play the lute, Guilhem, and you shall do all the singing. You may draw all the eyes, as doubtless you know well how to do. I will seat myself in your shadow and, by God, I will wear my hood!"

A FEW HOURS and a hot bath later, Will leaned against an archway and let his eyes drift around the long, low taproom. The stone-built undercroft with its heavy arches boded well for good acoustics. The number of unwashed sailors and associated strumpets it contained did not. The place was not precisely full of dockside rabble—there was a leavening of foreign merchants and assorted travelers—but the conclusion was unavoidable.

There would be no troubadours' songs that evening. Lordly lyrics would not only go entirely unappreciated by this tavern crowd, they might also invite the disposal of soggy fruit in their singer's direction. But a minstrel was nothing if not versatile. With that principle in mind, they had practiced plenty of bawdy ballads and dance tunes onboard the ship. Will drew a deep breath. Now he must do more than practice. It was time to try whether a knight could pass as a low jongleur.

He glanced back at Alain. The youth was hunched on a stool between Will and the wall, lute cradled on his lap. He was tuning its strings for perhaps the fourth time since entering the taproom. The rushlight glinted off his hair—or at least, as much as was visible beneath his hood. It peeped out more visibly than before, seeming to have acquired more bounce and air since the lad's visit to the bathhouse. Short, soft curls gleamed with reflected gold.

Will shook his head. As if he cared what a man's hair looked like. It was just his companion's cursed secrecy that made him so curious.

Will ruffled his own hair back—again—and surveyed his audience-in-waiting more narrowly.

He only hoped no one acquainted with him had wandered into this dockside drinking establishment. Alain was not the only one who wished to go unrecognized—a fact Will had not seen fit to tell his companion. Some things were too tender and newborn to expose to another's scrutiny. He would allow his dream to grow a little, see whether it had a chance to live first, before admitting it to any other besides Benedict. Should someone recognize him in the guise of a minstrel singing ribald tunes for sailors, it would only render it that much harder to return to his life as a knight. Should he choose to do so.

Perhaps he really wanted someone to recognize him.

Their host chose that moment to intrude, presenting them with two mugs of ale and a meaningful look.

"Something to wet your whistles," he grunted. With the evident implication that those whistles needed exercising, and soon.

Will raised the mug to him and drank. The vessel quivered slightly in his hand.

By God, was he nervous? He, Sir William de Fauconberg, concerned about entertaining a cellar full of sailors?

He inhaled slowly and then turned to Alain.

"We shall begin with 'The Monk and the Maiden,'" Will informed his companion, and, without waiting for a retort to match the grimace that appeared on the youth's lips, Guilhem the Minstrel began to tap his tabor to an insistent beat. He only hoped Alain's lute would follow in its wake.

IT WAS MANY tankards later when Guilhem the Minstrel and his trusty lutenist were finally able to desist.

Will had lost count of how many sticky ceramic beakers the host had served him. The fellow seemed to think that so long as he kept tipping ale down their throats the music would continue. He seemed not to factor in the evident side effects of such lubrication.

Will laid aside his vielle—he had handed Alain his tabor and had him tap a danceable if basic beat upon it while Will had set his vielle to rattling out a series of tunes that would set a cripple's feet to dancing. And it had worked. Now he judged his audience pretty well too drunk or exhausted to be bothered stamping the floor to dust any longer. Pray God the innkeeper did not press another ale upon him. Will's bladder could take no more.

"Just got to pay the alley another visit," he muttered to Alain, and Will wove an unsteady path through the thinning punters to the well-frequented side door.

The Scottish sailor who'd taught him the song about the seal-woman clapped him on the shoulder as he passed, nearly knocking him sideways into an arch. The fellow bellowed something, to which Will grinned and raised a hand in reply. He supposed the fellow had spoken in English, but it wasn't any variety he was familiar with. He *had* taught him the song about the seal-woman, hadn't he?

And as he gave his bladder some blessed relief, Will grinned up at the few stars he could glimpse above. *By God, they'd done it.* He and Alain had set this hairy, unwashed, and thoroughly loveable mob to roaring out choruses and staggering about the flags in an approximation of dancing. *They were minstrels.* The host had poured ale down them until Will's gut was awash, merchants had tossed stray pennies into his hat, and no one had shouted out that he was a masquerading knight and Alain was…well, whatever he was.

Will felt a wave of affection for the youth. Ah, Alain knew not his potential, but Will would coax him out of his shell, set that voice to soaring, yes, even teach him how to drum the tabor with more finesse. Will pushed himself off the grimy wall and ducked back inside the tavern. He wanted to share the joy. Besides, his reclusive companion might be getting lonely.

Will found said recluse fending off a serving maid. The girl had crouched down by his stool, thus affording Alain an unparalleled view down a well-tenanted bodice. But it seemed the lad was not in the mood to appreciate the landscape. Will grinned. Well, it behooved a knight to come to the rescue.

"Is my lutenist not consuming enough of your establishment's fine brew, fair maid?" he inquired with one hand leaning firmly upon an archway. He discovered that *establishment* was a surprisingly hard word to get one's tongue around.

The girl gave him a little smile and patted Alain on the thigh. She let her hand rest there.

"I was just saying how well he plays the lute, sir. I have a little gittern. I thought he could give me a lesson or two."

Will swallowed any number of replies that sprang to his lips. *And what lessons will you offer in return?* being only the most circumspect. He had observed the panic in Alain's upraised eyes.

"Perhaps tomorrow, sweet maid. My minstrel has had enough exercise—" damn, he meant *music*, "—for one night. His lordly pallet calls."

The serving maid took the hint and wandered away to gather the ale beakers from a bench nearby, although with no evident haste and with many glances cast their way.

Alain raised a brow at Will. At least, Will thought he saw such movement under the lad's hood. "An occupational hazard, Guilhem?"

Will grinned down at him. "Oh, you have no idea, fair youth. Welcome to the wonderful world of minstrelsy." Not that he had such a deep acquaintance with it either. "But perhaps if you had sung, she'd have realized you are unlikely to take advantage of all she had to offer."

"God have mercy," Alain muttered. "I expected you to draw admirers, but me? She couldn't even see me…I hope."

Will drew his fingers through his hair with a languorous gesture. "Oh, you flatter me, my minstrel." Then he grinned. "Got to admit it, Alain, I'm a tad surprised you're the one fending off the fair sex tonight. Where are my legion of admirers? I usually score one or twelve. I reckon it's your air of innocence that does it. That, and the superlative skill of your fingers of course." He affected a leer and wiggled his own.

"Are we done for the evening?" Alain asked somewhat pointedly. He stood up, lute in hand. "May we retire?"

"By all means, my hero. Behold!" Will flung out his arms. "We are the victors on the field. We have triumphed, Alain. We are minstrels! We may retire to our bower covered in glory."

That raised a smile to his minstrel's lips. Will's curved in return. Oh, the world was a wonderful place, and this ale-reeking basement was the most heavenly corner of it all. By God, he was a troubadour.

It seemed only natural to fling his outstretched arm about his partner in music. The youth had done well tonight. More than well. It was Alain's first performance, so far as Will knew, and he had exhibited every sign of stage fright before his debut. It took a moment for Will to realize that the figure he was embracing in ale-tinged exuberance was standing stiff as a corpse. A trickle of awareness filtered through. *Bum boy.* Had Alain overheard after all?

Will let his arm drop, but not too abruptly. No need to appear guilty. What was going on in the lad's head? He patted Alain's shoulder and stepped back. Tried a rueful smile.

"Fear not, Alain, I have no taste for men. You are safe from me."

The youth ducked his head and didn't answer.

And Will recalled Benedict's strange insistence that he swear to protect his bastard brother's body. Alain did seem uncommonly delicate and pretty for a man from the little Will had managed to glimpse of him. Why, even he had noticed the sweetness of the lad's mouth. Had Alain attracted unwanted attention from some of his elder brother's men? Or worse, things may have progressed further than mere attention. No wonder he acted strangely at times and particularly in public.

The subject of his thoughts began to head toward the stairs.

Then Alain stopped and glanced back.

"Are you coming, my minstrel?" That sweet mouth tweaked as it echoed Will's phrasing. "If you are not after my bum, then I would appreciate your company among those who may have more discerning tastes."

Will's brows rose. Well, it was an offer of peace, and Will's brain was too pickled to consider the matter more tonight. A bedchamber full of snoring sailors crooned its siren song above, and a minstrel with a golden voice wanted Will to sleep guard beside him. Who was a well-sozzled Guilhem to refuse?

MAYBE SIR WILLIAM declared himself uninterested in her posterior, but Azalais still felt distinctly self-conscious as she mounted the steps to the dormitory. The knight followed behind her. They both held tallow candles, and his was probably illuminating a fine view of her derriere. Admittedly, she had not made a study of male backsides, but surely hers departed from them in curve and sway?

She entered the dark and sailor-smelling dormitory above. Armpit and second-hand ale were only the more fragrant notes in its bouquet. Azalais shuffled along the bare boards to their respective pallets. They were set far too close together. At least on the ship, she'd been able to curl up in a corner away from wherever her companion chose to sleep. Not tonight. The innkeeper intended to make as much money from his prime establishment as possible—each pallet lay at most an arm's length from the next.

I have no taste for men. What was she to make of that state-ment? She supposed she ought to be grateful, but instead, she was confused. One implication was that his taste inclined toward women. That was good, wasn't it—so long as he thought she wasn't one. But how long could she hide it from him? Perhaps she would give herself away in her sleep. When the light of morning crept over her sleeping face, would Will wake to find himself facing a woman? What then?

The worst of it was—a tiny part of her welcomed the thought. By heaven, was she mad? Oh, she knew from where that madness emanated.

She crouched down by what passed for a bed and poked at it. She'd managed to avoid fleas on the ship by some miracle, but she didn't have high hopes for this hostelry.

"Make the most of sleeping quarters that don't move to-night," a voice murmured behind her. "Tomorrow we shall sleep on a bed bound for Bordeaux."

"I'm not so sure this bed doesn't move," Azalais retorted in a whisper, prodding the pallet again. Observing it closely in the candlelight. Then his words sank in. "What, have you found us a ship? Without consulting me?"

"You were too busy bathing yourself this afternoon, O Alain. I wandered off and found us a ship instead. Or at least I assume you were bathing in there, but given the length of time you spent …"

He never bothered to finish the sentence but laughed low instead.

So, this William not only thought her a youth, but one pos-sessed of precocious appetites? She didn't know whether to laugh or be outraged. But she *had* seen a quantity of rather scantily clad women arrayed about the bathhouse. It had prompted her to bar herself against all comers in an expensive but blessedly private cubicle. She had no desire to pay for extra services, male or female. Besides, she'd needed to wash her clothes.

A crunch of straw as her companion arrayed himself on the pallet adjacent. She did not turn to look at him. She wasn't sure she could keep her expression under control. It was not the ale—she'd drunk no more than one beaker of the stuff. Nor was she particularly put out about his finding a ship.

"You've purchased us a passage to Bordeaux? We leave to-morrow?"

"Tomorrow, O Alain. And straight to Bordeaux. No bobbing in and out of every harbor on the way. Prince Edward demands supplies for his campaign, and the man's not known for his patience."

Straight to France and minstrelsy for good and earnest. Trav-eling in intimate company with this performer. Her stomach contracted.

"There's room for me in the hold?"

"Some. The ship's well-laden, the master says. Our prince

requires prodigious resupplying in order to devastate Spain. But knowing your predilection for staying out of sight, I did inquire. There is room enough."

"Thank you," she whispered. "Good night, Guilhem."

She puffed out her candle and lay down fully dressed. There were rustlings behind her as her companion removed various items of clothing, but she kept her back firmly turned. She stared into the gloom and tried to ignore the man behind her.

She was positive she wouldn't sleep. It wasn't just the quantity of strange men sprawled about her sleeping quarters. She held tight to the notion that Will's presence would keep them at bay. No, her innards were in a state of turmoil for other reasons, too. Part of it was elation.

She had passed her first test as a minstrel. *She could do this.* And somehow Guilhem still thought she was a man. Those two items were astounding enough, but what really startled her was this—it was Alain who had had to fend off female attention, not Guilhem the Minstrel. Were all the women in the tavern blind and deaf? The men, too? Even she, Azalais the would-be nun, had felt it. His presence.

The smooth, dark honey of his voice. The way his music tingled inside her, melting inhibitions like ice in the midday sun and stirring all kinds of wayward, irrational sensations inside. Now she knew why the Church preached against minstrels. This particular one was sensuality incarnate. When he performed, his hands, his body, his eyes all urged one to throw restraint to the wind, to dissolve with his music. With him.

Oh, he wove a dangerous magic with his voice and fingers, this man who lay so close beside her. And that way lay madness. Utter ruin.

A hand landed on her shoulder. Azalais jumped. By God, she very nearly screamed.

A chuckle. The hand gave a light squeeze and removed itself.

"Sleep safely, my minstrel boy. And trust me when I say you did well tonight."

Chapter Five

A SHADOW SHIFTED at the corner of sight. Azalais's fingers stilled on the lute strings. She glanced up, casually, and let her gaze wander the hold.

She'd thought she was alone down here, aside from the rats and innumerable barrels and bales of army supplies. Apparently, arrows for the renowned English longbows were transported in barrels.

Azalais had quizzed her companion on the contents of the ship's hold. Sir William had fought in France, she knew, and she was curious. But he was surprisingly tight-lipped about such matters—surprising because her brother's men were ever ready to flap their jaws about military matters. Robert's, that was. Not Benedict's men, of course. He only had nuns.

But no, she saw nothing out of the ordinary. Not that one could see much in the hold, what with the lack of light and the tightly packed cargo. Probably the constant rocking of the ship had shaken some item or other loose. She was just nervous.

For William—was absent. He was off to glean what information he could from the captain, he'd told her. The situation in France was constantly changing, and this captain was a Gascon. He would know more about his homeland than Sir William, who had not trodden French soil for over a year. Guilhem the Minstrel would play for the captain while he dined and then discuss matters French with him over a cup of good Gascon wine. She had declined to join them. She would have had to remove her hood.

So Azalais turned attention to her lute again. Guilhem had suggested she try coaxing more volume from the instrument. True, a minstrel needed to be heard, but there was a fine balance to strike between noise and sweetness of tone. She was experimenting with different finger placements in his absence. She inclined her ear to the instrument and began to pluck the strings again. Louder.

Perhaps that was why she didn't hear the man approach.

A figure settled against the bale in front of her. Azalais's fingers froze.

"Don't cease your strumming for me, minstrel," he said.

She took a deep breath and tried to calm her hammering heart.

"Oh, it's you," she said.

He was one of their musical admirers—a familiar face down here in the hold, at least as far as she could see his face. When the cog's sailors were off duty, they often sifted down here to lounge upon bales and listen to her and Guilhem play. She didn't mind, or at least not when Guilhem was present. After all, she must accustom herself to performing before an audience. She had even sung for them.

This one had frequented the hold more than most. She recognized him by his balding pate and his habit of relieving himself of itches in sundry private places. Like now, when he scratched his groin.

"I was only refining my plucking technique, good sailor. Nothing worth listening to."

She laid aside her lute and then stood to retrieve its leather casing. If she ceased to play, then perhaps he would leave. She had been cornered by strange men before and had no wish to repeat the experience. Her fingers quivered.

"Sing for me then, songster."

Azalais turned. "Come back when my companion is here, sir. There will be music aplenty later. Not now."

The fellow smiled. "Your man's playing for the captain. I heard him. He'll be up there a good while yet."

Why had she not gone with Guilhem? The risk of discovery before the captain suddenly seemed an unimportant matter. Azalais's breath turned shallow. Maybe this fellow was only a harmless lover of music. Or maybe he wasn't. Her fingers crept to her belt, and the dagger it held.

"I am sorry to disappoint you, sir," she said. "But you will have to come back later. Even a minstrel cannot play all day."

She let her hand rest upon her dagger more obviously, hoping he caught the movement and read its message.

"A minstrel has other ways of earning coin than playing." The fellow patted a purse at his waist. It gave a metallic jangle. Then the hand slipped lower and gave his nether regions a leisurely scratch. "Give your fingers a break, lad. While your minder's singing ditties to the captain, how about you earn some coin for yourself? I'm a generous man."

There were strange pins and needles invading her legs. Oh, she knew minstrelsy wasn't a respected profession, but *this*?

"Sir." She tried to keep her voice steady. "I thank you for your kind offer, but I regret I must decline." She gripped the dagger's hilt openly now. "You have mistaken my trade."

The fellow shook his head. Scratched again, as if in bemusement.

"Reject me, eh?" *Scratch.* "I make you a decent offer. Besides, I reckon you take it up the arse regular enough without coin."

He took a step toward her.

"Sir! I am armed, and my companion will be most displeased if I am...am maltreated. We are paying guests on this ship. Do not attempt anything unwise, I beg you."

"Guests, be buggered. You're minstrel scum, the both of you. I'll do you good and quick, and you won't squeak of it to your minder-man neither, or you'll find yourself nudged overboard one of these dark nights. So just you put away that knife, and maybe I'll pay you after all."

O, God, not again. Not again! She'd thought men only behaved this way toward women. But this one called her "lad." Heaven save her, he wouldn't think her a lad much longer unless she could stop him. She pulled out her dagger. Light licked over its blade as the weapon quivered in her grip.

"Get out," she hissed. "Or I will use this. Do you want to be gelded?"

"Put it away, minstrel. You'll only get hurt. Just take the coin for Chrissake and bend over."

He took another step toward her and raised his hand.

"*Guilhem!*" she bellowed and darted sideways. She put a barrel between herself and the creature and leveled her dagger at him. "*Guilhem, get down here!*"

The sailor lunged, but she kept the barrel between them. He tried a grab over the top of it, but she swayed out of reach. Another grab, and she jabbed her blade at him. It struck his hand and he yelped.

"*Guilhem!*"

"By God, I'll give you such a plugging as you never felt before, you little turd. I'll have you walking crooked for a month." The fellow was most definitely not smiling now.

A few more dance steps around the barrel, and still no Guilhem. *He couldn't hear her.* He was playing or singing, and the ship was droning out its endless complaint. She had to sort this out for herself.

But how? This lout was bigger and stronger than her, and even if she got lucky with her dagger, killing a sailor would likely get her strung up herself. Perhaps she should just do as he said and bend over.

O, God, no. The very thought... The memories washed over her like a physical force. They rooted her to the spot for one horrible instant. A moment too long. The fellow had lunged again. He caught hold of her arm. She stared at the weather-beaten fingers on her tunic sleeve, seeing another hand entirely. Her legs had turned shuddering and boneless.

The hand gripped tighter. It tugged her forward, and she reacted.

He had hold of her left arm, thank heaven. Her dagger was still in her right. She jabbed it down.

It hit flesh. There was a howl. The arm was jerked away, and her dagger nearly flew with it. She managed to close her fingers around its hilt in time. The sailor was gripping his arm, but he did not seem inclined to retreat.

Then came the sound of polite clapping.

What?

Azalais's head jerked up, her hood slipped back. And there was Guilhem leaning against a bale, clapping.

"Good strike," he said. "But pray don't let me distract you. Oh, and do keep your eye on your opponent, Alain."

At which point the sailor grabbed her about the waist.

All thought vanished. Azalais transformed into a kicking, scratching, stabbing fury. Her dagger bit backward. After one strike that certainly sank into flesh, the fellow dropped her and staggered back. Azalais whirled on him, dagger leveled.

"Leave!" she barked at him.

The balding man bared his teeth first at her, then at their lounging audience of one.

"I offered coin," he snarled at Guilhem.

"And by my friend's reaction, I gather your offer was rejected," came the mild answer. "Do not force a bargain where none is wanted."

"Greedy bastard, you want him all for yourself, eh?"

"Not in the least, good fellow. You mistake my proclivities. Now, unless you wish to afford my companion more blade practice, I suggest you depart. Now."

WILL CONTINUED TO lounge against the bale, eyeing the sailor with what he hoped was calm assurance. Alain continued to level his dagger in the fellow's direction—if "level" was an apt term for such a shuddering grip. The youth looked distinctly unimpressed by the sailor's advances. With his hood back, Alain's features seemed somehow different than Will recalled—younger maybe, or perhaps just transformed by fright. Praise heaven Will had heard Alain cry his name. Or had he just felt it? The captain had certainly looked startled when his minstrel stopped mid-bow stroke, mid-stanza. Apparently, the boat master had heard nothing amiss. Will hadn't stopped to explain. He had just bolted.

And found this.

The balding beast evidently had an itch he had a strong desire to scratch. The bulge beneath his belt had subsided since Will had announced his presence—not that Sir William of Fauconberg was in the habit of examining other men's crotches—but the fellow's pride wouldn't be so quickly deflated. Will would prefer to dissuade the lout with a few punches rather than have Alain perforate him more permanently. His companion's minstrel career would be over before it began should the latter occur. Of course, Will would also prefer not to endanger his vielle fingers, but the sailor was lingering with a bullish obduracy that did not bode well.

Then a bell clanged overhead.

The sailor twitched. He looked from one to the other, mut-tered a few choice expletives, and then declared: "Change of watch. I'll go where I'm wanted. Wasted enough time down here with minstrel scum."

And stumped up to the hatch and out.

Will drew a long-overdue breath.

Alain wrenched up his hood one-handedly and swung upon Will. "Why in Christ's name didn't you help me, Guilhem?"

The youth's voice was higher pitched than usual and distinct-ly wobbly.

"I thought I did," Will replied mildly. Then seeing Alain's

brows rise, he added, "It's bad form to interrupt another's fight. You were doing well enough. Although," he mused, "whoever taught you to hold a knife needs gutting with it. I'll have to remedy that sometime. Not the gutting—" He smiled. "Your dagger technique, I mean."

Alain did not seem inclined to put the weapon in question away. It continued to quiver in his hand.

Will stepped toward him, but the young man stiffened. "Shh, it is over now, Alain. Stand down," murmured Will, placing a hand upon the lad's white-knuckled fist. The hand jolted beneath his. Its trembling quivered up Will's arm.

"You have had man-trouble in the past, I see." Will did not pause for confirmation. He knew he was unlikely to get it. "But rest assured you are safe from me, my minstrel." He tried a grin. "I love you for your heavenly music, Alain, not your beautiful bum."

He could not see his companion's expression. He only felt the fist tense under his. So much for humor diffusing a situation. A complex fellow, evidently.

Alain drew a ragged breath, and Will was startled by an urge to draw the youth into his arms and to hold him there until he ceased trembling. Perhaps he would have if he wasn't certain Alain would misinterpret the gesture.

"Why do men do this?" A quiet, quivering voice. "Am I never to be safe?"

Ah, he had been right not to embrace him. Will lifted his hand from Alain's for good measure. It seemed words must do what touch could not.

"Not all men, Alain. You are safe with me. I will not handle you in that manner, I swear to you."

The dagger was lowered. Slowly.

"I'd give that blade a clean before you sheathe it," Will murmured. "Sea air's bad enough for steel, but blood has a powerful rusting effect. I trust you did not hurt our friend too much?"

Something between a snort and a sob answered him. "I did

not, more's the pity." A pause. "So how do I clean this thing, Guilhem? *And* sharpen it? It jagged on his clothing. When I stab a man, I want to pierce him straight through. And I will take you up on your offer to refine my technique. When will we—?"

"Shh, my warrior. Let us confine your bloodthirsty urges to dry land. I do not fancy directing your stabs while the floor beneath us heaves like a fishwife's breast. Wait until France and, in the interim, let us murder some music instead. Perhaps the *Chanson de Roland* will suit your mood?"

Chapter Six

BORDEAUX, AT LAST.

Azalais was on deck, leaning over the gunwale, hood clutched tight under her chin. The wind was not quite so blasting since they swapped the sea for the River Garonne, but she was taking no chances. The less of her on view, the safer she felt.

The low banks slipped by, and the signs of habitation increased: rubbish on the wide, slow river; fishermen and ferrymen in small, bobbing boats; and, growing ever larger, the walls of Bordeaux dominating the river lands. The chief city of Gascony and the core of English control in France. The voyage was nearly over.

"Does it meet expectations, my minstrel?"

Azalais jumped. She knew he was up on deck, too—she wasn't sure she'd have ventured up here without him, not being keen to learn swimming courtesy of a rejected sailor. Or worse. But she hadn't seen the knight approach. One of the disadvantages of being muffled in a hood.

"It is nothing like Yorkshire," was all she could think to answer.

Guilhem chuckled. "I should hope not. The wine would taste a deal less sweet if it were."

"What do we do once we're on shore?"

"We find ourselves an inn for the night, then acquire ourselves some nags and head east. Is that not the plan?"

"Horses?" Azalais frowned at the approaching city. "Do minstrels ride?"

"Not horses, O Alain. *Nags.* Nothing too fancy for penniless itinerants. In fact, the more mange-ridden said nags are, the better. Besides, the Prince's army probably stripped Bordeaux of all half-serviceable steeds when it left for Castile. But ride we must. As I recall, your father is held captive many days' travel inland. Should we linger too long, our dear countrymen may return from ravaging Spain and complicate matters for us."

Complicate. Yes, she could do without complications. Azalais's nerves were strung tightly enough already with the constant need to hide her gender. The linen band flattening her too-feminine chest chafed and was rank from days of wearing. During the voyage, she'd relieved herself over a pot in the darkest corner of the hold, and her monthly bleeding had been a nightmare in management. Now, she was about to leave the dark haven of the ship's hold and travel in broad daylight with this knightly minstrel.

Who swore he would not touch her. No, *him.* It was Alain who was safe from Sir William de Fauconberg, not Lady Azalais. She knew how warriors treated women. Even would-be warriors like her brother Robert.

But William had given his word to Benedict, too. Ben had told her. Would that be enough to protect her?

The cog bumped up against the dock, was made fast against the tug of the current, and a plank run to shore. Time to leave the dubious safety of the supply ship to Bordeaux. Not daring to look at Guilhem, Azalais secured her lute across her back, picked up her bag, and wobbled down the gangplank for her first step onto French soil. One step closer to her father and the man-free haven of a nunnery.

THEY HAD BARELY left the harbor before she heard the music. It was music that was *designed* to be heard—a single, piercing pipe accompanied by drumming. Guilhem paused, too. They both turned, and Azalais nearly smiled. They were like two hounds scenting a hare—musicians hungry for music.

"Shall we?" Guilhem said.

She did not ask for clarification, simply nodded. Then followed as Guilhem swerved left along the cobbled thoroughfare.

It was a lone minstrel, and by some sorcery, he was playing two instruments at once. Azalais halted mid-street and stared. The fellow sat on his cloak on the cobbles, back against the city wall. He wielded a small pipe with his right hand, while his left was busy with the drum on his lap. The fingers on the pipe flickered like dragonflies over a pond, leaving a trail of notes in its wake that a bird might envy. His left hand beat an intricate rhythm. After some moments of fascinated observation, Azalais registered the piper's odd posture. One leg was bent in a V before him, while the second stuck straight out, its hose knotted off at the knee. There was no calf, ankle, or foot for the hose to cover.

"Haven't you seen a man play a pipe and tabor before?" Guilhem murmured. There was a smile in his voice.

"He must be two men in one to play such instruments together," she said in frank admiration.

"No more than you or I when we play and sing simultaneously. But he has some skill, does he not?" A pause. "I would guess he was a soldier once. But no longer."

She heard an odd twist to his voice and glanced up. But Guilhem was already moving away from her. He had a coin out and was approaching the piper.

The fellow halted at the end of a stanza and glanced up expectantly. Guilhem crouched down beside him, handed him the silver, and started speaking. Azalais could not catch the words. Something about Guilhem's last comment held her back from the pair.

The conversation continued, her companion evidently asking

questions. The piper lifted his drumming hand to point. Guilhem discovered another coin in his purse. It changed owners and the knight rose.

"Come."

Then Azalais had to scuttle to keep up with Guilhem's sudden pace. It was as well the streets of Bordeaux were thinly populated, or she might have lost him altogether.

He paused at a junction of two streets to consider.

"Guilhem, wait!"

He turned to her, brow raised. The sparkle of wickedness that usually lit his features was absent.

"Walk slower, I beg you. My legs…the ground…they do not seem to understand each other."

"Ah." A flicker of a smile. "My apologies, O minstrel. I had forgotten you were but fresh off a boat. Your sea legs have not left you yet—" He broke off, staring above her head.

Then she understood. Legs. She had never considered before how fortunate she was to possess two.

"Did he lose his in battle?" she asked softly.

Guilhem stiffened. For a moment, she thought he would not reply.

Then, "I did not ask. Almost certainly so. Yes, I have seen that happen, and worse."

Azalais was struck by an urge to put an arm around him, this man whose knightly role it was to kill or at very least mutilate such men as they had just met.

But Guilhem had already turned and began striding up his chosen street. At a more reasonable pace, praise heaven. And Azalais hurried after him.

➤➤➤◄◄◄

THEY HALTED BEFORE an imposing building midway along the street. It was built entirely of stone of a beautiful, pale gold hue, evidently the abode of someone with more wealth than was good for their eternal soul.

"Whose house is this, Guilhem?" she demanded. "Why are we here?"

He turned to her with something like his old expression. That laughing look that crinkled the corners of his eyes, flared his brows, and spoke of untold depths of mischief. Azalais's gaze diverted to the cobbles.

"This, my innocent, is one of the finest houses of accommodation in all Bordeaux. I would hesitate to name it a mere hostelry or inn. Be of good cheer, for tonight we shall take our rest on feather beds and dine upon the finest Bordeaux wines and beef."

Her gaze flicked back to him, just for an instant. He was watching her, and it was broad daylight. Worse, her face and body seemed inclined to disobey strict instructions to react to him in but a neutral manner. It was his performative power, she knew. She couldn't help but react. Guilhem knew just how to draw his audience out, to make them *feel*, to magnetize them with his presence. She had seen it in London, even in their occasional sailor on board the ship. And Azalais was his most constant audience. She was not immune, but at least in the dark hold, it could be concealed.

"Surely this is no place for the likes of us then, minstrel scum that we are?" she bit back.

"Ah, that rankles, doesn't it?" A hand was laid on her shoulder. Azalais tensed. "He had it wrong, that sailor. That slug from the salty depths. Believe me, Alain, he was a bitter man, for he aimed to pluck a star from the heavens and failed. We are no minstrel scum. We are artists of love. We are poets of pleasure. We are troubadours come into our own in the land of the *langue d'oc*. And tonight, we will play before the most discerning ears Bordeaux has to offer."

Her face, even angled away, must have sketched a picture of incredulity, for the knight chuckled.

"Or something like that, at least. My friend with the pipe advised me that Bordeaux charges minstrels a princely twelve pence for the liberty to perform on its streets. I do not fancy relieving my purse of so much for a mere day's sojourn, especially as most of Bordeaux's knights and associated rabblery are now south of the Pyrenees. Yet my fingers itch for music, Alain. *Real* music. The piper suggested we try our luck in an establishment catering to merchants and minor nobles. Their population here is not so diminished." He swept a hand toward the imposing edifice. "Thus, our lodgings for tonight. I hope."

Azalais looked down at her clothing. She saw a tunic and hose in dull browns, complete with saltwater staining and other varieties of grime less mentionable. The ocean had at times been rough, particularly on her stomach. She doubted she would be permitted to so much as set foot inside this elegant building, let alone perform before its clientele. And then there was her hood. Certainly, it was no fur-lined item of fashion. She only prayed that, if by some slip in judgment on the proprietor's behalf they did entertain this house tonight, she could find a dark corner to play in. A very dark corner.

AH, THIS WAS more like it. Will strolled into what in any normal establishment one would call its taproom. This "taproom" was rendered positively opulent by a hearth fire *sans* choking quantities of smoke, thanks to that novelty of architecture, the chimney. It served wine instead of endless English ale, and the rich scent of grapes seemed to emanate from the very beams.

Its trestles were covered with white linen, and the people who took their ease about them were dressed in a manner that would have seen them knifed and stripped at the dockside den Guilhem had last played.

This evening they would play courtly love songs—no, *canzos* now he was in France—for the delectation of this well-heeled crowd. At least, they would if Alain deigned to show his beardless face.

The youth had been more reluctant even than in London to sing for his supper.

Will muttered a choice blasphemy. He did *not* want to play alone tonight. He wanted his companion with the magical fingers and golden voice but said companion had offered up a barrage of excuses why he simply could not do so. What the hell was his problem? Will had assured Alain that he had a voice to make the seraphim jealous. Besides, he had added, their proprietor had agreed—after some persuasion—to hosting *two* fine troubadours, not one. They might find themselves on the street should they not deliver. Finally, when Will had solved Alain's latest objection by offering up his best tunic to render the lad presentable, Alain had conceded—but only if Will left for the taproom directly. Alain swore he would follow forthwith, appropriately clad.

Yet now Will was halfway down his second cup of wine.

When Benedict had first proposed he take on this task, Will's chief fear had been that Alain couldn't play. His first doubts had been dispelled by the young man's performance at the nunnery. Then he began to worry whether the fellow could sing. Perhaps he could not hold a tune, or his voice was still breaking and he would perform a *canzo* half in soprano, half in bass. Why else would he refuse to sing in the graveyard?

A fresh thought struck him. Will sipped his wine and eyed the door, awaiting the appearance of a slight figure with a lute tucked under its arm. The door remained empty. Will frowned, trying to recall when his own voice had evicted him from York Minster's choir stalls. Surely Alain was old enough that his Adam's apple would have put paid to his angelic tones? He was tall enough, yet no trace of hair dusted his upper lip. Christ, was the fellow a eunuch? It might explain some of his evident run-ins with men.

Will choked on a mouthful of wine. It was dark and tannin-rich and much more flavorful than he was used to. It occupied his throat with a vengeance.

A hand whacked him on the back. Three times.

"You want me to do *all* the singing, Guilhem? Leave off the red juice. You will croak like a crow if you keep this up."

A broad smile took possession of Will's face. He choked a couple more times and then subsided.

"All part of the plan, my tardy minstrel." Cough. "Christ, do you think this fine establishment will sink so low as to provide me some water?"

Alain padded off in search of the low liquid, and Will focused upon swallowing for some moments. By the time Alain returned, Will was at least partially in control of his senses. But only partially. Will blinked twice. His eyes were watering, and he wasn't sure they properly registered the apparition approaching. Had Alain sent a barmaid in his stead? The firelight shimmered upon loose curls of a golden brown. The belt about the apparition's waist outlined distinctly feminine curves beneath.

Beneath *his* tunic. The one William had loaned Alain that he might cut a suitably dashing figure before this audience.

Will blinked again.

"Here. Have some water. Let's hope it will not turn your innards likewise to water. I've seen what they toss in the Garonne around here."

It was most definitely not a barmaid. Alain edged into the comparative shadows by the wall, dipping his head, and Will gripped the mug and attempted to arrange his thoughts.

Eunuch or just a rather pretty young man? No wonder Benedict had been so insistent on protecting him. And he had forced Alain to reveal his charms down here for all to see. Well, the least he could do now was to allow him to linger in the shadows.

He raised his mug to his companion. "If I partake of the mighty Garonne, then I doubt we'll travel any farther than Bordeaux." He took a long draught and considered. "Tastes like well water to me. *Sans* an infusion of turd, as I hope. So, shall we play?"

THEY PLAYED. BY God, did they play. Will was positively drunk on music. His audience was entranced and their proprietor more than pleased. But the moments that shot Will to the giddiest heights were those when he and Alain sang together. The lad's pure descant echoed Will's refrains as a bird singing with its mate, mingling and weaving between his deeper tones.

They sang songs of wild longing and unrequited love, troubadour *canzos*. And then, every now and again, they added a leavening of something more cheerful. It would not do to strike his listeners entirely into a despondency. But they ever returned to suffering lovers. Somehow his vielle yearned toward the melancholy, the unrequited, and Alain made no objection.

Will glanced sideways at his partner in music. The lad's eyes were raised slightly above audience level, seeming to gaze beyond them and into some unattainable land. His face was transfigured. Beautiful.

His vielle stuttered over a familiar phrase. Will forced himself to focus on his fingering. Alain simply carried on singing his solo, trusting his accompanist to recover.

The youth trusted him.

Will's bow sawed the strings with rather more force than necessary.

God above, what had got into him? Had the music infected him with some Bacchic madness that he was even registering Alain's beauty? He took a deep breath and centered himself on his bow, its delicate hum over the strings. Alain was a beautiful *musician*. That was all. Will most definitely had no fancy for men. It was the music seducing him. Nothing more.

William persuaded his gaze to drift out over the audience, offering a smile at those who caught his eye. Perhaps the intoxication of his companion's soaring, yet slightly husky tones reflected in Will's expression, for some among the audience smiled back, and those smiles simmered with invitation. Will did not care. *Fin'amor* flowed from his vielle strings. He would make love to one and all with his music. No, with *their* music. By God, it would be a tavern-wide orgy.

He grinned at that. The thought was something of a relief. It wasn't Alain. It was just the music.

Alain slowed a little toward the end of the last stanza, the lyrics with bittersweet finality, signaling completion. Will followed in kind, permitting his bow to draw out the last note with ever-softening poignancy as Alain bowed his head as if in prayer.

Silence. Stillness. Then a few tavern occupants clapped, softly, as if reluctant to break the spell and murmuring conversation gradually resumed.

"What next?" Will inquired of his motionless companion. "Have you the stamina for more?"

Alain raised his head, shook back soft curls, and smiled.

"Whatever I choose must wait. You have admirers, O Guilhem."

Will flicked his companion a wicked half-grin. "Of course I do, my minstrel. I am surprised they have restrained themselves thus far."

He looked around.

Two women approached, hand in hand. Ah. He recalled their faces from earlier. Gazing at him. Smiling. No, "smile" did not begin to describe their expressions.

He looked back at Alain. "Are you sure they are *my* admirers, sweet minstrel? Recall London?"

"Oh, I am sure," the youth said with a grimace. "Look sharp, Guilhem. The hounds are upon you."

At which point, the question of the next song became irrelevant. Will found himself commandeered, herded in a rustle of silk and French chatter to the fair ladies' nook of the tavern, to be seated most snug between the cooing pair, while their maids melted discretely into the background. He had time only to shrug a laughing apology to Alain and wave a hand that he play on should he desire. He was not abandoning the boy—they remained in the same room.

Besides, it was time to redirect his *fin'amor*-stirred attentions to subjects more fitting than his minstrel companion. The passing madness must be purged.

AZALAIS WATCHED HIM go, a woman attached to either arm. They had not dragged or coerced him away; Guilhem had needed no persuading. He had simply left her with a grin—and a particularly wicked one at that. He was a man, and he scented womankind. God, was he getting hard in his hose already? The image arose unprompted and far too vivid.

She swore aloud, screwing her eyes shut. Oh, she knew precisely what a man's prized possessions looked like in such a state. And, by heaven, they were ugly. Nothing but raw meat and hair. But what was uglier still was the impulse that drove them.

She must distract herself. Time for her most complex lute solo. So, she bent to the instrument and dwelt with energy upon each and every note. No lyrics this time. No words of love and longing.

She played it twice, but it was still over too soon. And as soon as Azalais lifted her head to acknowledge the scatter of applause, her gaze sought out Guilhem. Oh, he was not applauding her. He was not even aware of her existence. Instead, he was hemmed about by two sumptuously dressed women and was doubtless considering how best to sumptuously *undress* them.

Time for another performance, only this time she would sing, too. She raked her memory for some appropriate lyrics. Ah yes. And she rippled her fingers over the introductory notes of Bernart de Ventadorn's immortal *canzo*:

I despair of women; never again

Shall I have faith in them;
I mistrust and fear them all
For I know they are all alike.

And hoped it was only in her heart she altered the "women" to "men". She would prefer not to advertise herself as a girl—or as a man whose fancy might run in similar directions.

The only problem was, Bernart's bitter words could not drown out her thoughts. Indeed, they seemed to amplify them. Betrayal. That was the only word for the feeling that clenched its fist about her gut. Throughout the evening, a golden thread of connection had seemed to grow between Alain and Guilhem, *canzo* after *canzo*, stronger than on the ship or than in London, for now, they were both playing the music they loved and giving their all to the performance, attuned to each other as never before.

She had even dared to appear hoodless, exposed before this audience, for *him*. And there had been a moment—one heart-stilling moment early in the evening—when she had thought he saw her as she really was. He had gazed at her as she approached and a little frown had drawn his arching brows together, quickly chased away by…appreciation? Admiration? Whatever it was had vanished in an instant. Yet it had stolen her breath.

Because for an instant, she had *wanted* him to see her as she was.

God, what an idiot she was. The betrayal was in part her own. Guilhem was only acting as men always did. At least he was not forcing himself upon his chosen victims. Azalais suppressed a shudder and focused all her attention upon her current *canzo*, making each note ring mournful and true. Until the song ended with Bernart's declaration:

I shall renounce and give up singing,
And hide myself from joy and love.

Azalais pronounced the words with purpose, owning them—more so than Bernart himself. The troubadour had not truly meant those lines, she knew. The world would have been poorer of music if he had. She would not renounce singing, but certainly, she intended to hide away. In a convent. Wykeham Priory only awaited her father's permission. Safety. Seclusion from men.

She lifted her eyes, signaled a serving maid to bring her more wine, and then of course, her gaze slipped of its own accord to her companion's corner of the room.

And her heart stuttered.

Guilhem was standing, but not with the purpose of making his way back to her. Quite the opposite, he was departing the tavern room altogether.

He was not doing so alone.

Azalais watched as two silk-and-fur-clad women, trailed by their maids, ushered Guilhem the Minstrel out of the street door and into the night. Then the door closed on the darkness with finality.

It was some time before Azalais remembered to breathe.

Chapter Seven

T HEY RODE THROUGH sunshine and silence.

It was a troubadour's own spring day—buds were bursting, birds were caroling to their true loves, a soft breeze caressed their cheeks—and they were riding into the land of the *langue d'oc*, music's own heartland.

And Will's companion seemed impervious to all its charms. Alain had barely spoken since they left Bordeaux. Now, if Will turned in what with some exaggeration might be called a saddle, he could no longer sight that city's spires. Even its smoke had smudged into the blue distance. Will had done his best to chat cheerily, but it was like pushing a boulder uphill. After a series of monosyllabic responses, Will had mentally shrugged and turned his attention to the beauties around him. Perhaps they might inspire the lyrics for a new *canzo*?

But inspiration flitted past him like tiny birds, impossible to catch.

Something was nagging at him. It was like an itch on a toe that he couldn't scratch for the leather encasing it. He would try to draw his fellow minstrel out again. After all, they had many days of travel ahead of them. Will did not fancy plodding all that way beside a mute ghost. A precedent must be set. Besides, he missed bantering with the youth, aggravating him and teasing him out. That aside, there were a few answers regarding this odd mission of theirs Will was curious to extract from his companion.

"Tell me, Alain, now that we have traveled some miles, do you find yourself content with your choice of mount?"

The hooded head shifted minutely, seemed to study its mode of transport's tufty mane. Then the shoulders beneath the hood lifted.

"It will do."

Further silence. Unacceptable silence.

"You insult your noble steed, man. Why, I would have you wax lyrical upon its many peerless attributes." Will leaned to pat his own mount upon its shaggy shoulder, although admittedly, he had some difficulty locating said shoulder beneath the abundance of mane. "Take my fair charger, for example. It is a superlative animal. Rarely have I had more ease in mounting a horse. Why, from a standing position, all I need do is to swing a leg over its haunch and I am on. As for falling—should my trusty steed rear, I would barely bruise a buttock, let alone break my head, the distance to the ground is of so little account. Behold, my prime danger in bestriding my destrier is that I might stub my toe."

And he pointed his dangling boot in demonstration. Its tip trailed a gentle gouge in the dirt road.

That earned him the briefest of chuckles.

A pause. Then a miracle—Alain ventured a comment of his own.

"We have yet to test their paces," his companion said. "I worry that, should my pony attempt a gallop, I shall find myself as seasick as I was on the high Atlantic."

Will grinned, as much in relief that Alain saw fit to utter two full sentences as at their content. Then it struck him—the tension he had sensed between them since Bordeaux had set him on edge.

Well, that was only reasonable. They had many performances before them, and Will must travel cheek by jowl with this odd youth into some decidedly unsettled territory. His edginess was absolutely nothing to do with those moments that crept over him. When Will found his every sense attuned to his companion—absorbed by the intensity of Alain's music, the flicker of feeling across his shadowed face, the shift of his supple figure, or his soft breath in the night. Of course, such attention was only natural. It was prompted by his admiration of Alain's skill and a continuing curiosity about him. Not to mention Will's assigned role as protector.

Hmm, odd youth. That reminded him.

"Then I shall strive to ride upwind of you should you gallop, my minstrel. But I have little true concern I shall wear your breakfast. You ride well." *For a bastard*, he did not add. Poor men did not ride, not even upon shaggy ponies. How had this low-born side-shoot acquired his many accomplishments? Sir Robert must be an indulgent sire—which perhaps explained his bastard's desire to ransom him. "Tell me, Alain, however did you learn to speak French so well? It cannot be solely from singing. God knows, the language you exercised on the horse dealer never featured in any troubadour lyric."

Will grinned at the remembrance. He had learned a few choice French phrases in that exchange.

"My mother was from these parts," Alain replied.

Then the youth's shoulders tensed. Perhaps another might not have noticed it, but Will was becoming…well, disturbingly attuned to his companion.

Will considered the young man, head to one side. Alain could not see his expression, for his hood was tugged so far over his face he was in danger of riding into a tree.

"Sir Robert has a fondness for Frenchwomen, then," Will said lightly. "Ben's *mater*, too, came from this land. I recall him saying so, for the wretch always had a better grasp of the tongue than I."

That earned him no reply. Still, that was one mystery solved—if only marginally.

"You are half French, then," he went on. "It is no wonder you sing like a troubadour born. It will be a pity when your voice breaks," Will said.

And then wished he hadn't.

Now he'd shoved his riding boot well and truly down his throat. He'd been intending to avoid *that* topic at all costs. Just in case. So, he opened his trap and shoved the boot down it some more. "I mean, your voice…well, it complements mine quite delightfully, my minstrel. The high and sweet against the low and mellow, the trilling lark in concert with the crow. I have not gained such pleasure from the mingling of voices before. But tell me, how do you find your native land now you are in it? Is it as you expected?"

Will cursed himself silently and prayed that Alain would respond. This damned awkwardness between them was making him blather.

The hooded head shifted a little, seeming to take in its surroundings.

"It is very flat. I thought there would be more vines."

Will laughed. It sounded too loud to his own ears. "We ride between the rivers, Alain. This is the floodplain between the Garonne and the Dordogne. No vine likes a regular bathing. They grow summer wheat here, only, and some pasture. But fear not, you will see hills and vines in such inebriate quantities that you will sicken of them yet."

That statement was evidently considered and then—praise heaven—it was followed by a question of Alain's own.

"We follow the Garonne inland?"

"For the most part, yes. But the river winds, and it would double our distance to follow its curves too closely. Still, there are many towns along its banks. We will not want for accommodation and opportunities to play."

"English-held towns?"

Will considered the route in his mind. He had traveled much of it before, although in a different capacity.

"In theory, yes," he said. "Although their inhabitants have developed a strange aversion to the English of late, or so our boat master informed me. The prince taxed Gascony heavily to raise his army for Castile. It has not improved local feeling toward him."

"Is that why my brother insisted you accompany me? To protect me against locals?" snapped the hood. "If so, he was mistaken. As you point out, Guilhem, my French is better than yours. I could pass as a Gascon. You could not. Your *u*'s are abominably English."

Ah. That theme again. Something inside Will twisted. Even now, his minstrel wanted to leave him. What could he say? That Alain produced a most unfortunate effect upon men, himself not excluded? That it was not precisely the youth's Frenchness that caused Benedict concern?

"Do not let the peace of this road deceive you, Alain. We are still within the shadow of Bordeaux. This corner of Gascony has seen no war. It is still firmly under English control. The farther east we travel, the more ravaged the land will be. Poverty and war breed desperate men, and not all of them will have marched south to Spain. Such men will not stop to discover whether you are French before robbing you."

Or worse. No need to give Alain nightmares.

"Well then, you'd better do as you promised on the ship, Guilhem. Teach me to handle a dagger."

Will sighed most pointedly. "If you wish it, my minstrel. If you wish it. I am not saying it is the answer to all woes, mind you. But if you bear a blade, you may as well know how to skewer a man with it. But bear in mind, he is generally not so cooperative about the matter as your evening meal."

IT WAS A sun-streaked woodland glade, secluded from the road and situated east of the village of Branne. It was Azalais who had urged they enter the wood, and she had been rewarded by this semi-level clearing between the budding birches. She hobbled her pony and left it to wreak havoc on the wildflowers.

Then she slipped her dagger from its sheath with a steely whisper.

Her companion had likewise secured his mount. He patted it on its furry rump, then turned to her. Three actions followed: he raised an eyebrow at the dagger, he produced a sigh, and he ruffled back his hair.

He is such a peacock. His every action is produced as if for an audience. Such were her rational thoughts. Beneath them—and only just submerged—lingered a far-too appreciative audience of one. It wanted to ruffle that hair for itself.

"Well, we are here," she said. "Shall we begin?"

She had waited nearly two days for this. Guilhem had stubbornly refused to stop by the exposed roadside to wave daggers around. Passers-by might get the wrong idea, he claimed. Alain must contain his bloodthirsty urges until they happened upon a secluded stretch of woodland.

And now they had found the requisite landscape, and Azalais was beginning to question the wisdom of her decision.

True, she craved the ability to defend herself. In fact, she nursed a secret ambition to sever a certain man's…well, that was all in the past. It would not happen again. She raised her dagger. She would make sure it didn't happen again.

But right now, it was the thought of Guilhem focusing his attention upon her, examining her movements, even touching her. A shiver traveled up her spine. No, that must not happen.

The peacock sauntered over the flower-dotted sward toward her and said, "I see you are itching for action, my murderous minstrel. To the end that *you* are not murdered, I shall begin our lesson with two observations of invaluable value."

Guilhem slipped his own dagger from its sheath with an entirely unnecessary flourish and twirled it between his fingers. When it ceased its movement, it was pointing directly at her.

"First," the dagger pointer said. "While your current grip admittedly offers the greatest reach, Alain, it delivers little force of blow and limits your modes of attack. Let me suggest you reverse your grip, like so."

And Guilhem flipped his dagger so that the blade pointed downward from his outthrust arm. Then he made a few downward chopping motions of said arm, left and right.

"See? In this manner, the arm gains more force on the thrust." Then Guilhem smiled and reached out to pincer the muscle of her right arm between his free finger and thumb. "With pigeon wings such as yours, my lad, I suggest you maximize the mechanics of your blows."

Azalais snatched her arm away. "My *pigeon wings* are my concern, minstrel. Keep your hands to yourself."

Guilhem shrugged gracefully and withdrew. "You specified daggers, my minstrel. If you desired hands-free combat, then you should have nominated the sword. Not that you appear to have one, of course. A sword keeps an opponent at arm's length. The dagger, however, begs a body to wrestle with blades."

"What?" She tensed. *Wrestling?* "The whole idea is that I keep men from mauling me," she declared in a low voice. *Men like you,* she didn't add.

A positively evil smile lit her companion's face. "Oh, I doubt they will maul you with a hole in the chest—or the neck, or the head, or whatever body part takes your fancy. But we will come to that in good time. First, we must mend your grip—"

And he reached out and took hold of her dagger hand. Azalais turned to stone. Unfortunately, it was a decidedly sentient stone, whose sensations all concentrated upon the extremities of one limb. It had been bad enough when he tweaked her arm a moment ago through a layer of fabric. But now those warm, strong musician's fingers closed over her own naked hand. Skin on skin. He gently reversed her dagger grip. A few adjustments to her fingers, and then he released her.

"How does that feel?" he asked.

The truth was unspeakable. Azalais clenched her teeth and reminded herself that those hands had more than touched the skin of two French women back in Bordeaux. And managed a shrug.

"It will feel strange at first, but you will get used to it," he assured.

She did not think so. Nor did she intend to get used to it. She had evidently not thought through her ambition to perforate too-tenacious men. It involved unforeseen contact with the worst threat of all.

He was watching her—or at least he was trying to. She kept her hooded face averted and made a show of wriggling her fingers on the hilt and assaying a few stabs in imitation of his.

A moment later, her hood was tweaked back. Soft spring air cooled her neck and stirred her hair. Azalais squeaked in outrage and instinctively brought her dagger hand down, straight at Guilhem's too-near chest.

It was batted aside with seeming negligence. Her fingers loosened, and the dagger hit the turf with a thud.

A sigh. "I think we had better replace your blade with an appropriate-length stick for now, Alain."

Azalais crouched to retrieve her dagger, taking care to turn her back upon her tutor-in-weapons.

"My second observation was going to be: you should remove your hood. But perhaps that ought to be my third," said the voice behind her. "I would also have you bear in mind, Alain, that it is inadvisable to turn your back on an opponent."

A soft step behind her, and a length of cold metal laid itself against her throat.

The flat of a blade.

The chill of it seemed to enter her very blood.

"I did not know you were my opponent," she whispered, moving her throat as minimally as possible.

But, of course, he was her opponent. He had always been. He was a man. He preyed upon women just as every other man did, witness Bordeaux. He used them for his pleasure and then discarded them.

The sliver of steel removed itself.

"Stay watchful, Alain. You do not always know who your opponent is. Do not blinker yourself with your hood—and most certainly do not turn your back."

She snatched up her dagger and whirled about, rising as she did so. She had her blade in the prescribed grip and her teeth were bared. She drove the dagger down in the manner he had just demonstrated. At him.

"Tsk."

This time her arm was batted aside, one of her legs was hooked out from under her, and his left hand planted itself on her chest and shoved. Lightly, it was true. But Sir William still laid his palm on her bound chest and pushed.

Azalais tumbled back and lay still.

It wasn't the soft sod that knocked the breath out of her.

She stared up at him.

It was the look on his face.

"TAKE YOUR TUNIC off," he barked.

Alain stared up at him, eyes huge in his too-delicate face.

"No," Alain whispered.

Will found he was breathing hard. A jagged feeling prickled his fingertips, spiked up his arms—the feeling that always appeared in the aftermath of a close fight. The world beneath his feet was shifting.

He wanted it solid again.

"Take it off!"

Silence.

Then a small, small voice: "Why?"

That voice told him nearly everything he needed to know. It quivered, but it did not break. It would never break.

"I could force you, Alain. You know that." A pause. "But I will not."

A shudder ran through the youth's frame.

"So, *tell* me instead," Will demanded. "What would I see if I lifted your tunic?"

"Linen," whispered the boy.

"Why? Are you cold? Must you wear a tunic beneath your tunic?" Will knew he was clutching at straws. But anything—*anything*—was better than what he suspected. His dream was crumbling by the heartbeat. Then a slightly more solid concept occurred. He seized upon it. "Do you wear your valuables bound to your body? Is that how you hide the ransom?"

But it had not felt like hard-edged metal or gems.

Something flickered upon Alain's face. He wanted to agree, Will realized. But would it be the truth? It could be. After all, it was only wisdom to keep the location of a small fortune a secret. Even from one's trusted traveling companion.

"I wanted to tell you before now, Guilhem," the small voice managed.

"Tell me what?" Will fought to keep his voice soft, reassuring. He sank down before Alain—but not too close. "I will not steal from you, I swear it. Your ransom is safe from me."

Just tell me.

For Alain's face was transforming before his eyes. That pointed chin would never wear whiskers. The smooth, pale neck was unmarred by any Adam's apple. Nor would it be. Will had never looked upon his companion's face so closely in daylight. *No, it couldn't be.* Alain had just bound the ransom by much linen to his skinny torso. That was all Will had felt.

"It is not the ransom, Guilhem." Amber eyes held his. They were fringed with brown lashes. Quite beautiful eyes, like pools of honey.

Oh, Christ.

"I think you know what I hide already, Sir Knight. And it need not change anything. After all, you swore a solemn oath to my brother, and my father still needs ransoming." The amber eyes had hardened. Their owner rose to a crouch as if readying for a fight. "Well, knight… what do you say?"

Will's thoughts were twigs in a torrent. What could he say? The only words that came to him were quite preposterous. They could not be true. Pray God they weren't true. He said them anyway.

"I think," Will said slowly, and the words seemed pulled out of him like a rotten tooth. "I think that your name is not Alain, O Alain. I think it is A…"

The name escaped him.

"The name you are looking for is Azalais," she said. "Azalais de Keldy."

✦

Chapter Eight

"**I** WILL NOT go back," she said. "You cannot send me back."

Actually, he probably could.

Azalais's heart was pounding in her ears. She stood abruptly, took a couple of steps back. The knight rose more slowly. Azalais fumbled for her dagger, to realize it still lay in the grass, out of reach. Not that it would make much difference even if she could reach it, given recent evidence. All she could do was wait for his reaction. There was no reading his expression. Guilhem's face was quite blank. The arched black brows did not quirk with sly amusement. And those dark, all-seeing eyes were fixed upon her face.

Seeing it for the first time.

"You are not a bastard," he said, voice flat.

"I would prefer to be a bastard. And a man." It was true. And then—because he still had not moved or burst out in angry accusation—she added, "I would prefer you to continue as if I am one."

"But you are *not* a man, Azalais de Keldy. *Lady* Azalais, if I am not mistaken. What in hell was your brother thinking?"

"He trusted you, Sir William. He made you swear. Was he wrong?"

She had told Benedict why she must flee. She had told him everything—every awful detail—anything to convince him to help her. To persuade him not to send her straight back to Robert. She had told him all that, and still, Benedict decreed she must travel with this knight. A knight, of all loathsome creatures! Now the test had come. Was Benedict wrong?

"*Of course, he was wrong,* you… O, God, I cannot even call you a minstrel anymore. He was most heinously wrong to set you loose in France on a fool's errand and in men's clothes. And with me!"

"I would have gone anyway. Alone. The only part Benedict had in the plan was to enlist you. He did so against my will. So, leave me, knight, if I offend you. You have got me thus far, and for that, I am grateful." Her voice trailed off.

It struck her then that she did not want him to leave, even now. Poor, deluded fool that she was. It was the music, of course, the unutterable joy of joining musical souls with another. Well, doubtless she could find that in the nunnery, too. She was far safer leaving him now. Now he knew her for Azalais.

"I cannot leave you. I swore to keep you safe."

"Well then, let us continue as we were, Guilhem. I am your minstrel companion."

"Impossible," he snapped. "O God, *why did you do this to me?*" Then, as if that divinity had abruptly cut the strings that held him upright, Guilhem collapsed upon the turf, a loose collection of limbs. His head was in his hands, his hair turned into wild tufts.

Azalais seized the moment to reclaim her dagger, half-hidden in the grass. She stared at the blade a moment, watching it quiver in her hand. Then she looked at Guilhem. He seemed not to notice.

She wiped the blade dry on her tunic. Then she adjusted her grip as he'd shown her, tried a few feints again.

"You can put that away," he said, voice muffled. "I am not going to attack you."

She considered the blade, reluctant to obey, even if out of principle. Still, not much chance she'd have of fighting him off with it, given recent performances. So, she slipped it back in its sheath.

"So, what *are* you going to do?" she asked.

THEY RODE. HE must think.

They descended the small track out of the woods and when—all too soon—they reached the road that shadowed the Garonne, he reined in.

"Why do you hesitate, Guilhem?" came the soft voice behind him. "Our route is to the east."

"The further east we go, the greater the danger to you."

"Yes, but my father is to the east."

"Your father," he muttered. And stared at the road. He was beginning to realize where his duty lay.

She began to edge her pony around his. He flung out a hand and seized the animal's rein. He and the goddamned girl were brought practically knee to knee.

"Wait," he snapped. Her knee shifted minutely away from his. Christ, he couldn't think. East or west? What was he to do with this…this *female*?

"Let us at least travel east to the next town, Guilhem. We can discuss matters further there—if you wish." Said quietly and carefully, yet he heard—or was it only felt?—the tremor beneath her words.

That tremor decided him.

A deep breath.

"Until the next town then."

They rode east.

THEY REACHED LA Réole some hours later. It was a town of reasonable size and boasted a half-reasonable inn, and Will flung himself off his mount and strode to its door, trailed by a silent Alain. No, *Azalais*.

"A private bedchamber, if you please," he demanded of the aproned woman who met him inside. "No, *two* private chambers."

The woman's brows contracted. Then one of them rose as their buxom owner surveyed the beings that demanded these costly private chambers of her. Doubtless, she beheld two disreputable minstrels, and one a mere youth. Will cursed under his breath. If he had been accoutred as a knight, the woman would not hesitate. But then, if he had appeared as a knight accompanied by a young man, then he would have only requested one chamber. A knight slept with his squire in attendance. He did not dish out silver that said squire might recline in his own private bower.

He would have to get this damnable Lady Azalais appropriate lady clothes just to prove she was one. Oh, and then scrape up a lady's maid for her, too, so that her honor might not be compromised. Had her bloody brother taken leave of his senses?

"I have but one private chamber, messieurs," their innkeeper announced, and cited a most unhealthy sum for the use thereof.

Will winced. And then he swore. *One* bedchamber? God, that was worse than none at all. Better to sleep in a common dormitory rather than bed down alone with a highborn damsel.

"Is there another inn in this town?" he demanded.

The innkeeper shook her head, setting her dark curls quivering in the process.

Will's head was set to burst.

A tug on his sleeve. *Her* hand—that too-delicate-for-any-man's hand—had his tunic between finger and thumb and was steering him away from their hostess. Toward the open door.

"Excuse us, madame," the high-born-lady-dressed-as-a-boy said. "My companion and I must discuss matters between us. There seems to be some misunderstanding. Give us a moment, if you please."

The aproned-one lifted her hands in a manner most French did and turned back to her more comprehensible customers. And Will permitted himself to be led out the door.

"WHY DO WE not perform for our lodgings, Guilhem?"

They were by the ponies again. One of them had relieved itself on the cobbles, and the aroma was the perfect complement to Will's mood.

"We can be minstrels for one more night, can we not?" Her voice was not exactly coaxing. He tried to focus. What was it—persuasive? Yes, but something more. There was real feeling to it, he realized. With infinite reluctance, he looked at her. He'd been avoiding doing that. To look at her—*her*—was to face the dissolution of a dream, one he'd dared to nurture this last handful of days.

She was watching him, her hooded head lifted to his. The waxed fabric of that hood slipped back over her hair and for once she did not tug it back. She was not hiding from him anymore. Amber eyes met his. He registered a delicate, slightly uptilted nose beneath, and then those lips. But it wasn't their softness or sweet shape that tugged at him. It was what he knew they could *do*: sing like the lark ascending, like a heavenly angel, and yet with the slightest husky edge to her voice. A huskiness no angel would own to. And she wanted to sing with him. Tonight. That was what her look and tone told him. She wanted their music, perhaps almost as much as he did himself.

To sing together for the last time.

His breath turned shallow.

"The innkeeper saw two minstrels, Guilhem. I saw her look at my lute." She reached back to tap the instrument encased on her back. "We can still negotiate."

"It is unseemly," he muttered.

She frowned.

"What? That I play and sing? You heard my name, did you not, Guilhem? My *real* name. Do you know why my mother named me Azalais? It was my mother's choice. I was only a girl, so my father permitted my mother to label me. So, she named me for a *trobairitz*: for two *trobairitz*, in fact. Female troubadours. Women have been minstrels, as you well know, and two of them were called Azalais. How is it *unseemly* that I become a third?"

Ah, how fittingly named she was. Her mother had been French. Had her mother played, too?

But that was beside the point: "The age of the troubadours is long past, Lady Azalais," he said. "Nor did your namesakes ever perform in low taverns and wander about the countryside unattended. You know how minstrels are regarded. Have you forgotten your friend the sailor?" She shivered at that, tightening her lips. "It is unseemly that you, a gently-born damsel, should appear as a man before these commoners."

And his gaze dipped with meaning to her hose-clad legs. By God, her tunic barely covered her upper thighs. Admittedly, the hose that wrapped those thighs was baggy—deliberately so, he now suspected—but it was still scandalously indecent. Worse, far worse, he felt himself stir at the thought.

And then Azalais began to laugh. It started as a chuckle but soon gathered strength. And quite lost control.

His loins subsided. It was impossible she had noticed, but nevertheless, they shriveled under the mere suspicion she might have. *He had given his oath.*

She was grasping her pony for support now. Shaking. Was it still laughter?

"I never took you for a prude, minstrel man," she managed. "Well? Did you insist those tarts in Bordeaux kept their clothes on? Oh, I can just picture it—*just bend over, mesdames, let me adjust your skirts. We don't want to reveal too much.* Oh, that explains it all. I thought you were not gone long." Definitely a touch of the manic about the laughter now. "But I ask you, Guilhem, who is going to know? About me, I mean. I will engage in no pissing contests. *You* only found out because you groped me where you ought not."

"And others might do so, too," he retorted. "And what tarts in Bordeaux?"

And then recollection struck him. *Those* tarts. Well, ladies really. But that was another story and a more complicated one than she suspected. He could not tell her, yet she evidently thought the worst of him. And why would she not?

"I shall rely on you to dissuade them, Sir Knight—from groping, that is."

"Recall I am not a knight. Not here and now."

"Any more than I am a lady. So let us both be minstrels and have done, Guilhem!"

It was a thought. A tempting, insidious thought. And he lingered over it just a heartbeat too long. She saw.

"I cannot always be in attendance, *my lady*," he growled. "I must sleep or piss at some point, I suppose. And what if we are set upon by a group? Some men like a bit of young man's arse, as you have discovered. What if such lad-loving brigands set upon us? Will they hesitate when they find your bum belongs to no man?"

His words had the desired effect. The laughter died. The hand that grasped her pony's mane, however, continued to quiver.

"Then the solution is obvious—you will have to teach me how to handle a dagger."

He closed his eyes.

"God above, is that a good idea? Look what hap—" No, he would not go there. "A dagger will not stop a determined man, my lady."

"But I would wish to try, Guilhem," she said quietly. "I will not be taken as a helpless female thing again."

Her words fell like stones. *Why in hell were they even discussing the matter?* He opened his eyes and looked down at her with all the sternness he could muster.

"Lady Azalais, you will have no need to defend yourself because you are going to stay here. Here in La Réole and as a woman. I will find you a female companion and some suitable clothes. And then I will travel on—alone—to ransom your father."

Chapter Nine

AZALAIS TOOK A firmer grip on her pony's mane. There was no flicker of amusement upon Sir William's face now. His dark eyes bore into her.

She had dared to hope he might value her music sufficiently to continue as they were. She thought he felt it, too—the golden thread that connected them when they played. But it seemed not. Or maybe their connection was nothing special, just something that happened when any musician played with another. Guilhem was simply used to it. He could find another like her any day—another dozen, no doubt.

But *she* could not. And she never would again. If she married, her husband would doubtless forbid her to dally with any minstrels that strayed her way. And the nuns of Wykeham sang only plainsong. She might play her lute in the loneliness of her marital bedchamber or chaste nunnery cell, but she would never commune in music with another. She accepted the solitary fate of monastic life—it was the destiny she had chosen, and Azalais thought she was content to have it so. But if she must wed …

"No!"

Her hand was a fist upon the pony's mane, and the knight was still watching her.

"What aspect of my decision do you object to?"

"All of it, you officious fiend! I entered on this task to save both my father and myself—and my brothers and you do nothing but subvert it!"

The black brows rose.

"You do not trust me with the ransom, my lady?"

"Stop calling me that. I am nobody's lady. And it is not a matter of trust. Well, not wholly. I will not be left here like inconvenient luggage while you gad on your minstrel way with the entirety of my future and probably get set upon by brigands for your pains. Why, they're as likely to fancy your arse as mine, Sir Pretty Knight. If I am to lose my future, at least let me be there to see it!"

She wasn't sure that last bit made sense, but the outburst was worth it just to see his face—to peel back that façade for a moment. Oh yes, he knew he was pretty. No, far more than pretty, if truth be told. But the odd thing was, she got the impression he did not really like the fact.

"I swore an oath to your brother," Sir William gritted.

"What, that you'd protect me? Yes, I know. He told me."

"And safeguard your chastity," he added.

Azalais's gaze sank to the cobbles. Oh. Of course, he had. She should have figured that out from the first. She had told Benedict why she had fled Keldy, and why she could not return to Robert's dubious protection. It was the only reason he had agreed to help her with this quest. *Of course*, Benedict had done what he could to shield her from further harm, even from this man he supposedly trusted.

She took a deep breath. "But if you leave me, you can't protect me."

"If I leave you here, with a chaperone and in secure lodgings, you will be far safer than as a youth on the road."

"I will not stay. I must ransom my father. That's why I am in France."

"Then let *me* do that. You do not have to present the ransom in person. In fact, it would look passing strange if you did." The dark eyes narrowed. "Surely your father would recognize you, even dressed as a man? My lady, he will not be best pleased." He glanced down at himself with meaning. "Fathers have been known to assume the worst of me, Lady Azalais, and that on the basis of but a brief time spent in their daughters' presence. Not entire weeks."

She almost laughed at his conceit. Except that it wasn't conceit. He was fascinating, and he knew it.

"Listen to me, Guilhem," she hissed. "I will not stay behind. I must ransom my father. It *must* be me."

"Then you leave me no choice. I will escort you back to Bordeaux." He drew a deep breath. "Do you understand what it is to be a knight, Lady Azalais? I have given my word. I swore on the cross—on Benedict's cross. A knight is worth nothing if his oath cannot be trusted."

"You were happy enough to escort a young man—a bastard across France," she retorted. "Azalais de Keldy is worth less than an ill-begotten lad. I have no value save as a pawn in marriage. Continue to keep your word to my brother, Guilhem. Help me ransom my father."

"You are mistaken, my lady," he said softly. "You are worth far more than a nameless man. And I begin to suspect that this ransom—wherever you have secreted it—is composed primarily of your own property. The money that will enable you to marry."

"The money that belongs to my future husband, you mean," she snapped. "God in heaven, will you cease to worry about propriety? *I* shall travel all the way to my father as a male, and appear before him *as* a male, and only then—when he recognizes me—will I reveal myself to you for the first time as a female. *You* will be astounded. *He* will be stymied. Will he accuse you of buggering his daughter as a male minstrel through France? Besides, by then, I will have just handed over most of my dowry to free him, and he will have no choice but to grant my wish to enter a nunnery."

JUST WHEN WILL thought he'd come to a cast-iron decision, she tipped him off balance again. It was her dowry she intended to give up—it was her choice and her mission. Who was he to take that away from her?

But all in order to *enter a nunnery*?

Will examined his minstrel companion afresh. Looking down, he registered a piquant face, a delicate arrangement of high cheekbones and a pointed chin, even if the jaw was a little set right now. Those honey-colored eyes were fixing him with a mutinous expression. Her pale, near-luminous skin seemed lit from within by outrage. And the rest of her? It was hard to tell beneath her loose layers of clothing and the breast binding. His fingers tingled at the thought. They recalled the feeling as he'd pushed her away, his hand to her chest. A density, a softness that shouldn't be. No, the sensation had gone beyond reason. His fingers had simply instructed him that *this was no man*.

Now his eyes told him the same thing. They also told him that it would be a crying shame to lock Azalais de Keldy away in a nunnery.

Of course, many beautiful things were rightly dedicated to God. Music, for one. Stained glass and soaring cathedrals, too. But not Azalais, surely? And not her music.

Christ, what was he thinking? Or *not* thinking, more accurately. Something other than his brain was making the most irrational suggestions to him.

"Well?" the would-be nun demanded with a most un-nun-like tone. "Have you made peace with your proprieties, Guilhem? Do you see a woman before you or a man? I am Alain the bastard minstrel. This is my quest and my future. I will not be set aside."

If only she *were* still his minstrel-man.

And all the hopes—no, the outright fantasies he had entertained these last few days came back to slap him in the face with a mailed gauntlet. His minstrel could play. Alain had an instinct for slipping his voice like a swooping swallow over and around Will's deeper tones. The youth's fingers coaxed more volume from his lute now, and still, Alain never ceased to explore, to stretch both his musical boundaries and Will's own. Making music with Alain was an intoxication, an increasing addiction, and in the last few days, Will had begun to wonder whether the bastard of Keldy might continue to travel with him once he had rescued his father. With Alain by his side, Will thought he could finally cut all ties, burn all bridges, and throw knighthood away. For a life of minstrel wandering.

"Answer me, Sir Knight!"

William found he was still standing there, a mute monument in the center of La Réole. The voice breaking in on his thoughts forcibly reminded him that neither of them had moderated their voices for public discussion. They were speaking in southern French, true; they had done so ever since Bordeaux. They were French minstrels, after all. Speaking English would draw unnecessary and potentially hostile attention. But they were standing in the town square opposite the inn, and the volume and intensity of their interchange was attracting some quizzical glances.

Will came to a decision. He untethered his pony. It gave him a reproachful look. It thought it was done for the day.

"Come. Let us walk," he said. "I believe we have matters to talk over in greater privacy. If you will, my lady." An ironic bow.

And to his enormous relief, she complied.

THEY WALKED OUT of La Réole. Rather than recrossing the bridge to the southern bank of the river and incurring yet another toll, Azalais trailed Sir William along a lane that hugged the northern bank of the Garonne. He was merely leading his pony. He evidently did not plan to go far. So, Azalais tamped down her many objections and arguments—for the moment—and followed her erstwhile companion with wary attention.

To find her gaze lingering upon her companion's posterior. It was a warm spring day, and he had, earlier, divested himself first of his cloak, then his doublet, and now he walked ahead of her clad in a sleekly fitted tunic and hose. A leather belt was slung about his hips, accommodating a dagger upon one side and a sword upon the other. A purse clinked faintly in front, hidden from this angle. But she could see his hindquarters far too clearly.

He had quite beautiful buttocks.

The thought entered her head with no warning. Azalais stuttered to a halt in the dappled lane. Guilhem paused and looked over his shoulder. A dark eyebrow lifted but, before he could inquire, she jerked her chin that they should continue. They walked on.

But once planted, the notion would not depart. Her eyes would not leave well alone. They registered that Guilhem's tunic reached to his thighs, as decency and fashion dictated, but that with every long-legged step, the fabric shaped itself about the muscles thus engaged, tautening about trim contours, and then loosening a tantalizing instant later. It meant she could never quite get a sense of the whole. Oh, but she wanted to. Her hands yearned to explore those contours, to feel their shapely solidity, to—

This was the utter height of idiocy. Sir William the Womanizer was about to incarcerate her in an inn and run off with her father's ransom. Azalais de Keldy had far, far more important things to think about than what lay beneath this peacock's tunic.

So, she wrenched her gaze from her companion's buttocks and directed it firmly onto the hoof-trampled soil before her—and thus completely failed to notice that said companion had halted until he laid a hand on her arm.

Azalais squeaked.

Guilhem chuckled and immediately released her.

"Fear not, my lady, I was not making free with your person. I was merely ensuring you did not walk into my pony's rump, thus earning yourself a hoof to the face for your troubles." Then in an undertone: "It would be a crime to despoil such lovely features."

"Any more of a crime than for Alain to receive a hoof in the face?" she retorted. "It is the same face, Guilhem. It has passed as a man's so far, and it will soon belong to a nun."

He cocked his head, observing her far too intently. "I always thought you were a remarkably pretty man," he murmured. "I did not mind. It is good for the minstrel business, you know. Men and women both like to be serenaded by a beautiful youth."

"And more than serenaded upon occasion," she snapped, but more for want of something to say.

He had called her beautiful. A beautiful youth, yes, but beautiful. It shouldn't affect her in the least—but it did. No one had ever called her even passingly attractive before. Her brother—Robert, that was—derided her lack of womanly curves. He informed her that she rode abroad too much, so wearing away her feminine softness. Oh, Azalais knew too well the sort of curves Robert's tastes ran to. It was probably just as well he didn't admire hers.

And Lord Leonard, he had never called her beautiful either. Well, that was fine, she never wanted him to call her anything. Not ever. She did not want to hear his voice ever again—unless it was to beg mercy as she wielded a dagger upon his... She shook her head as if to dislodge a bee. No, she could definitely do without *that* image.

"Come." Guilhem had led his pony to a nearby sapling and looped its reins about the trunk. "We have matters to discuss, Lady Azalais, and it is better we do so out of view of passersby." He indicated a grassy sward among the trees. It sloped gently down toward the river and was shielded from the path by a few willows. "Will this suit?"

By the time she'd secured her mount, he had removed his saddle blanket and smoothed it upon the grass.

"My lady." He indicated the blanket. "Pray make yourself

comfortable."

"Guilhem—will you desist! Cease acting the courtly knight with me. I am Alain, your minstrel companion. Nothing more."

"Lady Azalais, you are a gently-born damsel who should not even deign to seat herself upon a sweaty saddle blanket on the grass, let alone linger with a disreputable minstrel among the spring flowers."

Oh, he would infuriate her to murder. The thought seemed to transmit itself to her fingers. They found themselves grasping the wired hilt of her dagger.

She advanced on him, stalking through the dandelions with bloodlust in her heart.

Guilhem, crouched beside the blanket, lifted his eyebrows, and raised two empty hands.

"Sir William de Fauconberg, there is nothing to discuss. This is my quest and my future. You swore to help me, and I will continue as Alain. I *will* ransom my father."

"Or you will perforate me, my lady?"

"I never swore to protect *you*," she said, lifting her dagger free of its sheath. She held the blade downward in her fist, just as Guilhem had instructed.

He did not move, save to angle his head slightly to one side, observing her with a devil's glint in his dark eyes.

"Would you strike an unarmed man, my lady?"

"If he keeps on calling me *my lady*, I will."

Her heart was thundering. Surely this was how it worked? One threatened an opponent with violence—a naked blade, no less—and they were compelled to submit. Or resist. Not just crouch there with a smile in his eyes. What now? Must she follow through with her threat? What if she wounded him, killed him even? Even in the light of her failed attempts earlier that day, it was possible. After all, he had held a dagger then, too. Now his hands were empty.

"That would be most unchivalrous of you, my lady." Those last two words were spoken with velvety emphasis. Like a caress—a silken slap on the cheek.

It snapped her last shred of reserve.

Azalais lunged forward. She drove the dagger down.

And down.

And still further, oddly enough. Some part of her registered the judder of her calf where his leg kicked out to tip her off-balance. Then there was the flick of his arm against hers, batting the dagger hand away, grasping her wrist. Followed by the impact of the turf against her shoulder and ribs. And finally— horrifyingly—his body on hers, the scent of crushed grass in her nose as her opponent pinned her against it, and then stillness. Nothing but the sound of water flowing and two people breathing rather quickly.

WILLIAM STARED DOWN at her, his pulse in his ears. His breath came short and shallow. It was nothing to do with exertion, for he had barely shifted position. But *what* a position he now found himself in—one delicate wrist captured in either hand, his legs pinning hers. Not that he needed to secure his captive, it seemed. She lay quite still, eyes huge, watching him, her mouth slightly ajar.

"Indeed, that was most unchivalrous of you, my lady," he murmured. "It is as well you are not a man. I would have to call you to account."

A shock ran through her at his words. He felt it, for it transferred itself to him, shivering up his legs, his arms, to meet somewhere in the middle. God give him strength.

"But you are most assuredly no man, my lady," he went on. "No more than you are a bastard minstrel." William drew a deep breath. His body had forgotten to attend to the matter by itself. "I think some part of me suspected all along."

It was probably the same part of him that was currently reminding him quite forcibly of its presence. And his neglect of it.

Still, she made no reply. Her hair spilled out in short loose waves upon the grass, glinting like gold where the sun caught it. Eyes like honey-sweet depths that he might drown in, lose all sense of himself within—stared up. He could not read her expression.

"Lady Azalais, I swore to your brother to protect your body, your spirit, *and* your chastity. This is why you cannot accompany me any further east." Another breath. "This—" he said.

Will let himself sink down, resting upon his elbows so his forearms could continue to secure hers.

So, his face could dip lower—until his dark hair mingled with hers—and his lips touched hers.

Just the softest graze, a mere meeting of skin on skin. Nevertheless, it sent a jolt through him, ferocious as summer lightning. Her lips quivered like butterfly wings.

And before he knew what he was at, Will was dipping lower. He hadn't intended to. He only meant to make a point. A brief demonstration. But somehow his fingers were tangling in her hair, and his mouth was compassing hers. No mere grazing now—he took full possession of her lips. It was not outright invasion—never that, for there was something fragile about this man who was a woman, something about her need to remain a man.

So, Will held himself back, kept his tongue to himself, and simply learned the shape of her with his lips. A heavenly beautiful mouth, whose contours produced such angelic sounds. His lips caressed hers, worshipped hers. For the first and what must be the last time.

For this had to end. He must finish this now, while he still could. He must leave this would-be nun in peace. It was only a demonstration.

She stirred beneath him then. Just a tiny movement. He felt her lips shift under his—and Will stilled, waiting. He would let her wrench away, threaten him with a dagger, and roundly revile him. He had made his point. No more.

But her lips were not moving in protest. They did not shout at him or twist away. They were responding. *By God, they were responding.* Her chin tilted up, and she opened her mouth to his. Welcoming him in.

Thought evaporated from Will's head. There was only her mouth, the silk of her hair, the shift of her legs beneath his. Two minstrels singing a wordless song—a duet most perfectly in harmony. Two mouths responded, one against the other.

His tongue brushed hers. An explosion of heat in his gut, and she twisted against him. Oh, not in resistance, but in echo of her mouth. *Their* mouths. Her tongue snaked against his, luring him, inviting him. She wanted this—she wanted *him*—and by God, he was entirely willing to oblige her.

It was the pressure in his braies that finally did it.

As his mouth melded with hers, his body leaned in to do likewise. His groin brushed up against her thigh and hardened to an almost unbearable solidity. A jolt shuddered through him, and suddenly action became an utter imperative.

His oath. His word as a knight. Or was he an amoral, despicable minstrel?

He managed it.

Will flung himself up and away. Somehow, he propelled himself back—to a semi-sitting position on the abused grass. He had done it. He was no longer touching Azalais, no longer even looking at her. He was staring skyward, unseeing, and hauling in air.

And after a such few breaths, he produced one sentence, "And that, my lady, is why you must not continue with me to the Chateau de Bruniquel."

$$\sim\!\!\ast\!\!\sim$$

Chapter Ten

S HE WAS TEMPTED to continue lying there. The ground, at least, was solid. Nothing else was. Besides, she wasn't sure she could meet her companion's gaze.

Clouds and thoughts scudded over her. *He* sat nearby.

Lord Leonard had never kissed her. But if he had? It would have been nothing like that. She knew it instinctively, inarguably. The very thought of it…a shiver rippled through her. Lord Leonard's hands, his grasping fingers, the overpowering remembrance of—

Azalais rolled to a sitting position, arms wrapped about raised knees. For want of something sensible to do, she looked about for her dagger. A small part of her mind noted she was making a habit of discarding it amongst the flowers and that this was a habit that ought to be broken. She was evidently in dire need of Guilhem's tutelage.

She located the dagger. She scooped it up and stowed it back on her belt. The heft of cold steel gave her sufficient bravery to answer him.

"No. That is why I *can* continue with you, Sir William," she said quietly. She hoped he detected no quiver in her tone. "Because you stopped."

A rusty chuckle. She did not look in its direction.

"Have you any idea how hard it was, my lady? To stop, I

mean."

His voice was like a vielle bow over the taut strings of her nerves. It made her vibrate.

"Then why did you start?" she snapped. "Surely mauling me on the mouth is against your oath to my brother, too?"

He turned to her. She felt it. It was pure instinct to look up, to meet those dark, slumberous eyes, and then let her gaze slip to his mouth.

His mouth.

It moved. "Well, not exactly," it said. "And as for why I started, my lady, I would remind you that it was you who attacked me. I merely defended myself. In light of our disagreement, I believed a little demonstration was in order."

"Demonstration! What, do you disarm all your foes in such a manner, Sir Knight?"

A chuckle. She did meet his gaze then. She could not help it. Sir William lounged there on the grass with his dark hair flopping over one brow, his eyes warm with amusement and the embers of desire.

"Indeed, it would make for a novel technique. But no, I do not kiss my fallen foes, Lady Azalais. Only you. And as for my demonstration, I wished to test the potency of something I have long felt in your presence, perhaps from the start."

"What?" She studied her hose-covered knees. One of them sported a grass stain.

"Lady Azalais, I do not tend to be attracted to men. I believe I told you so at one point."

She nodded once, not trusting herself to speak.

"Nevertheless, I found myself watching you. No, more than watching."

The vielle bow of his voice was caressing her again. So soft and skillful.

"At first I thought it was just curiosity," the voice went on. "I was intrigued by your secrecy, your insistence upon a hood. Then I thought it was your music, my minstrel. For you make magic with your lute strings, you see. And your voice—" His own hesitated.

Azalais could not move. She could barely breathe.

"Your voice, my lady, it stirs me. Almost unbearably at times. I began to entertain ideas that…well, suffice to say, that would contravene your brother's idea of protection. And yet while I thought you a man, I believe my admiration would have remained just that."

A tremor trickled down her spine.

"So, I needed to show you the folly of continuing under my protection." His voice was like rich. "And I needed to prove as much to myself. As a result, it is evident both my oath and your safety are best served by you remaining in La Réole, and under chaperonage."

He ceased speaking. She felt his gaze upon her, but she refused to meet it. Her thoughts skittered like autumn leaves. Only one notion remained steady, a horrible constant.

She must tell him what drove her from Keldy. After all, the knowledge had changed Benedict's mind. Perhaps it would work on Guilhem, too. Oh, it would be hard. The shame and the fear rose like vomit in her throat even as she considered it. She never wanted to relive those moments again.

But her companion must know the whole.

Then he would let her travel on with him.

AZALAIS LIFTED HER head and met his gaze.

"Listen then, Guilhem, and I will tell you a story. But this is no fairy tale or courtly romance. And I do not yet know what the ending will be."

She looked at him steadily. She could do this. He must be made to understand.

He had evidently caught the gravity of her tone. The laughter faded from his eyes. He inclined his head.

So, she drew a deep breath—and began.

"There was once a girl, a noble lady if you will, who grew up in a small stronghold on the edge of the North Yorkshire moors."

Just an anonymous girl. After all, courtly tales frequently fail to mention their female characters' names. Why not this one?

"Her mother died when she was young, though the girl honored her memory—and her native language and love of song. She remembered nights when her mother sang her to sleep, and days when she recited poetry in the *langue d'oc.* The girl's father was often away, fighting in France. Nor did he remarry after his wife's death. Oh, sometimes he had women, the girl knew, but they were liaisons only, with women of low estate. He used them and cast them away, as men do."

Lord John de Keldy had tried to be discreet, Azalais knew. He had not intended her to know, but Keldy was a small place. People talked, especially about the lord of the manor. Azalais did not exactly blame her father—well, she did, but it was a lesser species of blame. Men had mysterious urges, it seemed. At least Lord John paid the women for their troubles before he abandoned them.

"So, the girl was left to grow up motherless, largely lacking female company in a castle full of men. But there was one woman to whom she grew attached—a maid from the village of about her own age, who served her and acted as a chaperone."

Meg had been her constant companion. Azalais had taught her to ride so the maid could accompany her on horseback rambles. And Azalais had protected Meg, too, in her way. The castle was full of men-at-arms and the like, attached to either her father or her elder brother. There were male servants, too, of course, but they were not a problem. They were mostly village folk who would never lay a hand on Meg.

The men-at-arms felt no such prohibition. Azalais knew this, for she had observed their behavior. No serving maid the castle hired remained there long. Once, Azalais had encountered one of the men-at-arms in the stables when she had come for her horse. He was not alone. He had a maid upon the straw-littered floor. Azalais would have intervened—the maid's movements and her cries did not indicate that she was there of her own free will—except she had arrived too late. The fellow already had his braies down. The movement of his thighs between the woman's legs indicated even to an innocent Azalais that the matter was beyond repair.

But not beyond reparation.

She had run for help. She had found her brother Robert and tried to haul him to the scene, demanding that the man be punished. Robert had merely laughed and told her that men would be men. It was only a peasant woman, said he. Then he had looked at Azalais, his eyes narrowing, and told her to watch out for herself instead. *Don't meddle with things you don't understand, or you'll find yourself meddled with, little sister—and who would marry you then?*

When she had returned to the stables, a whip in hand, they were both gone. She never saw the maid again.

Azalais had acquired a dagger shortly after. It was not for eating with.

"Your story, my lady?"

The quiet voice nudged aside her thoughts. Unpleasant thoughts, but she must gird herself. There was worse to come.

"The manor was not a rich one. It was too close to the moors for that. So, the girl's father and elder brother decided to try their fortunes in war. They acquired men—dregs from York and further afield—and took them to France. Money was made, French possessions were looted, Frenchmen were ransomed, and then disaster struck."

"The lady's father was captured," said the quiet voice.

"You follow my story, Sir Knight." Of course, he did. He knew this was no fairy tale. "You guess correctly. The lord was captured on the edge of English territory in France. It is not only the English who know how to squeeze men for money. No one kills a nobleman if they think him worth a ransom. The local lord thought the girl's father was worth a tidy ransom. The girl's brother, however, disagreed."

"Did the brother negotiate? Ransoms are often set too high. A lesser payment might have been agreed," Guilhem offered.

"Oh, this brother did not intend to part with *any* of his hard-looted inheritance, Sir Knight. It was bad enough that he had to permit his sister's dowry to leave his hands if he was ever to marry her off. But his father? Why, the old man would likely die soon enough. Men often do as a result of imprisonment. So why bother parting with a ransom? After all, if his father lived after release, his dutiful son would be deprived of control over the lands that would be his upon his father's demise. Where was the advantage? Of course, he left his father to rot."

"What of the honor of his family name—his duty to his father? Is he not ashamed to be known as the man who abandoned his sire?"

There was a curious lack of judgment in Guilhem's voice. Azalais might have wondered at it, but she had a story to tell.

"As for honor or shame, the son claimed to be trying to raise the money. The ransom was too high, he said. The manor was poor and could not pay. He must have more time. And so, two years passed, filled with excuses, and still, his father did not die."

"How thoughtless of his papa," murmured Guilhem. "And yet, it was the elder son's duty to find the ransom or to negotiate. Whatever made the daughter think she could do it?"

"You are leaping ahead in the story," Azalais said. "But yes, she can do it. She must, for she will not go back to the castle on the moors while her brother still holds it. And it is a woman's sad fate that the male head of her family controls her life."

"It has ever been so," said the knight.

Azalais narrowed her eyes at her audience of one. "Has God not granted women free will, Sir William? Am I to have no say in my own future?"

"I did not say it was right, my lady. I just said it was so. I, too, strain against society's dictates."

"And do those dictates include giving your body to a man who disgusts you? For the rest of your life?"

His eyes were somber, hooded. She might have thought they showed compassion—but who was he, a man, to feel compassion for a mere woman? Men used women. They used them as items for barter or for their bestial pleasures.

"I am spared that at least," he murmured.

"This girl was not," Azalais said bleakly. "Her brother had a friend—a wellborn and wealthy friend from lands closer to York. This friend came visiting her brother to go hunting on the moors. He saw the girl."

Azalais swallowed. Oh, to hell with it. She was fooling no one with this show of anonymity. She was mostly trying to distance herself from the story she told, not her companion. It wasn't working.

"Let me be blunt, Sir Knight. My brother—my loving brother Robert—made sure his friend saw me, for he had designs on this prosperous, well-connected lordling from York. But I did my best to avoid him. I saw he was just like the others, only higher born. He swaggered and he swilled wine. He boasted of his prowess, but he had no concept of true chivalry."

"I get the feeling this girl was unimpressed with men in general," the knight commented.

"Do you wonder she craved the nunnery?" Azalais retorted. "Their idea of fun was beating each other senseless in preparation for war or galloping about the countryside to slaughter any animal that appeared before them, and mauling women whenever they got their hands on them. And when they got drunk enough to think they could sing—" Azalais shuddered. "O, Christ, they set the very dogs to howling in their kennels."

A chuckle.

"Indeed, I have met the type, my lady. Would it help if I assured you not all men are of that stamp?"

"Perhaps. Benedict is nothing like his brother. But Ben took holy orders."

"Not all decent men are tonsured," her listener murmured.

Decent men. Knights. Two incompatible concepts.

And like a demon summoned, Lord Leonard's face materialized before her. His thickset body, too, all shoulders and no neck.
His animal smell. The apparition was shading out William's
presence. It seemed to grow larger, more solid by the second.

She flinched back. No, she would not name the demon. Even
thinking of him raised his specter. So, she reverted to anonymity.
This series of events happened to someone else. She hurried on
with the tale before courage left her altogether.

"The girl's brother wished her to wed his lordling friend. His
task seemed straightforward, for the lordling required little
encouragement. Why that was, the girl had no idea, for she
discouraged him at every turn." Azalais set her jaw. It was
becoming hard to force the words out. "Oh, the lordling was
pantingly keen to get the girl to the marital bedchamber. That
much was plain and by God, it disgusted her. It was the slavering
beast that stalked her every nightmare."

A movement distracted her. Her listener had acquired a sky-
blue scabious from the grass and was pulling it to pieces.
Systematically. Petals scattered on his lap.

The detail drew her back to the present. She could continue.

"Only two things obstructed the brother's fine goal of the
marital alliance—the girl and her absent father."

She glanced at Guilhem. He was still focused on the flower.
His lips were compressed. She could not imagine any music
spilling from them now.

"Doubtless you know that only a father—if he is alive—has
the power to gift his daughter in marriage. Perhaps you know
that marriage may only be performed if a woman says *I do*. She
has that much free will. A brother cannot compel his sister to wed
in absence of these criteria. Only if his father was dead could he
hope to force her hand, for then he would be the guardian of his
sister's body."

The knight's head indicated assent. He did not look up.

"So, the brother decided to try another way. He must place his sister in such a position that she had no choice but to give her assent. She must be forced to say *I do*—however reluctantly."

WILLIAM COULD FIND no more flowers. He had shredded all those within easy reach. But his fingers must do something. His breath seemed caught in his chest.

"Azalais, you do not have to go on," he said. His voice sounded harsh in his own ears.

"But I must," she said. "It demonstrates why I must travel to the Chateau de Bruniquel. My father must know who it is that frees him."

He did not reply. To say that nothing would convince him it was a good idea would only aggravate her. This tale was hard enough for her to tell already.

She spoke on, her voice determinedly neutral. As if she spoke of another but herself.

"So, this lordling began to follow the girl about—with her elder brother's encouragement. He appeared in the stables when she went to saddle her horse. He crossed paths with her on her rides. He cornered her in odd angles of the castle."

Oh, he could picture it all too clearly. A fine specimen of knightly behavior. The subtle art of courtly love. William had seen it before—men who lacked the finesse to woo the objects of their desire—or whose lady loves spurned them for good reason—who then fortified themselves with wine and pursued their desires with ham fists. And worse.

He could picture it, and now—for the first time—he felt it, too. What it was like to be the creature pursued, hounded like a fleeing doe. And her foul brother had permitted it. No, the wretch had egged it on.

"Why in hell didn't Benedict intervene?"

"He had no power. He was not at Keldy. He is a younger son and a monk, at that. In absence of a father, the eldest brother has custody of a sister."

True. But it still didn't excuse him.

But Azalais was speaking again. "The girl took her maid with her everywhere now. *Everywhere.* The maid slept beside her at night, she accompanied her to the garderobe, she rode by her side. But it was not enough. It was a mistake."

The tale-teller fell silent. William cast her a sidelong look, not wanting to affright her. She had her arms wrapped about her legs, and those legs were drawn tight up against her chest. She was bundling herself up, making herself as small a target as possible, protecting herself against the world—against men.

Why in hell would she wish to continue traveling with him, thus leaving herself vulnerable to further attack?

"The lordling had offered marriage," Azalais spoke tonelessly. "The girl's brother had induced her to hear him out. She had listened to the lord's declarations and had declined, with courtesy at first. She said she would not dream of wedding while her father was still held captive. After all, her marriage depended on her father's permission."

A breath.

"So, her brother began to order and threaten. He made good on those threats—he gave the lordling his permission to...to..."

"You do not need to continue, Azalais," he said again, very softly.

He wasn't sure *he* could bear to hear any more. Not without needing to eviscerate this Robert and his pet lordling. And his minstrel—she was mere feet away, holding herself in as if, should she let her arms drop, she would fall into pieces. Will found himself battling an urge to wrap his own arms about her, to cradle her golden head against his chest and shield her from the world. As if he could. It would be the worst possible thing he could do at this juncture. She would think him as just another knightly thug, hungry for her body, grabbing her against her will.

"I do," she said. And before Will could reply, she hurried on. "The lordling, he followed the girl and her maid onto the moors. He came upon them unawares, he and his man-at-arms. Again, he asked the girl to wed him. Again, she said no—and so he seized them."

Azalais shuddered—a convulsive moment. Practically a sob. Will found his hands had formed fists.

"He held the girl," Azalais whispered. "And his man-at-arms grabbed the maid. The women both screamed, but no one could hear them. They fought, but the men were too strong. Then the lordling demanded that the girl marry him. Still, she said no, so he gave his man-at-arms a command." A shuddering breath. "And the man-at-arms lowered his braies."

Will began to shred grass. A cow would have nothing on him for the destruction of greenery. Dirt began to accumulate under his fingernails.

"The fellow displayed his wares, the…the *instrument* of which men are so proud. The lordling asked the girl again. She said no— for surely he would not permit his man-at-arms to sully his intended bride? The display of foul manhood was only meant as a threat. But no, at a further nod from his lord, the man bore the girl's maid to the ground. Shrieking and kicking. He pulled up her skirts. He knelt between her legs. The lordling, meanwhile, saw fit to make free with his hands upon the girl he held."

A pause. Then Azalais looked up. She looked directly at Will, and her eyes were chips of golden flint.

"And the girl cried *No!* and *Stop, for pity's sake!* all at the same time. She had seen this happen before, you see. Men forcing women. She could not live with herself if she permitted it now."

"You will marry me? the lordling asked. *"You swear it? On your maid's body? On your own?*

"I will," said the girl. *"Just let her go. Do not let it happen. For God's sake, do not let it happen.*

"The man-at-arms had paused, you see. He had the maid pinned. He was ready, but he had not committed the crime yet.

He looked at his lord, and it was the look of a rabid dog. The lord called his dog off. The dog snarled and slavered. So, the lord commanded him to fondle himself instead, and he did." Azalais shuddered, a movement of pure revulsion. "The creature pulled at his member until it, too, slavered and spat—over the bare legs of the poor maid. And all the while, the lording held the girl he wished to make his wife and rubbed her against himself."

She fell silent. Will noted her chest rise in quick little movements, her fingers clenched. He waited.

"After that, he let us go," she said at last. "But he told me he would hold me to my promise. Should I renege, he would rape my maid himself, and he would do it before my eyes. If that proved insufficient, he would perform the same act of negotiation on me. To prevent this, I must marry him the next day."

She shrugged. The little attempt at nonchalance twisted something inside him.

"So I ran. I took my maid back to her father's home that very afternoon, and—once darkness fell—I took my lute and my dowry and I ran. To Benedict and Wykeham."

Silence again. Will let the moment lengthen, stretch. He would let her collect herself before bothering her with questions. Besides, he wasn't sure which ones needed asking most. Or if he could ask them without letting his fury show.

Eventually, she spoke again, over the gurgle of water, the rustle of willow leaves, and the thud of his own heart.

"And that is why I must continue to Bruniquel with you, Guilhem. I do not truly trust my father, you see. He is a man. He, too, wars for money and uses women. Just like Robert and Lord I, Robert's friend. I am not certain he will support me over his firstborn son. But if he sees me deliver up my dowry for his freedom, if he is made to feel grateful *to me*, he may take my part. In the first flush of his freedom, I will make him swear to enter me into a nunnery. After all, I will be dowerless by then and quite unmarriageable. A hoyden who has wandered France as a minstrel. He will have no choice but to enter me into Wykeham. And there I will play music and remain safe from men."

Chapter Eleven

AZALAIS HAD TOLD him just about everything. Now it was up to him—to reject her reasons, to manipulate her, to think that he as a man knew best, or to continue. With her.

She had rolled her dice—now it was his throw. And sweet heaven, she was not the stuff of which gamblers are made.

"What you ask of me is dangerous, my lady." He paused. "Too dangerous."

"Then leave me to travel alone if you are so concerned for your own skin, Sir Knight. I release you from your vows to my brother."

Those expressive black brows rose. *You cannot*, they said. And his mouth continued as if she had not uttered a word.

"We may meet men who possess not even the scruples of Robert and his friend, men who abuse men as they do women. I do not know where you have hidden the ransom—"

And by God, he would *not* know.

"—but should we be robbed or set upon, our attackers will undoubtedly find it. You stand to lose everything, Lady Azalais. Your disguise, your honor, your dowry, your very life. My protection is no guarantee of safety."

She had told him everything and still, he would reject her. The knowledge was like her own dagger twisting inside her. She had dared to hope he was different, that if he knew everything, he might respect her—her decision, her judgment, her desperation. He was not. He did not.

"You are a coward, William de Fauconberg," she hissed. "Leave me then, coward. Crawl back to Bordeaux and play with your pretty ladies. I release you."

She was shivering. *Coward* was the very worst insult you could throw at a knight, a man whose fighting ability was central to his being. She had seen men fight to the death in her father's castle yard over that word. She needed to wound this knight, to knife him where he would most feel it.

She girded herself for the explosion.

"Perhaps I am," he murmured. "At least, I believe my father would agree with you. And I admit it, my lady, I *am* frightened. Terrified." Even softer. "For you."

Damnable charmer that he was, she refused to react. He would try to win her to his way of thinking instead.

But he wasn't finished yet. "I am frightened that I will watch you die. Or see you dishonored. Or even that I might forget my oath and do the dishonoring myself."

Azalais ground her teeth. There was such a thing as too much honesty. He was slapping her in the face with those excuses. He was trying to turn her into a quivering coward herself.

"But," that voice continued, stroking her tight-strung nerves, making them worse. "If it is your wish, Lady Azalais, if you are not to be dissuaded from your course, I will consider myself bound."

Her nails dug through the weave of her hose. They excavated little holes in her knees.

"What do you mean?" she whispered.

"I will bind myself to you," her tormentor said. "And I will do as you ask. We will continue as minstrels, and you will continue in the guise of a man. And I will protect you to the best of my cowardly ability. If that is what you wish."

><<

NOW SHE WAS following him back along the banks of the Garonne. To the inn at La Réole. The thought occurred that it was *she* who should take the lead. After all, by some strange turnabout, he had accepted her command. He was the man-at-arms, the bodyguard, and she was the knight on a quest.

Except she was not. Nor was he. They were minstrels.

Still, she could not quite believe it. This was some trick. He was a subtle man. Maybe he intended to fool her into complacency and then lock her in a chamber in La Réole. Or maybe he would continue on with her 'til they reached a wild and secluded nook—only to rob her and rape her himself. Then pass the whole thing off a brigand attack.

Except if he planned to do that, he might as easily have taken her on the grass this very afternoon. And he had wanted to; she had felt it. That solidity against her thigh. Just like Lord Leonard, pressing his animal urges upon her.

Except that he hadn't. And it wasn't because she had fought him off. Far from it. Azalais's cheeks warmed, and she prayed her companion did not turn. Something had possessed her as his lips had moved over hers—and it wasn't Guilhem. It was as if some spirit had taken her over, evicted all thought, all free will from her being, and transformed her into a creature of pure feeling.

Azalais hadn't directed her lips to respond—they just had. She had no idea what she was doing. How could she? She had never kissed a man before, not like *that*. The very notion her tongue might reach out and slip around his and...no! Such a thing had most certainly never occurred to her. Something else had taken over, urging her to react in thoughtless abandon, to slip her tongue between his lips, to jolt to the hardness he pressed against her. It turned her own body traitor against her. It undermined her common sense, her resolve, and it threatened her very quest. Indeed, it was very like demonic possession.

Except Azalais wasn't certain any priest could exorcise this insidious spirit. Worse, she wasn't sure she wanted one to.

So, she trailed after Guilhem, drained from telling her story, from battling him, and from the maelstrom of his kiss. Not knowing what she felt.

They walked their ponies as before, reins in hand. And as before, she found her gaze lingering about the base of his tunic, lured by the contraction of muscle below, the slight shift of the belt about his hips, the supple grace of his stride. Those buttocks would accompany her eastward, their owner had promised. That same owner who had just pinned her to the grass, disarming her, holding her prisoner, taking his pleasure of her lips without permission.

The heat from her cheeks suffused downward, sending odd little flames flickering in her belly. *By heaven, the man was a knight. He was just like Lord Leonard and Robert. Even her father. He used women, and he threw them away. What was she thinking?*

She walked on. The sun was sinking before them. The world burnished and softened. It turned mysterious and magical. She might cross between the mundane world and fairyland in such a moment. All was becoming blurred.

He was nothing like Lord Leonard.

Leonard had threatened rape to get his way, with that end a lifetime of bondage in which her body would be at his disposal. Until he tired of it and turned his urges upon another. And another.

Guilhem, by contrast, had kissed her in warning. A warning against himself. When his words had proved insufficient, he had demonstrated in actions why she was not safe with him.

And it had had the opposite effect.

For he had stopped. Guilhem had halted their kiss, and certainly not because he wanted to.

That flame curled within her again, unwilling to be doused. No, it urged her to fuel it, stir that delicious heat into a true fire. An all-consuming blaze.

It was undiluted idiocy. She could not continue to trail behind this charmer. Just look what thoughts his posterior inspired in her overheated head!

Azalais increased her pace, tugging her pony along to draw alongside her minstrel companion.

"So, concerning the inn," she announced. "I propose we sleep in the common room as poor minstrels ought to. And *you* shall negotiate with our hostess that we play for that privilege."

He looked at her. She kept her eyes on the path ahead, on the golden light they were advancing into. Its glow would conceal the color on her cheeks. She hoped.

"Safety in numbers?"

"Safety in disguise," she countered. "Besides, I need to play. My fingers crave the lute. I must sing."

It was true. Her feelings must be given vent. They had been tossed about like a stick in a torrent today. That was the very purpose of music—the expression of feelings that could find no other release.

By God, she would give the inn's inhabitants something to listen to tonight. She had a demon to exorcise.

WILL NEED NOT have worried that the innkeeper would be suspicious at their change of plan. The woman expressed herself entirely delighted to swap their music-making for bed space on the inn floor and some pottage and wine. The inn did not stretch to providing a separate dormitory for impecunious guests, she explained, leaning forward to rest a plump hand on his arm. The tavern's hall simply served as a communal sleeping room once the drinking was done.

Indeed, the only difficulty was in peeling himself away from the woman's proximity. She seemed bent on confiding her life's story to him, how her husband was away with Prince Edward to fight the Spanish—him and half the men of the district, *par Dieu*—and it was up to his poor lonely wife to manage the inn in his absence. Well, at least the number of tavern fights had decreased in the absence of so many soldiers. La, but it was a positive treat to entertain a minstrel—no, two minstrels—of such evident quality.

And all this without having heard him sing a note, Will mused, carefully steering his eyes away from a bosom of bounteous proportions that seemed determined to edge itself into his field of vision.

Thank Christ the woman soon found herself obliged to rustle off to serve the evening customers. His minstrel companion did not need to see him on such friendly terms with an admittedly attractive woman. He—no, *she*—would only think the worst. It was what accorded with her past experience, today's included.

Said companion had already found herself a stool and was now bent over her lute, ear cocked to the strings as she adjusted its tuning amidst the tavern racket.

"Well, my lady—what is your musical will tonight?"

The golden head jerked up at his words. Safe in her dim corner of the tavern, she had discarded her hood.

"I am no lady, recall?"

He chuckled. "I can barely hear my own voice in this hubbub, *my lady*. None of these locals will catch a syllable. Your secret is safe with me."

Damnation. He should have chosen a different word. The one thing he could not promise her was safety.

A complexity of emotions lit her eyes for a moment. Quickly doused.

"Well then, out with your vielle, Sir Minstrel. We need more volume than a mere lute can muster tonight. The locals of La Réole need some rousing *pastorelas* to aid them in digesting their pottage, and I have a craving to sing Marcabru's *Shepherdess and the Troubadour* as our entrée."

He mentally tipped his hat to her. Of course, she did. Not

only were *pastorelas* popular for their lashings of innuendo and roistering rhythms, but this particular one had the tart shepherdess putting the troubadour firmly in his place.

The troubadour who wanted to kiss the pretty shepherdess, oh, and then go on to do so much more.

So, he extracted his vielle in knightly obedience to his lady's command, checked its tuning—and Azalais's preferred key—and launched upon the opening strains of *The Shepherdess and the Troubadour*.

She sang, and the hubbub soon died to a munching murmur. After Marcabru's *Shepherdess*—sung with a verve with which he had never heard it rendered before—Azalais commanded more *pastorelas* from him. Then there were requests from the audience, duly played. Requests for *canzos* and *sirventes*. Never anything less than troubadour fare, for this was the land of the *langue d'oc*. The minstrel and his boy did not need to leaven their *canzos* with less lofty ditties. They could serve up a solid diet of troubadour songs, each of them beloved by their audience.

And throughout it all, William of Fauconberg watched his co-conspirator in music pour her soul into the dingy, smoke-stained room.

And cursed himself and his situation, even as he let the music sweep him away, lift him to a higher plane.

He had not lied when he'd said her voice moved him. At times, near unbearably. He'd long since come to trust her sense of pitch, the way every note emerged with effortless accuracy. That was the least of her skills. It was what she did with those notes and the words they carried that stirred him—the soaring expressiveness, the way she toyed with the melody, making it her own, and the delicious huskiness to her deeper, more intimate tones. The huskiness that reached right inside of him.

Tonight, all that seemed magnified. His minstrel boy's voice filled with all the feelings agitated in the course of the day. Emotions churned up like mud at the bottom of a pool. Defiance, determination, and searing loneliness. And beneath all, a yearning for...for what?

Will shook his head, nearly dislodging the vielle from his shoulder. The music was getting to him, turning him fanciful. Of course, that was its power—it expanded the soul, it fired the spirit, it urged men to deeds of bravery and blinding love. Perhaps it did so to women, too. Looking at his lady now, he could well believe it.

For her face was alight. Alive. It was a shifting tableau of passion and fire. Her amber eyes caught the taper light, reflecting an almost golden glow. Her short hair, which he now knew to be a dark blonde in the daylight, was sheened red-gold by the flickering flames.

Well, his Lady Azalais seemed fired to bravery at least. But never love. After all, she was fleeing from the very possibility of love. She would flee all the way to a nunnery. In the light of her story, who could blame her? And what had he done, Sir William the Charming, wielder of sweet words, but confirmed her in her belief that all men were beasts?

Rutting, ravening beasts.

He gritted his teeth. Thank God the current *canzo* had reached its conclusion. Without glancing at his companion, Will laid down his vielle with a purpose. He loosened his shoulders, well-exercised from wielding bow and vielle. He needed wine. He needed a moment to compose himself.

Evidently, their lady innkeeper had read his mind. That lavishly displayed bosom, luminous in the low light, was moving toward him. Preceding it were two perilously full beakers of wine.

"My sweet songbirds, you must be parched," their hostess crooned, presenting first Azalais with a cup, and then pressing the second—and a good deal of herself—into Will's outstretched hand.

Will saw Azalais's eyes widen, and he edged back, inviting some air between himself and their attentive host. But the lady would not have it. She stepped close, inveigled an arm about his waist such that her bosom nudged against his upper arm, and proceeded to steer Will toward a nearby trestle. Azalais was commanded to follow.

"Food, my blackbirds," said their hostess. "You must eat before you fall over."

A serving maid swiped the trestle with a damp rag and furnished it in a short time with three trenchers and a good-sized bowl of pottage.

Azalais took a seat and inspected the stew, poking it experimentally. Will was too busy trying to disentangle himself to do likewise. He wasn't having much success. So rather than struggle too obviously with his hostess, he gave up and simply sat.

"There's meat in it." His conspirator-in-song sounded surprised.

"Of course there is, my lamb," the hostess cooed. "Only the best for my songbirds. A minstrel needs meat, does he not?" Will found a hand warming his leg. The hostess had plumped herself down beside him on the bench. "With so many men away at the war, there's too few to shepherd the sheep, you see. So, we enjoy a nice bit of mutton for a change instead. Better than letting the brigands eat it."

The hand did not remove itself. Nor did the generous thigh that pressed against his on the bench.

"Brigands?" prompted his minstrel companion. "We travel east from here, madame. Are we likely to encounter trouble?"

"Only riffraff that weren't fit for Spain," said their hostess. "Poor things. Broken men. Men shook up by war or maimed and ill. They pick off our sheep and terrorize the shepherds, sweet youth, but they'll never bother such a fine strong man as you have here."

Will cleared his throat. He did not wish to alienate this useful source of information—not to mention provider of bed and board—but this was getting out of hand. Indeed, her hand seemed to be making progress up his thigh.

"I believe this is your own meal, madame," Will murmured.

"In all courtesy, we cannot deprive you of it. Pray serve us whatever you give the rest of your customers."

The hand stroked his thigh under cover of the trestle.

"Oh, don't worry your handsome head about that, Guilhem—wasn't it? It's not every day I get a minstrel in this dreary place. Go on, let a girl feed you up. You're not stealing my meat off me. Look, I'll take a bite of it, too."

And she leaned toward him—if it were possible to get any closer—and proceeded to spoon a quantity of stew upon her trencher. One-handed.

Will was beginning to worry she would conduct her entire repast by means of one hand. Indeed, the pressure upon his thigh continued to shift. It crept perceptibly upward. It seemed that particular hand had plans that did not involve a trencher.

Christ in heaven.

Will stumbled to his feet, a decidedly awkward operation given the proximity of his bench to the trestle and a large bowl of hot stew. Not to mention the lush body pressed to his. One slip and he might end up in her commodious lap.

"The garderobe, madame. Or latrine, or what have you?" he managed. "Where might I find it?"

Azalais was looking up at him, the oddest expression on her face. Amusement? Bemusement? Probably both. Just so long as it wasn't distrust.

Beside him, his hostess rose, too. The hand found his arm again. O Christ, now it had his waist instead.

"Let me show you, good minstrel," the woman cooed.

He tried to protest that her pottage would congeal. Just point him in the right direction, please. It was, of course, fruitless. The lonely innkeeper's wife would show him her midden in the dark, whether he liked it or not.

And all the while, Azalais watched.

At least his fellow minstrel had no way of observing that which eventuated as soon as they had achieved the chill of the night air. His hostess evidently found herself in danger of catching cold. It was the exposure of so much bosom to the night air, doubtless. Thus, that bosom was pressed up against Will's doublet in no time at all, the plump arms wrapped about him, and—for the second time that day—Will found himself kissing a woman.

Only this time it was through no choice of his own.

Oh, she was well endowed, this innkeeper's wife. Her mouth tasted of sweet red wine, and she was flatteringly hungry for him.

Except he didn't share that hunger.

Will unglued his lips from hers and gently unlatched her arms.

He held her hands for a moment, only in part to prevent them wrapping about his person again. The bosom heaved in the starlight.

"Madame, you do me much honor," Will murmured. "Pray return to your pottage. You will excuse me. I require the latrine with some urgency."

O, God, that was no lie. He required the privacy of a piss in the dark and with no hand but his involved in the operation.

And heaven be praised—the innkeeper's wife, doubtless well acquainted with the effects of wine upon men, pointed him in the appropriate direction and vanished back into the warmth of the inn.

AFTER THEIR MEAL was downed and one innkeeper was detached from his side, his minstrel companion required Will to sing to her accompaniment.

It was probably a mistake. There were fewer drinkers now, meaning their hostess found herself at leisure to become their most attentive audience. She kept catching his eye. Surely the woman did not consider the lyrics of longing and pent-up desire with which he filled the long, low room were aimed at her?

So, Will shifted his gaze from the audience to the boyish creature who accompanied him. She was sat upon a stool, while he stood, the better to open his lungs. Her lute sang in constant, rippling undercurrent to his words, her sweet voice joined his in the refrain. Ah, those moments were the best—when her voice joined his in swooping melodic reply, a contrast in notes yet so perfectly attuned to his deeper tones. While she sat, one with her lute, he could look at her without her knowing it. He could safely direct the words of his song to this androgynous angel—her hair short, her bosom, tight bound, and her lips so sweetly kissable. And sing:

Alas, I thought I knew so much about love
And how little I really know
For I cannot prevent myself from loving
One from whom I shall reap no benefits.

And nearly stuttered in mid-*canzo*, the words rang so true.

What in God's name? Should he avail himself of their hostess's not-so-subtle invitation after all? Benedict had sworn him to protect a very angel of music descended to earth and here was Will, considering his minstrel companion in a most unholy manner. She wanted to be a nun, for heaven's sake. She was halfway there already, with her cropped hair and angelic tones. Perhaps he should assuage his misplaced urges upon someone who would evidently welcome them.

So, he glanced up at their hostess and sang:

And when she took herself from me, she left me nothing
But my own desiring and a wanting heart.

The Frenchwoman smiled most sweetly back at him. Oh, she was attractive, with her mass of dark curls and her generous proportions. He could see that. Another time—sometime in his not-too-distant past—he might have responded to her. But now?

She left me nothing but a wanting heart.

It was not his hostess he serenaded, although it should have been.

So, William of Fauconberg, masquerading minstrel, sang on, dividing his attention between a Frenchwoman and a minstrel-lad—with an occasional glance for the rest of the taproom. And when the end of the evening came, it was inevitable that they had barely bagged their instruments before their hostess was upon them. No, upon *him*.

Quite literally.

"Monsieur Minstrel, you steal my heart," was breathed into his ear. "Such singing. Oh, my loves—" This spoken loud enough for two. "It is a crying shame to house such songbirds upon my grubby tavern floor." Then, lowering her voice to a decidedly French whisper, a whisper destined for his ear alone: "In fact, I have a nice bed you might rest your bones upon, monsieur. You alone, I regret. There is no room for your sweet companion."

And there it was. The invitation he required, nice and clear.

Before he could second-guess himself, Will looked at Azalais. Her face was angled toward them, the light of a nearby taper bathing the delicate planes of her cheeks, dancing over her lips. Those lips he had kissed.

He felt himself stir. Harden.

Could he?

By God, now there was a foul proposition. He would bed this generous Frenchwoman and all the while he would be picturing his fellow minstrel. Beneath him. On top of him. The very thought was an insult—to his hostess and to Azalais.

His lady-minstrel's eyebrow lifted. Will hated to think what she read upon his face.

A plump arm wound around his waist. It stroked.

Will steeled himself and said: "Madame, your offer is generous—more generous than I deserve—and this poor minstrel is most truly grateful. But my companion has had some unfortunate experiences of late. I have sworn to sleep by his side."

And that was that. William of Fauconberg only prayed his hostess did not decide her bed was big enough for three.

Chapter Twelve

"WHY DIDN'T YOU go with her?"

They were riding again, following the south bank of the Garonne through a drizzling morning, having survived the previous night on the floor of La Réole's sole inn with no more than a little stiffness and perhaps a few fleas. Azalais scratched her leg experimentally. The fabric of her hose was none too fine. It did not fit her role as an impoverished minstrel to go sauntering through France in best broadcloth. Was that something digging its teeth into her skin or just the scratchy wool?

But she was prevaricating. She had asked Guilhem a question, and she needed to know the answer—she just didn't want to look at him when he replied. Well, it was raining, and it was necessary to keep her hood well up. He, too, had his hood and a waxed cloak wrapped about him against the wet.

The relative anonymity of rain and hood had emboldened her to ask the question that had been nagging at her since last night. Now she was beginning to wonder if she would have to say it again.

"Guilhem?"

No answer.

"You haven't actually sworn to sleep by my side, you know," she continued. "And even if you had, you might have gone with her for…for, well, however long it takes, and then come back to watch over me if you felt so obliged."

"Christ, Azalais—" he said. "Some men do not feel compelled to rut with every woman they see."

His voice died away.

"Unlike some men of my acquaintance, you mean?" she finished for him. "But she wanted you, I think. Our hostess, I mean. You would not have needed to use force."

"Yes, she wanted me." The words sounded a little strangled to Azalais's ears. Then came a brief laugh. "God knows, the only force required was in keeping her off me."

"But she could not have taken *you* by force," Azalais said. She stared at her pony's ears. The furry items flicked every now and again to disperse the gathering drops of rain.

"Probably not."

"And her bed would have been more comfortable than the floor."

"Indubitably."

A pause, filled with damp clopping, the patter of rain on leaves, and the ever-present murmur of the river.

"But *why* did she want you?"

A chuckle. It turned into outright laughter.

"For a minstrel who sings so persuasively of love, my lady, I would have thought you'd know the answer to that. Or should I be insulted? Is my person so objectionable that you cannot imagine what our hostess might see in it?"

She nearly snorted at that, but such noises were not ladylike. On second thought, she *should* have snorted.

Instead, "The songs I sing were mostly written by men, Guilhem. They sing of how *men* feel, not women. Besides, I do not believe our hostess was after love. Not precisely. She saw you as an object to be desired, much as a troubadour views his lady. I simply wonder that you did not respond."

As for his objectionable person, that required no answering. He was not insulted.

"You sum the matter up well, O, Alain. Indeed, I *was* the

object of that delicious lady's desire. The only obstacle was that her appetite was not reciprocated. By me."

"Unlike in Bordeaux."

Silence.

"Or is it that two women at once is more to your taste, Sir Knight?"

She hadn't intended to say it aloud. Azalais shrank a little deeper into her hood. And waited. After all, she was a little curious.

"I do not believe your brother would approve of this line of inquiry, Lady Azalais."

Likely he wouldn't.

"You do not answer," she countered.

"I do not."

She dared fling a quick look his way. It showed he was riding with a kind of concentrated stillness. His chin was angled directly forward. Immovably so.

"Oh, for God's sake, listen to me, Guilhem! I will shortly enter a nunnery. Once there, I will be chaste to my dying days. That should be enough to please Benedict. *Or* I will be forced to please my other, less-considerate brother, and I do not believe chastity is part of that bargain. In the meantime, I would know of what I sing, at least in theory. I believe you have some knowledge of the subject. Considerable knowledge."

A pause.

In which Azalais hearkened to the thudding of her heart and wondered what possessed her to so brazenly address the matter eating at her. Perhaps she *was* possessed. Or perhaps it was because she trusted him. He had sworn, and he could keep his oath. He had broken the kiss off. He would not treat her as her brother's men treated women, or as Lord Leonard would so dearly like to treat her.

Then he spoke, so quietly, she hardly caught the words above the soft sounds about them. "You sing of love and yearning, my lady, and yet, you know not of what you speak."

"Yes."

"And you think *I* can enlighten you? That I have considerable experience in the matter of what? Base lust? Desire? Or yearning?"

So, she had managed to insult him after all. That was unexpected. Her brother's men—and Robert, too, for that matter—were all too happy to crow about their amorous conquests. Azalais just hadn't wished to listen. Their descriptions bore no resemblance to poetry. Nor did the women they spoke of ever appear to crave their attentions—certainly, they hadn't welcomed such acts as Azalais had observed. Unlike like last night or in Bordeaux. Those women had wanted her minstrel-knight, that was plain. It was a phenomenon quite new to her, yet it was hinted at in the handful of *trobairitz* lyrics, those songs sung by long-dead women. It was just something she'd never really believed to be true.

Now something inside her whispered maybe it was possible. A tiny flame that curled deep down—a faint hope, a flickering warmth.

"My lady, what is it that you want from me?"

Soft words, distinctly wary in tone.

They framed a good question. Unfortunately, it was one she couldn't formulate a coherent answer to.

But the tiny flame flared in response. It told her what it wanted on a level that was deeper, more primal than mere words. And what it wanted was unthinkable. Certainly, she could not voice it.

So, she changed the subject—or at least, she appeared to.

"Our hostess at La Réole talked of brigands, Sir Knight. It concerns me." That much was no fabrication. The thought prompted her to glance left and right along the road edges. Trees dripped. Beyond them, the Garonne's current bore a small boat downstream. Nothing else moved, praise heaven. "She spoke of broken men, Guilhem—outlaws reduced to snatching sheep. If they attack poor shepherds, then what is to say they will not try us? I fear she was flattering you when she said no one would dare attack you."

Guilhem chuckled. "Flattery is not in your repertoire, at least. So, you doubt me, my lady?"

"I doubt myself," she retorted. "You disarmed me yesterday as easily as you would swat a fly. Should two or more brigands come upon us, you might find yourself too occupied to look out for me. I would have you tutor me further in the use of my dagger. That, Guilhem, that is what I want from you."

For the moment.

※

THE RAIN CEASED before midday. Will was rather hoping it wouldn't.

Worse, the clouds began to part, and an intermittent sun shone through, turning raindrops to tiny diamonds on every bush and branch. Soon the diamonds were evaporating or trembling to earth, and small birds appeared to snatch spiders from their spangled webs and trill about the general joys of spring.

Will found such joyfulness ill-judged.

By the time they halted for a midday meal, such as it was, the grass was nearly dry enough to sit on. Damn it all to hell.

If it had kept on raining, they might have kept on riding, squelching their damp way to the next town for a roof to ward off the elements. That roof would inevitably shelter many other souls, and Will could focus on them rather than on his companion. He certainly would not be called upon to tutor them in the art of eviscerating men.

Will chewed the last of his bread and cheese and washed it down with a mouthful of wine. He brushed the crumbs from his tunic, rose from his seat on the grass—and sighed with enough theatricality to earn him a lead role in a mystery play.

"You are certain you want to do this, my lady? Nuns do not play with knives, and I doubt your Lord L would approve of a weapon-wielding wife."

"But minstrel-men do," she retorted, hand resting upon her still-sheathed dagger. "Especially when they travel with—"

He thought she was going to say something along the lines of "irritating companions," but after a moment she finished with "—goods of great value."

It was a solid reason, he had to admit. And there was sense in teaching her some elements of defense. It was just…well, dagger play inevitably brought opponents into bodily contact, as he had demonstrated just the previous day. He did not think she would have forgotten that particular lesson. As for himself, well, he had dreamed of that kiss last night as he lay within an arm's length of his fellow minstrel. He had relived it in all its dizzying sweetness—except in the dream it had not ended at a kiss.

Oh, it was determined to culminate in far more than a meeting of mouths, and the rest of him was nothing loath. In fact, it was only by a supreme act of will that he had wrenched himself from sleep to lie shivering on the tavern floor—and not with cold—listening to her soft breathing close by. Undisturbed breathing, thank God. In his dream, Will had most definitely disturbed her. And himself.

It was a warning to keep his lady at a goodly distance.

But now she was unclasping her hood and cloak. She hung them from a nearby tree. Then she turned to face him clad in her loose tunic and dull hose. The dagger glinting in her palm gave him all the answer he required.

She was holding it incorrectly again.

He produced a second sigh to rival the first.

Then he gifted his cloak to a tree and stepped toward her. But not too close.

He slipped his dagger into his left hand, the better to act as a mirror to her right-handed grip.

It would be so simple to just reach out, take her hand in his, and adjust her fingers upon the pommel. But he would not. He would demonstrate instead.

He drew a breath and began.

"There are four primary strikes in the dagger-fighter's repertoire, my lady, three in which the blade is held downward in the fist, and only one in which the blade points up. These four strikes are the basis of all else, so we will master them first. Watch. I will demonstrate."

He did—in slow motion, focusing upon producing the perfect strikes for his lady's bloodthirsty elucidation.

Right, left, up, down.

All the while he was acutely aware of her gaze—examining him, gauging his every move.

He set his teeth and demonstrated three times, following the same sequence each time. Of course, no fight replicated the pattern of a drill, but they would worry about that later. They could mix up the sequence once she'd mastered the basics.

"Your turn, my lady."

She had adjusted her grip on the dagger. Now she raised it cautiously. She tried a stab right and then left at chest height. Then cocked her head at him.

"Shall I demonstrate again?" he asked.

She nodded.

Right, left. Two slow backhand stabs in her direction, but at a safe distance.

She watched him closely, and then she moved. But not to strike. Instead, she came around to the left side of him. Close enough to touch. Will froze.

"Do it again," she said.

He instructed his muscles to do so.

He could practically feel her breath on his neck.

"Why are you using your left hand?" the breath asked.

A valid question. No man or woman admitted to left-handedness if they could possibly help it. Judas the Traitor was left-handed. It was the mark of the devil.

He explained it was to aid her when she faced him. "Besides, a knight usually has a sword in his right hand. If he holds no shield, then a dagger makes an excellent accessory for his left."

"Should I acquire a sword, too, Sir Knight?"

She was so close, she only need murmur. Will did not turn to look at her. He must not.

"No. A sword requires more strength and control. Because of its weight and greater reach, it takes longer to master than the dagger. Besides, I doubt you'd find one at short notice around here. All the swords of southern France are migrating to northern Spain as we speak."

"Show me the strikes again." And she laid her hand on his forearm.

Will startled.

A soft laugh. "I promise not to attack you, Sir Knight. I just wish to feel the action of your arm as you strike. Please—show me again."

He did: *right, left, up, down*. And all the while the weight and warmth of her hand burned like a brand through his tunic.

It branded him an oath breaker—at least in intent.

Then she stepped away and he breathed again. She turned to face him. Slowly, she put her dagger through the moves he had shown her—*right, left, up, down*.

"That is better. Continue like so, my lady. That is the first drill. Now practice it until your muscles know the movements and your head does not need to instruct your arm."

Yes, continue practicing solo and at a safe distance from me.

So, she continued, and occasionally she asked him to demonstrate again—but only from a distance. And he watched her.

No, he drank her in.

Only a day ago he had thought her a man. The very notion was impossible now.

Yet, she was still the same slender figure clothed in drab brown, breasts bound, hair, page-boy short. And he could admit it, now that he knew her for no man: he had been beguiled by her even when he thought she was. At least then the concept of meddling with a youth in his care had been beyond contemplation. It had merely confused him mightily. It had not tempted him to act.

Focus, Will.

He did not have to persuade himself to focus on the figure before him. No, it was the manner of focus that needed adjusting. He narrowed his eyes upon her arm, the hand on her dagger, the sweep of her blows.

Ah, she was getting the hang of it. Her strikes had become more confident and much more forceful.

"Now mix the sequence up," he instructed. "Try *up, down, right, left.*"

He demonstrated. She imitated.

She fumbled a little on the shift of grip between *up* and *down.* It was only natural, but it caused her to scowl at her hand.

Will grinned. For once, he was not the one causing the offense.

"Watch closely, my lady."

He demonstrated the half-circle shift required between backhand and forehand grips. Slowly at first, then faster.

"Now you're just showing off," she accused.

"Oh, no. *This* is showing off."

He spun his dagger a full circle in his left hand between strikes. Repeatedly.

She was shaking her head at him, free hand on hip. Smiling.

"Poseur."

"At your service, my lady." He bowed upon a downward strike, sinking upon one knee, then struck up from that half-kneeling position.

She laughed outright. "You prove my point."

He shrugged. "It is a valid strike, my lady, and a useful one if you are knocked to one knee."

"Stop groveling on the grass, Sir Knight, and help me spin my dagger!"

He rose with a grin.

"As you will, my lady. But bear in mind you should never shift your grip from backhand to forehand in the middle of a fight.

In the midst of a flurry of blows, that is. But certainly, to change grip is a useful skill." He cocked a brow. "And most effective for showing off, too."

He demonstrated the half-turn shift.

She tried again and fumbled again. And swore.

"Come and help me!" she demanded.

He gave her a questioning look.

"Put your hand on mine, Sir Knight. Guide me through the motions."

He did not move.

"Please?"

Oh, it was a bad idea. Not only would he have to cup his hand over hers, but the rest of his body would have to align with hers—and much too closely.

But what could he say? *No, my lady, I am afraid if I touch you, my groin will get the better of me? My lady, let me confirm in your fear of men.*

And as he stood there, hesitating, she stepped toward him. She slipped in front of him, her back to his front, and aligned herself to his right side. Her shoulders were a mere finger's breadth from his chest. Short, golden curls tickled his chin, and Will ceased to breathe. Her scent, so warm and close, set him teetering on the brink of madness. Such insanity would erase his oath, his honor, and all sense of self-preservation.

And while he teetered, his pupil took his unoccupied right hand in her left, and laid it, tense but unresisting, over her dagger hand. His right arm overlaid her own. It tingled to her warmth. By means of her left hand, she curled his fingers over hers.

His abandoned left hand turned nerveless. The dagger dropped from it to the grass. All feeling had transferred itself to his right hand, alive with the feel of her fingers, slender beneath his. Fine-boned but made strong by countless hours at the lute. Trembling slightly. Or was that him?

"Show me, Guilhem." A whisper.

His groin tightened.

O, God, he was a beast.

He could barely think, but at least his hand had not forgotten its duty. It fitted itself to hers, finger upon finger. It encompassed hers so perfectly, his larger hand cupping her more delicate one from above. As if made for each other.

Her dagger moved. His fingers and hers released it sufficiently to allow it to drop a half-circle.

"Now up again," he murmured.

And with a slight flick, they urged the dagger in half-circle back up again. Ah, this was better. Will could focus on the dagger. By God, he would think of nothing but that damn dagger.

"Down," he said.

And the dagger obeyed.

"Then up."

And he certainly was. The challenge was to conceal it from her. She nestled so close to him that her slightest movement would bring their bodies together.

"Enough?" Will managed. His voice sounded rough in his own ears.

"Not really."

He stilled.

It was the way she said it more than the two words that comprised it. They sent a ripple of warmth trickling through him. A seductive, dangerous warmth.

He didn't ask her what she meant. He must be mistaken.

Then she turned in his arms and looked up at him.

Chapter Thirteen

I T WASN'T ENOUGH. Azalais wanted more, so very much more. More of that kiss, his weight upon her, and the way he had looked at her—eyes full of dark intensity as if she were the only thing in the world that mattered.

And now he was so close they breathed the same air. They were practically embracing. But not quite. Dare she? Ah, the memory of his lips on hers—soft and hard, gentle and furious all at the same time. She wanted them again.

Azalais swayed toward him.

Then paused.

Her minstrel was standing quite still, looking down at her. He made no move, either towards her or away.

What if she was just like last night's tavernkeeper in his eyes, offering an unwanted advance? Would he put her off with half-excuses while rejecting her in his heart? Would he smile politely and step away?

He kissed me willingly enough yesterday.

As a demonstration, remember? He was proving a point.

And the point was he wants to kiss me!

No, the point was you are a woman, and he has sworn to protect you. He simply demonstrated how vulnerable you are to the lusts of men.

Himself included?

Perhaps, as a passing itch. As a distraction, he has sworn to forebear.

Still, Guilhem said and did nothing. Merely breathed. She could hear those breaths—they were a little ragged sounding. His chest rose and fell so very close to hers. They had ceased to touch hands when she had turned. His hand had dropped from hers. Now the air was heavy between them where they *didn't* touch. It was a magnetic force urging their bodies together. Oh, and Azalais wanted to obey.

But if he pushed her away? In fact, now she thought of it, he almost certainly would. Either he didn't want her or, if he did, he would ignore that urge to hold true to his oath. His damned oath to her well-meaning brother. Worse, he'd then drag her back to La Réole—or on to the next *ville* of any size. There he would shut her up under chaperonage and leave her, a feeble, foolish woman incapable of commanding her own base urges. One for whom there was no better destiny than forced marriage or a nunnery.

Azalais searched his face—dark hair falling untended over his forehead; winged brows, no longer ironic; and eyes aglow with a fire she couldn't read. His lips were slightly ajar.

As if they wanted to savor hers again.

Her insides turned liquid at the thought. The wave of honey-eyed warmth threatened to thrust all her precious caution aside. All she wanted was to reach for him, sink her hands in his hair and draw his face down to hers.

Her hands began to move, fingers craving his skin. And then they stopped.

No, there was something else she wanted, too. The thought was struggling to the surface, nearly drowning in the flood of feeling—but not quite.

It was the magic of his fingers *upon his vielle*. The velvet of his voice in harmony with her lute. Music. Song. Would she toss it all away for a moment's mad craving? They were many days away from Bruniquel, Guilhem had told her. Days and days of making music as she had made with no other. With him.

Azalais stepped back, retreating over crushed wildflowers and fallen leaves. She stared at the ground, at her quivering hands. Anything but look into his face and see the judgment upon it. The rejection.

At least she had not said anything, or worse—tried anything. But doubtless, he had seen plenty. She could only pray he would be courteous enough not to mention it.

"Enough," she said. "Yes, it is enough for now, Guilhem. Come, let us ride. I need a tavern roof over my head before dark. We have dallied too long."

Or, more accurately, she had. For far too long. And now she needed to scrabble aboard what passed for a horse and ride eastward before Guilhem declared otherwise. She only prayed he didn't leave her in the next town they encountered.

HE SHOULD HAVE left her in the next town. Only it turned out that the next town was barely a village, a collection of huts only half-populated. Will supposed the menfolk were gone south with Prince Edward—to Spain in the hope of loot. The place looked like it was in dire need of silver. The tavern they stayed in let them play for their sleeping space on the floor, but Will could not imagine installing his lady minstrel there in any safety or comfort for the weeks it would take to ransom her father.

So, he sang with her there instead, just two lowly minstrels in a dingy village tavern, singing for thin potage and passable wine. At least his lady faced no danger of being recognized as such—the taproom was so dim he only knew the color of the wine he drank by the redness of its tang. Ensconced in that low-beamed and windowless room, he could almost imagine his partner-in-music was a young man—a slight, short-haired figure coaxing heavenly melody from his lute. Until he began to sing. And then, O, Christ, her damned voice seeped into his very fibers and set them on slow-burning fire. True, those tones were youthful in pitch, but surely no youth ever injected his words with such sweet longing or that sinfully husky edge.

She knew not of what she sang? By heaven, it didn't sound like it. Not to Will's ears.

He should have escorted her back to La Réole the very next day. But it was raining, and it was a solid day's ride back to the *ville*. Not that that made any matter. So, they rode on—eastward, away from the safety of La Réole, looking for the next settlement of any size. They only encountered villages. Villages he couldn't possibly leave her in, containing taverns they played in, slept in—side by aching side—and then rode on from the very next morn.

Some part of him knew he was making excuses. When on the third night he lay, staring up at a lightless tavern roof, listening to her breathe—he knew what his duty was. As a knight, he ought to see his lady safe. As one who'd sworn an oath to her brother, he ought to remove her far from temptation. His temptation. But he could not let her go.

It was her music, of course. Alain's music. *Why in hell did she have to cease being Alain?* It had been a dream come to life, of Sir William transformed into a wandering musician, yet never wandering alone, never without inspiration. For his minstrel companion inspired him. Alain was always trying something new—singing a sweet descant to Will's tenor, trying a fresh accompaniment to an old *canzo*, and running his fingers over his lute in strange and intriguing ways.

Except he wasn't Alain, and Will's body knew it full well. Oh, his pony had an awkward, bouncing gait at times, but that was not the reason why Will's loins were permanently sore these days.

Guilhem the Minstrel groaned—discretely—and rolled onto his side on the ungiving and dubiously clean tavern floor. Away from his sleeping minstrel-companion. Was this what it was like to be a monk? Was Benedict permanently tormented by his oath of chastity?

When she had turned to look at him in the forest clearing, her flushed face angled up to his, he had teetered on a precipitous brink. If she'd made just one move toward him—done anything that might constitute an invitation—his resolve would have crumbled. He would have drawn her to him, laid his lips against those sweet instruments of torture, and then...well, honor be damned.

And he would have been a despicable fool. He could only continue to travel with her if he kept his damned hands to himself. Just look at her past experiences! Besides, she was destined either to be a nun or someone else's wife. And then there was his oath. But more importantly, there was his music. No, *their* music. Will set his jaw in the dark and willed his nether regions into submission. By heaven, he would hold on to this minstrel dream for as long as he damn well could. It was a dream come true. *She* was a dream come true. Just so long as *she* remained to all intents a *he*.

"GOD, I LOVE this life!"

Azalais threw herself down upon the moss and leaf litter and lay there, gazing up at the dimming blue vault above. Spring leaves fluttered overhead, and a tiny brown bird perched on a twig, trilling a song of pure happiness.

Who cared if her hair was tangled with leaf litter and if it wasn't in the least becoming in a damsel to sprawl in tunic and hose upon the woodland floor? Last night, they had played for a well-heeled crowd in a sizeable town. Agen, Guilhem warned her, was possibly their last comfortable berth before they ventured into far wilder territory.

He had asked again whether she wanted to remain there, safe under chaperonage, while he continued into the lawless east. Of course, she said no. She had braced herself for argument—but it never came. Her companion had simply smiled that crooked smile at her and said, "As you wish, my minstrel." And that was it. What followed was an evening of soul-swelling music, a night on a real mattress, and now this—

"*This* is what I always dreamed minstrels do, sleep beneath the stars." She flung her arms out to embrace her surroundings. "Is it not idyllic, Guilhem? The moon will shine upon our dinner, the Garonne will lull us to sleep, and the owls will coo over us."

Guilhem chuckled. "They'll more likely shit over us," was his poetic reply. "Have you ever slept beneath your precious stars before?"

"What do you think? Ladies do not linger out of doors after dark, and they most certainly do not bed themselves down on the turf. Oh, I have always wanted to do this."

Guilhem was moving about nearby, making occasional rustling and clinking noises. Azalais turned her head to one side, observing him. He was strolling about the clearing, bending now and again to pick up branches or a sizeable rock. Every time he stooped, dark hair slipped down to veil his features. When he straightened, hands full of wood or stone, he found himself unable to ruffle the drooping locks back. Azalais's hands tingled. What would his hair feel like? Coarse like horse hair, or soft as a squirrel?

He glanced at her, one brow cocked. "I am pleased to oblige you, my lady. But I suspect you'll curse me for it in the morning. The cold has a habit of creeping up through the ground and entering your very bones. You'll feel as crooked as an old crone come dawn."

A host of responses crowded to her lips. *I'm sure you can soothe my aches away, Guilhem.* Or, *I know a way to keep the cold at bay.*

The upshot being Azalais did not trust herself to open her mouth. So, she shifted her gaze elsewhere as if to revel in the scenery. It was delightful, to be sure—a smooth sward of green, cushioned with moss and leaves and speckled with daisies. Dainty drooping birches. A few convenient boulders to seat oneself upon. It was a forest grove fit for a fairy queen. But Azalais was in no fairy-seeking mood. She would prefer to watch the man who was moving about this enchanted twilight space. He made picking up twigs look like a courtly dance—or perhaps a dagger drill in slow motion.

She had not touched him since that second dagger demonstration. In the past few days, they passed within a finger's breadth of each other a dozen times a day, but they never made contact. And when his eyes met hers, a frisson of awareness shivered through her. But that was all. They had both been exquisitely careful to keep their distance, Azalais sensed. But this was the first time they would really sleep alone tonight—just the two of them, without any drunken chaperones snoring nearby. Doubtless, he would sleep on quite the other side of the grove.

"Well, are you just going to recline there like a fine lady in her bower, my lady, or do you fancy gathering some firewood before it gets dark?" her minstrel asked.

Oh, *that* was what he was doing. Azalais scrambled up, her hair no doubt hedgehogged with twigs. A pity they weren't large enough to use as kindling. She had been playing the fine lady. It was time to think like a minstrel. The first thing any sensible person needed beneath the stars was a fire.

It turned out that even gathering firewood was a joy. Once Guilhem had pointed out that branches so green their leaves still hung off them were a recipe for nothing but smoke, she got the hang of it. And it permitted her to explore the woodland in quite a different way—examining the forest floor in detail, finding little sculptures of fungi or disturbing a dark-eyed dormouse. And she was working with him, accumulating the means by which they would eat and warm themselves—just the two of them—beneath a diamond-speckled sky.

Finally, she settled herself on a small boulder and watched as he arranged a hearth of stones and began to lay a fire. She was learning how to be a minstrel—how to fend for herself in the wilds. That it was pure pleasure to watch his hands move over stone and wood, his long fingers seemingly as adept at fire building as playing his vielle, was merely a side benefit. Only she wasn't sure whether she could replicate that fire building any time soon. Her attention was apt to stray, to wander to his hair—fallen forwards again, or the way tunic and hose adhered to his body as he crouched, placing sticks with the care of a sculptor.

Guilhem wasn't a heavily muscled man, she could see. Not like Robert or certain friends of his. But then Azalais had no taste for thuggish bulk developed solely for exercising violence upon other people. It wasn't as if her companion was a weakling… anything but. Instead, she perceived long limbs proportionately muscled, trim but not bulky. The very way he moved indicated strength mingled with agility. She doubted Robert would have the patience to crouch before a fledgling fire for so long. He would consider it beneath him.

Azalais snapped her lids shut. O God, she had been doing it again—watching him. No, "watching" was too mild a term for it. Observing him minutely, absorbing his every movement and contour. She had no more idea how to light a fire now than she had a day ago. Besides, what was the point? She would never be a minstrel—not like him. She did not need to know how to light a fire. Her knightly intended would not permit his wife to blacken her hands in a hearth, and even nuns had servants.

"You don't know how fortunate you are, Guilhem," she murmured.

"Fortunate? How so?"

Azalais's eyes blinked open. She hadn't expected him to answer. He had seemed so intent upon the crackling little blaze, she'd thought she'd spoken to herself.

He brushed his hands off and sat back on the grass. It was deep dusk in their forest glade now. The firelight alone illumined his face.

"To live like this," she said. "I have never done this before—this sleeping in the open. I've never needed to learn fire-making. A lady doesn't, you know. That's what servants are for."

She examined the flames rather than look at him. It was too intimate somehow, this gazing at each other across a campfire.

He chuckled. The sound was as warm as firelight. It blended with the crackle of flame and rustle of leaves. "I believe you overrate the art of fire-making, Lady Azalais. Ask any peasant child if they'd miss tending fires if they never had to do it again."

"It's not just the fire, Guilhem. It's the whole thing." Azalais reached her hands out into the night, encompassing the earth-smelling air and the sounds of the woodland coming to nocturnal life. "This minstrel existence. Spending the day in the open, riding through this beautiful land, and then evenings devoted to song. Troubadour songs, not dirty ditties for sailors."

His lips curved. They seemed painted by firelight, burnished and beautiful. She knew how those lips felt.

"Oh, troubadours have a fondness for dirty ditties, too, my minstrel. An innuendo cast in the *langue d'oc* still tickles men where it counts."

"Women, too," Azalais murmured. Not that she wanted to pursue that line of inquiry. Or did she? "But that is not my point," she hurried on. "It is the freedom I love. And the music."

The music with you, she did not add, although she ought to have. Now she knew why angels made music in heaven. Making music with another being was an experience not truly of this earth. It was a communion of souls.

Then a fresh thought occurred. Perhaps she didn't need Guilhem himself to access the angelic realm. Maybe she had just fixated on him because she'd been on her own for so long—she didn't know what it was like to make music with someone else. Just because he was appealing to look at did not mean he was anything special in the musical department. Perhaps any jongleur would do.

"Indeed. So, you feel it, too, my minstrel."

His words mingled and blurred with the crackle of flame. Nevertheless, they sent a tiny shiver down her arms. She held them out toward the fire—as if the warmth of wood could effect a cure. Ah, she was his minstrel again. He was her Guilhem. Good riddance to Sir William de Fauconberg.

But no, it was impossible. She was barred by femininity and nobility from this life. No such barrier was placed before him. He did *not* feel as she did. He might love this life, but it was his for the taking. For her, these few weeks were but a fleeting taste of heaven. Brief, tantalizing…and torturous.

"Which is why I say you are fortunate, Guilhem. So fortunate you do not know the extent of your own fortune." She held his eyes across the firelight now. She glared at him. "You love this life, too? Well, you can just reach out and make it yours, as simple as plucking a cherry from a tree. One bite and it is yours. As for me, men order my life. They tell me what I may do. Robert says, 'marry this lout,' while I pray my father will counter with, 'enter a nunnery.' Even Ben saw fit to arrange my life for me, and he gave me yet another controlling man—you—to oversee my life. Do you think any of them will say 'Oh Azalais, become a minstrel by all means! Ruin your status and reputation by strumming for a living'? I cannot defy them—if I fled, they would seek me out. And if they didn't find me, some other man would get his paws on me. So, you see *you*, minstrel-man, are supremely fortunate."

Azalais paused, her breath coming quick. She hadn't intended to say so much. Why bare her heart to him? There was no point. He was a man—a knight, for God's sake! He could never understand. Knights used women as pawns in marriage or sated their lusts upon them. Doubtless, Guilhem believed that was the proper way of things. He only tolerated her when he thought of her as Alain.

"I begin to think that if I were a minstrel, I would indeed be fortunate," Guilhem returned quietly. "But I am not one yet. Nor is it quite so simple as plucking fruit." Then his brows dipped. "Or maybe the comparison is apt—once the cherry is picked, it can never be restored to the branch. It is forever fallen. *I* would be forever fallen."

"Fallen? How?" She did not hide her disbelief.

"Fallen from knighthood, my lady. My kind would spurn me. My father would cast me out. Disinherit me. A wandering minstrel is not a son to be proud of, and no man would permit me to marry his daughter."

He spoke the words calmly. They were injected with no particular feeling. They seemed to have inhabited his mind so long their needle pricks no longer registered. Azalais frowned at the flames. He was *not* as constrained as she.

"I don't believe you," she said. "Knights and nobles need minstrels. They crave them for their feasts and entertainment. They value the news they carry. Your kind wouldn't spurn you— they would welcome you."

"They might welcome me as a minstrel, but they would distrust me as a man. If I commit myself to minstrelsy, I will never be accepted as an equal amongst those of noble birth again. Minstrels are rabble, Azalais. They are homeless wanderers of low morals, and they are not to be trusted."

"Your namesake was a nobleman of the very highest standing," she countered. "Guilhem of Aquitaine was no outcast, and his daughter wedded two kings."

"That was long ago, and Guilhem de Aquitaine was no vagrant player. He was a troubadour."

"Well, be a troubadour then! You sing and play, Guilhem, yet you are still a knight. You are the acknowledged son of a nobleman, are you not? It is not so unacceptable to be both."

Silence across the softly crackling fire. There. He couldn't argue with her.

Or could he?

"I am not a firstborn son, Lady Azalais. I am expected to carve my fortune out with my sword—or enter a monastery and have done with the world. I have no great estates to support the pursuit of song. The one manor I hope to inherit—should my father see fit—is barely enough to keep me in vielle strings."

She snorted at that. Pure exaggeration. How like him.

"I have little time, my lady," he continued softly. "My father has delivered me an ultimatum. I must begin to behave like a true knight or take vows of celibacy before the year is out. Or he washes his hands of me."

Chapter Fourteen

WILLIAM WATCHED EMOTIONS flit across his companion's face like flickering shadows. She didn't believe him, he could see. She didn't *want* to believe him. It gave her something to anchor her anger upon if my lady Azalais thought he was so much freer than she.

She was only the second person he had explained his dilemma to. Her brother was the first—Benedict, who had landed them both in this strange situation. And now Azalais's eyes were narrowed upon him.

"Your father wants you to behave as a true knight, you say. So how *have* you been behaving? What have you done that so offends him?"

Will plastered a grin upon his face. He leaned back upon the moss and leaves, lounging in a manner he judged sufficiently indolent and dissolute. He waved a limp hand. "I sing. I play music. I even compose poetry upon occasion. I consort with other such useless wastes of space, and, God forbid, I even take some pride in my attire." He surveyed his current clothing— stained and scuffed from travel—and produced a tragic sigh. "If you believe it of such a scarecrow as you see before you. But worse—far worse than all of these, my lady—is my refusal to return to the field of war. My dear *pater* wants me back in France, or better yet Spain, carving my fortune out of other men's flesh."

His companion's gaze flicked likewise over his clothing, and one brow arched in delicate disbelief.

"You are a knight," the lady replied. "England is at war and knights fight. That is their function. Why do you not? Surely you may both fight and play music?"

Another sigh. "My father's point entirely, dear lady. But you see, I have attempted that formula already. I have been a dutiful son and eviscerated Frenchmen in the service of my king. As a result, I found war is not all Roland and Lancelot and glorious deeds of chivalry. To be brief, I have found it is not my cup of wine at all."

He sealed his lips at that and fixed his gaze upon a burning log. Burning. Just like the homes he'd helped destroy across France, some with occupants still inside. Burning like the unholy fire of war that inflamed the men he'd fought beside, firing them to unthinkable deeds. Inhuman deeds. Even beasts were not so savage.

"My brother Robert finds warfare to his taste, whether he thinks it tastes like wine, ale, or water. I think he'd even drink it if it were blood."

Will unsealed his lips sufficient to reply, "It is."

"What?"

"Blood."

Will closed his eyes, but the vision of flame did not disappear. Christ. He shook himself, then opened his lids and looked directly at the girl across from him. He anchored his gaze upon her. Here was something pure and good, innocent of war, someone whose heart was given to music.

"No more," he said. "I do not wish to speak of war. I do not wish to think of it or see it. I do not even wish to sing of it."

She smiled at him. It was a gentle smile if a little uncertain. "Then let us sing of love instead," she said.

THEY DID, AND Will was never more glad to wield a vielle, to draw a bow that would harm no one, and to fill his soul with melody.

Azalais sang. At first, she selected old melodies—troubadour fare of centuries past. Songs of inaccessible ladies and languishing songsters. But after a few old favorites, she paused. She did not immediately launch into another. Instead, his minstrel companion frowned into the fire.

"Well, Alain?" he prompted. "Who is next? Ceramon perhaps, or the Comtessa de Dia?"

It wasn't Alain who raised her tentative gaze to his across the dividing flame.

"Neither. Nobody," Azalais answered, and his heart sank. He was not ready for sleep, nowhere near ready to give up song for the night—not with this divine nightingale for company.

"Nobody, that is, but me," she continued, her gaze dropping.

Evidently, Will's mind was not at its most agile tonight. Surely, she didn't mean…? No. It was all he could do to echo her words, "Nobody but you."

And saw a glow that had nothing to do with the fire feather her cheeks and turn her eyes to gold.

"What I mean," she said, "is I have been composing a *canzo* as we ride. Well, erm, you see I have slung some verses together and then cobbled up a tune to accompany them. It will be quite horrible, of course. A heinous affront to the ears. But, well…"

Will felt the most peculiar smile steal over his face. In fact, it was a collection of competing smiles—part relief that she referred merely to music, part mockery at himself that he thought it was anything else, and part reassurance for his companion, so obviously bashful at bringing a newborn song into the world.

She didn't look all that reassured. Will wondered what kind of extraordinary grimace he was producing, and quickly rearranged it into his usual half-smile.

"I understand, my minstrel," he said. "I, too, have been there. Sing, and know that I will not judge. All songs must start somewhere."

She gave a little snort. "Of course, you will judge, Guilhem. But I thank you for saying otherwise."

He opened his mouth to refute her, but she had already picked up her lute and had begun to pluck its strings. Focusing on it rather than him. Well, that was fine by Will. Now he could watch her at his leisure. He could contemplate this contradictory creature before him. This sylph-like girl dressed as a man, a lady who yearned for a rough minstrel life, a lovely woman destined to be a nun. And a songstress who sang of a love she had never known—and never would. Especially if she was forced to marry her despised Lord L.

Will found his teeth clenching. *Not his business.* His only responsibility was to protect her; he had sworn to aid Azalais in her harebrained mission. What happened after that was up to her father and her brothers, as was only right and proper. He unglued his jaw. All that was for the future. Right now, his charge was playing her chosen role to perfection. She was a minstrel bringing a new song into the world. And Guilhem the Wandering Troubadour was more than a little curious what his minstrel-lady would produce.

So, he trained his eyes on the firelit figure and focused on the melody she was picking from her lute. Her right hand curled to caress the strings, fingers flickering. It still seemed so strange to him, her technique of coaxing individual notes from the strings. Strange but beautiful. Like her. *No.* He closed his eyes and filled his ears with music.

Once he had listened to her play the melody a few times, he would improvise an accompaniment to it on his vielle as she sang. That was the plan. Indeed, it seemed a straightforward-enough tune—deceptively simple, even. Elegant and unadorned. But as soon as she began to sing, he had no thoughts to spare for accompaniment.

He abandoned himself to her words and melody.

She sang of spring, the troubadour's favorite season. At first, she sang of the beauties of spring—the awakening of the world after winter. A budding and blooming underpinned with meaning. Or was Will reading too much into the words? His minstrel-lady was probably just describing the scenes through which they rode.

But in the third stanza, the song shifted in tone. The singing slowed. The words spoke of an ending to spring, an end that came too soon. This minstrel's spring was but a fleeting season of joy, never to be repeated. The earth's rhythms were disobeyed, for after her spring came winter, and that season of sorrow would reign forever.

Forever.

The last notes of the lute hung in the air. Her voice had ceased. His minstrel-lady was studying the fire with a concentrated stillness.

What could he say?

"Play it again," he said at last. "Let me listen afresh."

She didn't answer but simply ran a thumb over her lute to create a simple accompaniment for her song. No more plucking this time—her voice picked out the notes instead. And she sang with such feeling—first of spring, then of the coming winter. Her tone was perfectly pitched and just a little husky. It set every hair on his nape to tingling. And this time he was sure of it: the meaning beneath the obvious sense of the words.

"Well?" she said at last. The last notes of the lute had been absorbed by the night, and the only sounds now were water and flame. "Is it so bad you cannot think what to say, minstrel? Fear not, I can take criticism. Just spit it out and have done."

"Bad?" Will felt a strong need to pick himself up by the scruff of the neck and shake his minstrel-self like a dog does a rat. Perhaps a self-administered slap to the face would suffice?

He closed his eyes to dispel the dream—not that it worked noticeably—then opened them to look directly at her.

"It was beautiful, my lady. Quite beautiful but sad. It pierced my heart."

It was her turn to blink. Then a little frown appeared.

"You flatter me, Guilhem. I do not want flattery. Tell me truly what you think—speak to a minstrel and not a lady. Where can I improve?"

"I do indeed speak to my minstrel-girl, not a tinkering court lady," he replied. "But let us play it again. Let me accompany you. I have the melody now. As I play, it may come to me where it may be tweaked."

Will looked across the flames at her and he didn't smile. He didn't need to. Perhaps the night formed protection enough that he could abandon mockery and charm. Or was it because she had revealed her innermost core to him—the heart of her music? He could simply communicate with her, musician to musician.

She gave a little nod, and he picked up his vielle.

They played. Will followed his songstress carefully, his bow echoing her mood and tone. She stared out into the darkness, and he never took his eyes from her. Yet while they played her *canzo*, they were as one. They were connected not by flesh or even look, but on some higher plane.

And he had no idea where her melody might be improved.

"THE SONG IS about you, is it not?"

They had played her creation through twice in its entirety, then he had suggested tiny amendments in rhythm and accompaniment, and they had tinkered with a stanza or two. Now the silence had descended again, and Azalais was feeling a need to bundle herself in her cloak and feign asleep. She couldn't bear the weight of his eyes upon her, the damnable intensity of them. Now that he wasn't smiling lopsidedly or brushing back his infernal hair, he seemed more present, more vivid, and far more of a danger. Music seemed to release something in him. She had seen it before in taverns, even aboard the ship. But never quite as tonight.

And now this question. He had not criticized her music or pooh-poohed her poetry. She'd almost prefer it if he did. Instead, he reached straight past metaphor and abstraction and identified the true meaning of her song.

"Yes," she muttered and busied herself with slipping her lute into its leather casing with most exacting care.

"This is your spring, is it not? This minstrel journey. This is your brief blooming before winter descends."

Azalais nearly let the lute drop to the forest floor. Guilhem had moved to stand beside her. He reached out a hand. She eyed it as if she had never seen such an appendage before.

"Come. We have sung enough. I do not wish to fill my head with any song but yours."

She gave him a wary look. Was the charmer back? But there was no teasing smile lingering about his lips. And still, his hand stretched out for her.

Thoughts slowed like honey. A tingling warmth crept through her instead. She took his hand.

He pulled her gently to her feet.

"Where do you sleep tonight, Azalais?"

She was melting. *This* was what she wanted. Guilhem was no Lord Leonard, no Robert either. This was what the songs described—this feeling, this unutterable longing. No fear or disgust. Just yearning. The need for his hands upon her, the touch of his lips. She didn't care for propriety or maidenly modesty. She only wanted *him*. Now was her springtime. After that, there would be nothing but winter. She needed a memory to carry into that bleak forever.

He had released her hand. He stood close by, awaiting her reply. Instead, she closed the gap between them, raised her arms, and twined her hands about his neck to draw him to her.

Guilhem turned to stone. But he didn't push her away.

"No, Azalais," he whispered.

"But—"

"I asked you where you slept so I could ensure you had chosen a good location. You have not slept outdoors before, have you?" Eminently reasonable words. Spoken by a statue.

A trickle of ice ran through her. She had gone too far. He didn't want her.

Then a counterargument filtered through, permeating without the aid of words. The body she pressed to hers was rock, yes, but it trembled ever so slightly. And some parts of it were more rocklike than others.

She gazed up into his face. His eyes were pools of shadow. Unreadable. "You do not break your oath if I give you permission, Guilhem. Benedict only acted to protect me, but this is what I want. It is what Benedict would want, too."

She felt the chuckle before she heard it—a vibration deep in his chest.

"Benedict is a monk *and* your brother, my lady. I sincerely doubt this is what he had in mind."

The glint of amusement vanished from his eyes, and still, he did not move.

"Benedict wants what is best for me." And then a thought struck her. In fact, it seemed so obvious she wondered why she'd never considered it before. "You know," she said slowly. "I think that's why he chose you, Guilhem. You are as little like L–, well, you are unlike any knight I have ever met. Perhaps he wanted me to discover that not all men are like…well, you know what I mean."

She felt him breathe. A tiny movement in a figure of rock.

"An oath is an oath, and your brother is my oldest friend."

"But if you were not bound?" she whispered.

A quake rippled through him. Her fingers twined in his hair. Ah, it *was* soft. Not kitten-soft, but more of a smooth, strong silk she wanted to bury her face in, to savor against her lips.

"It matters not." His voice was rough-edged. "The oath is given."

She was making a complete and utter fool of herself. He

didn't want her. He couldn't do it. This was not how men worked. She had been warned over and over from childhood that men weren't to be trusted. They were ravening beasts, wanting only one thing from a woman. They had no self-control when it came to their nether regions. Robert's men—Robert himself upon occasion—had only proved the truth of the matter. No serving maid was safe from them. No peasant woman. And now she was reduced to their level. She was accosting Guilhem, and he was only trying to keep faith with Benedict. It was too humiliating.

But she wasn't quite done with humiliating herself yet.

"This oath, Guilhem. What did you swear to my brother?" Then her brows dipped a little. A fresh thought edged into her befuddled mind. "You did not even know I was a woman then. What on earth *did* you swear?"

Chapter Fifteen

WILLIAM STARED DOWN at her—and willed himself to stay firm. No, damn it, not that variety of firm. To hold *true* to his damned oath, to Benedict, and above all, to Azalais. And Eve thought she had it bad with a snake whispering sweet nothings about apples in her ear. Apples be damned. He could resist a cartload. But this enchantress who wound her arms about his neck and raised her songbird lips to his? That was an entirely different sack of snakes.

Then her words penetrated.

She was right. He hadn't known she was a woman then. So, what *had* he sworn? Will had held onto the gist of his oath for so long that he'd never stopped to consider the words themselves. He cast his mind back. Benedict had said Alain had been hard used, hadn't he? That the boy needed protecting in spirit and body. But what had Will promised in return? Something flippant, no doubt, but an oath was an oath. He, too, frowned, raking his memory for…

Then he gave a shout of laughter.

The slight form pressed against his stiffened slightly.

"What?"

"Forgive me, my lady." Will choked back the second eruption of laughter. His temptress let her arms slip from around his neck and took a step back. The look she was giving him now was

161

devoid of amusement. He favored her with a lunatic grin. "I have remembered the words."

"Well?"

Will attempted to put his features in order and achieve some kind of gravity. It was an impossible task. Oh well, he may as well just spit it out.

"Lady Azalais, I gave your brother my solemn oath, taken on the Holy Cross he wears about his neck, that I would safeguard Alain's body from harm and his valuables from pilfering."

Will's lips twitched. They threatened revolt.

Azalais stuck her hands on her hips and glared at him. "And?"

"And I swore I would protect his posterior from plundering."

Will clapped a palm over his wayward mouth and watched his companion's brows shoot up, then sink. Then her mouth opened, failed to utter any sound, and subsequently closed. It was quite fascinating, the play of emotion upon the delicate face before him, flame-kissed and just out of reach. Which was probably just as well. True, he had sworn not to meddle with Azalais's delightful posterior, but that did not alter the underlying meaning of his oath.

He reached out and took her hand. Just her hand, he told himself. That is all. The moment of madness has passed. You will not succumb and nor will she.

"My lady, you are beautiful. And utterly desirable. Have no doubt of that. But I gave your brother my word, and however—" he gave her a lopsided grin, "—ill-chosen those words may have been, they still bind me. The meaning beneath them, I mean. I *will* protect you from harm."

"I did not ask you to harm me, Guilhem," she said softly. Then she offered a tiny smile in return. "Or my posterior."

Then she took his hand and stepped in close, pulling his hand about her—to place it on the banned region of her anatomy. His fingers contacted rough woolen cloth, and beneath it—the soft curve of a buttock. Unthinking, he shaped his hand about its surface. His fingers flexed to draw her to him, so he could lay his other hand upon her rear, or perhaps about her shoulders, then dip his face to hers, and—

He jerked his hand away, stepped back hurriedly—too hurriedly. He stumbled, nearly overbalanced. *She* had him off-balance.

But Azalais was speaking again. "Once we have ransomed my father, I will return to England. And there I will either enter a nunnery or marry a man I despise and fear. Winter, Guilhem. *This* is my springtime. I do not fear or despise you, and I wish to experience love—physical love, that is—at least once in my life. I want to know of what the troubadours sing, and who better than you—a troubadour—to show me?"

Just like that. Spoken calmly and reasonably, if with a slight underlying quiver. Thus, did innocent Lady Azalais de Keldy proposition him, a knight whose dissolute habits were well-matched by his current guise. And Will had no idea what to reply. He wasn't even strictly shielded by his oath. And there she stood—an enchantress in the flamelight, the flickering embodiment of his desire. Her short-cropped curls, the rough man's clothing, and utter lack of feminine adornment only emphasized her otherworldly beauty.

Will frowned, trying to work out what drew him so powerfully to her. If he could put his finger on the source, perhaps then he would have a chance at resistance. Oh, he discerned her delicate features, the full, soft lips, the eyes of amber, and he knew a lissom figure lay just under those loose clothes. It was a figure he craved to unwrap, to lay bare to the starlight, to explore with lips and tongue and fingers. Why, she had practically ordered him to.

But it wasn't just her physical beauty that drew him. Perhaps if it were, he could have resisted. It was the spirit that lit her eyes, moved her mouth, and sang through her very fingers. It was her music and all that lay within. There lay the true source of her beauty, and it shone through her every word and action.

Dear God, he ought to compose a *canzo* in honor of his inaccessible lady, not stand here gawking at her.

"I think that you are not entirely averse to me, Guilhem. Or am I wrong?" his lady murmured from far too proximate a distance. She had stepped up to him again, treading softly as if not to frighten a wild animal. Then she slipped her arms around his unresisting neck and raised her face to his. Again. "Kiss me, Guilhem. Kiss me like Lord Leonard never will—or any nun either, for that matter."

And without any conscious decision, Will found himself doing just that.

His arms looped about her, drew her to him, her slender curves against his taller breadth, and his mouth descended upon hers. No thought, just utter rightness. And her lips opened beneath his like a flower to the sun. They offered themselves to him, soft and untutored, yet so willing to learn. He kissed her, and she followed his lead, her lips shaping to his. Giving. Taking. Demanding.

William slipped a hand about her nape, threaded his fingers through short, soft curls, and slanted his mouth against hers. Deeper. More. Their two bodies moved against each other as if to become one. He could feel her heart thud against him, rapid as a bird's. And still, she kissed him, holding nothing back. Her fingers gripped his shoulders—strong, fine fingers. Oh, they could play him like a lute. His tongue reached, questing between her lips, to touch the very tip of hers.

A shudder coursed through him. It was an earthquake to unsettle his core. *O God, he shouldn't be doing this.* The thought was a bucket of cold water, and under its impact Will nearly managed it. He nearly pulled away, nearly managed to set her safely at arm's length. He knew he ought to. It was the right thing to do.

Then her tongue tasted his, inviting but a little unsure—and all reservation vanished. There was only her mouth, her hair, the form that molded itself against him, the softness of her against his aching hardness.

One of his hands had dipped back to her posterior. His fingers flexed, craving but fighting off the urge to press her against him, to show her how much he wanted her. As if she hadn't already worked that out. The problem was, if he did so, he wasn't sure where this would stop. If he *could* stop. So, he inched his hand upward instead—dipping it under her tunic, then up over the rough hose, over the braies to which the hose was attached. Until his fingers met warm, bare skin.

His minstrel arched like a cat beneath his fingers at her waist, yet her lips never left his. Will's groin jolted in response. O God, the mere touch of her skin—silken and warm, so alive to his touch. His tongue danced against hers, and his fingers continued stroking, adoring the living idol beneath his hands, until—

They encountered fabric. Linen, by the feel of it, barring his fingers from exploration and binding her tight. Will knew linen to be a comfortable fabric, one eminently suited to undergarments—but this linen stung his fingertips as if it were woven from thorns. And suddenly it seemed to exert the same effect on its wearer.

Will's hand fell away. Azalais's lips distanced themselves from his—left them naked and wanting. Their bodies still touched, but they were no longer as one. And he could feel the tension in her frame as clearly as if it were his own.

"The linen band," he murmured. It felt strange to move his lips to shape words. "Your binding," he said, stating the downright obvious but not knowing what else to say.

"Yes." Her voice was rough-edged. "It binds my breasts and pads my ribs. It turns me into a man."

He lifted a finger and traced a line down her back, down the outside of her tunic. He felt the outline clearly this time. The linen wrapping her torso from below her shoulder blades to the base of her ribs. Not just a breast-binding but a means of altering the shape of her entire torso. Clever.

And a timely reminder to him. Thank God.

Will drew a deep breath. He breathed in the mild night air

and the intoxicating scent of the woman who stood so close to him—but so far away.

He lifted his offending hand and brushed a wild curl from her cheek. Then he gazed into her upturned eyes, dark in the starlight, and said, "Lady Azalais, to repeat an earlier question: where do you intend to sleep?"

⋙✕⋘

A FRISSON COMPOSED of equal parts, need and terror, coursed through her.

"I—I thought—" Then she took a breath, turned, and pointed. "I thought I would sleep over there." Her baggage was a shadow beside a soft-looking expanse of leaf litter and moss. At least, it had looked soft by daylight. Now it was simply a patch of blackness dappled with stray moonlight.

His hand slipped into hers. "Come then, we should talk."

"Talk?" She gave a shaky chuckle. "Is that what you call it?"

"Yes, my lady."

And the hand in hers tugged her gently toward her baggage. Then he crouched down and felt about with one hand.

"A good choice," he murmured after a few moments. "Dry, free of rocks and branches."

A good choice for what? she wanted to say.

He reached for her cloak. It was folded on top of her baggage, a vague shape in the dim. He spread it upon the leaves and moss and then turned to her. His eyes were wells of darkness.

"Sit, my lady. Test your bed, and we shall discuss a certain pressing matter that has arisen between us."

She saw his lips quirk at that last phrase and goosebumps skittered over her arms.

Azalais sat, feeling his gaze upon her. Her every movement seemed alien as if her body was only partly under her control. And he seated himself by her, quite close—but not touching.

"Well? What is there to discuss, Guilhem?" It was meant to be a demand, but it came out as a whisper.

A soft sigh beside her. "Your request, my lady—that you wish me to help you discover that which the troubadours sing of— presents me with something of a dilemma," he said. "On the one hand, I am more than willing to aid you in your quest. You have deduced correctly, sweet Azalais. I find myself anything but indifferent to you. My body leaps to your command. And yet—"

He hesitated.

"Yet your oath binds you," she finished for him. "Your promise to my brother."

"Well, not exactly. Delicious as I find your posterior, my lady, I feel no pressing need to explore it as some men do. I am more concerned about certain long-term consequences of complying with your request. Has it occurred to you, my lady, that such activities might result in a child?"

Thank God for the dark, for the fact he was sitting next to her rather than opposite, and that the glow of the flames could excuse away any reciprocal glow on her face.

An innocent she may be, but she wasn't totally naïve. It *had* occurred to her, and it had not seemed wholly a bad thing. But she wasn't about to explain the intricacies of her reasoning to her companion. He was supposed to act entirely at the urging of his loins and to hell with the consequences. Consequences were the woman's problem. That was how men behaved, at least at Keldy.

Would he demand the truth? She raked her mind for an appropriate phrasing, some palatable way to say…

Guilhem's fingers trailed her cheek. They ran along cheek- bone and jaw, then gently turned her face to look into his. He smiled at her, and there was a glint of devilry in his eye. Or maybe it was just the reflection of the fire. Hellfire, perhaps.

"Fear not, my minstrel. I have a solution. It neatly solves two problems in one," he said.

And he kissed her again.

"SO, YOU PLAN to immortalize me in song, my lady?"

He murmured the question against Azalais's skin, just below her right ear. He had paused midway through trailing a line of kisses down the side of her neck, having already ravished her mouth with admirable thoroughness. Now his breath stirred the tiny hairs on her neck, prickling them almost unbearably.

But she didn't want to talk. She had far better uses for his mouth right now. When she didn't answer, at least not in words, he took the skin of her neck in his teeth and nipped. It was a bite a newborn kitten would be ashamed of, but it sent a bolt of fire through her. The noise she made in response was distinctly kitten-like, too.

"Well?" he growled, nuzzling her ear. "Answer me, song-stress. Are you making an inventory of my actions even now? Will my every move be recorded in verse? Will I walk into a tavern in some out-of-the-way hole years from now to hear myself described in song, blow by blow?"

She arched against him and laughed low. "Are you nervous, my minstrel? Don't you want your loins to be famous across Christendom? Or do you fear your performance will be judged somehow…lacking?"

Where did those words come from? She sounded like him. Azalais smiled. Too much bad company, for certain.

"You want to know of what troubadours sing," he replied against her earlobe, then nipped it for good measure. "I worry that you are simply conducting research, my minstrel-lady. I feel myself to be under observation. You raise the stakes. After all, if I am to be immortalized, I must produce a superlative perfor-mance." He traced the curl of her ear with his tongue. "But be warned, my lady—and it pains me to say it—I must ensure your research remains incomplete."

The words trickled through to consciousness. His lips were

still upon her ear. It was entirely distracting.

"What?" she managed. "Incomplete? How?"

It wasn't the most coherent set of syllables she'd ever uttered in her life.

And then the damn man removed his mouth from her ear in order to take her face in his two hands and look directly at her. Dark eyes snared hers. She could not look away. A fall of hair drooped over his brow, threatening to obscure his view. Without thinking, Azalais reached and did what she'd wanted to do ever since she first saw him—sifted her fingers through his hair, brushing the stray lock back from his brow. A hint of a smile crossed his face, turning him beautiful. No, more beautiful.

The smile vanished, and Guilhem spoke. "For the sake of both your honor and mine, Lady Azalais, we cannot consummate the act. Thus, my oath will be kept, and you will avoid falling with child. This is what I mean by incomplete."

Doubtless, her expression conveyed a whole host of responses, for her minstrel grinned and dipped his face to hers, his hands still cupping her cheeks. He kissed her as if he would devour every question before she uttered it—and perhaps he truly did so. The stroke of his tongue melted all words from her mind and left her with nothing to do but respond in kind. To devour him.

But the hands about her face were getting in the way—they kept her a little at a distance, and no distance at all was acceptable now.

She seized his wrists, but too late—his mouth left hers. He sat back. She nearly whimpered with frustration, but a last shred of dignity made her swallow the sound.

She tried words instead. "Incomplete? Do you mean to drive me quite crazy, Guilhem?"

"No," he murmured. "Only myself." And when she frowned at that, Guilhem raised a wicked brow at her. "Oh, I am not talking about kisses, my lady. Believe me, I intend to kiss every inch of your silken skin. I will peel these boy's clothes off you and array you naked upon the flowers. I will worship you with my mouth. And I am not talking about song, sweet minstrel. No, I will make you sing in wordless bliss."

Clothed as she was, her skin tingled as if lit by fireflies.

"Just so long as you are naked, too," she murmured in reply.

His eyes widened. And there, in the firelight, Azalais saw beyond doubt. It was like opening a door onto a furnace. There, blazing within Guilhem, was an inferno of desire. His face was alight with it. Her lips lifted. She rather suspected his body was, too.

"I doubt that would be a good idea," he said, his voice rough-edged.

But it still left her confused. For what else was there in the bodily transactions between women and men beyond consummation? That was what men wanted, wasn't it? It was all she'd ever witnessed, all she'd ever been taught to fear.

Remembrance flooded back, far too vivid. Lord Leonard's retainer. The livid, swollen flesh he had released from his braies. She blinked. Why did she have to imagine that now? She shook her head, but the image did not dislodge. That lout's overwhelming urge had been to shove his member between her maid's legs, it had been plain. Thank Christ he didn't. That pleasure denied, he had simulated the action with his hand. She gritted her teeth. The image remained. His bestial face—her maid's face—her naked, helpless legs. Were all men like that? Was that what Guilhem meant? But he was nothing like that thug or his master. Nothing. She hoped.

Yet, he was still a man. He had a man's apparatus.

Time to test the theory. Azalais let a hand stray toward her companion's lap. He could not see what she was about—one hand still cupped her face, his gaze was trained on hers. So, she dipped her hand between his legs—angled for ease of sitting—and her fingers found what they were seeking without the least trouble in the world. Her palm closed upon solidity, hardness, length.

A jolt coursed through her, a ripple of melting heat. But that was nothing to the reaction that rocked Guilhem. The hardness beneath her fingers bucked. Guilhem's eyes closed, and he uttered a groan that seemed to emanate from deep within.

"What is there beyond this?" Azalais said, and she could hear the swirl of emotions in her own voice—accusation, need, anger, and genuine query. *You are a man,* her tone said. *So far as women are concerned, you have only one aim. And this is it.*

When he didn't answer, she squeezed. Not hard, just hard enough.

"God in Heaven, Azalais." A hand descended on her own. It prized her fingers away, and all the while his eyes remained tightly closed. Only when her hand was safely in his did Guilhem open his eyes. Even then he didn't look at her. He stared over her head into the darkness and breathed deep.

"You want to consummate." She laid a distinct emphasis on that last word. "I am not entirely ignorant, Guilhem. You are nothing better than…"

"Shh, my lady." He laid two fingers on her lips. "There is more—far more—to the art of love than you have ever witnessed. Yes, it is true, a rather insistent part of my anatomy craves to be united with yours, but that alone is mere mechanical crudity. An animal action over in heartbeats. That is not what you ask for, my lady minstrel. Nor is it what you deserve."

He took a deep breath and met her eyes. Dark eyes, gentle, but simmering with banked desire.

"My lady, you do not have to do this. I understand your desire to be a nun. You have told me of one experience with men. Having met your elder brother, I suspect there have been others. Some men have no subtlety—that is their loss. Theirs, and the women they unfortunately encounter. Perhaps you have learned enough of love for tonight. Perhaps enough for a lifetime. I do not wish to add to your evil experiences of men."

She held his gaze.

"You will not, Guilhem. Of that I am certain. You are not a knight in the mold of my brother's men. You don't see love as a battle, as a matter of violent conquest. Physical love, I mean," she added, just in case he misunderstood. "I am willing to trust you. I want to know, Guilhem. Give me memories for my winter. Give me something to counter those I already have. And—"

She lifted a daring hand to his cheek. Warm skin. The prickle of stubble sent tiny shocks through her fingertips. The sensations, the moment itself, was too much. So, she turned a mischievous smile on him. She must diffuse the situation or she would combust. "Inspire me to song, Guilhem. Give me something to immortalize."

Chapter Sixteen

There he had it: an ultimatum. And she was smiling up at him with a mix of devilry and uncertain desire to pickle his heart. God, how he wanted to do this. For the first time, he could understand why men like her Lord L let their cocks take control. Will had always been one for the slow and subtle approach—as in a musical performance, a climax reached too soon is no climax at all—but now his groin threatened to make an oath breaker of him.

There was but one solution.

He laid his hand over the one on his cheek. He curled his fingers around her hand and lifted it in his own, raised it to his lips, and kissed her knuckles, one by one.

"Your will is my command," he murmured over her hand. And, by all that was holy, he would ensure it was. There would be no rough usage of this minstrel-lady. He would incur no dishonor upon Benedict's sister. He would make his songstress sing.

Then he lifted his gaze and captured her own. "The linen you bind about yourself—is it comfortable? You wear it constantly, do you not?"

She wriggled a little. "I wear it day and night. It is my armor, Guilhem. It keeps me safe." Her lips lifted. "It might even turn a dagger or two."

"I think it might." He smiled in return. Then he reached out and ran a finger down the center of her torso. His finger snagged on solid fabric. "But let me transform my minstrel companion back into a lady tonight. You will sleep easier for having no constriction, I am sure. Besides, I am curious to view you as a woman, O Alain."

She stilled. "It is bound tight—very tight. It...well, it chafes sometimes, and it leaves my skin somewhat—"

Will's heart twisted. He wanted to tell her that she was beautiful and that no little reddening or abrasion of her torso would alter that, but he suspected she would not believe him. Not yet. He would have to show her how lovely she was instead.

He stroked a stray curl back from her face. "All the more reason to relieve you of it, my lady. Let me see what I can do to soothe your skin. Turn your back to me. I will remain behind you until you say otherwise. After all, I may soothe without seeing."

She looked at him for a moment, lips unsealed as if to speak. Such finely made lips—made for singing and for responding to his. He wanted to kiss them again, but if he did so, there would be no turning her safely around.

As if reading his mind, his lady rose to a crouch and then to her feet. He echoed her movement and found himself presented with her back.

"It will be easier if I stand," she said. "I assume I need to take my tunic off? It is long, and I was sitting on it—"

So businesslike, as if this were a matter of mechanics. He knew where this sudden pragmatism was coming from.

Will moved to stand behind her. Gently, so as not to startle her, he wrapped his arms about her, invited her to lean against him. He nuzzled her neck and trailed a few kisses up it until felt her relax against him. "Do not worry yourself about the details," he murmured. "I will not do anything that you don't want me to. If at any time it becomes too much, just say 'no.'"

She melted a little further into him. "No," she said.

He froze.

That prompted a chuckle from her. "What I mean is I will *not* say no, Guilhem. Do with me as you will. I trust you, and—" She shifted her posterior a little more snugly into the region between his thighs. "I will sacrifice much in the pursuit of research."

Will closed his eyes and let slip a groan. *Her binding, man. Focus on the damn linen.* He forced his fingers to slip down the front of her legs, seeking out the hem of her rough man's tunic. He found it, grasped it, and began to draw it up.

"You must tell me if you get cold." He spoke against her ear, his head dipped down against hers so he could continue to drop kisses against the softness of her neck or nip her ear.

"I rely on you to keep me warm," was all she answered, and she lifted her arms as obedient as a child so he could shimmy the drab tunic up and over her head. He tossed the item aside and she shrank back against him—but not before he glimpsed her form by moonlight and firelight. A lithe and lissom shape deformed by a binding of linen wrapped around her torso.

He ran exploratory fingers over its lower reaches. It felt like good quality linen, thank goodness, but no fabric worn so constantly, so tightly, would feel pleasant after a time. "Where is it secured, my lady?"

"At the front." And she captured one of his hands and, lacing her fingers through his, guided them to a metal protrusion in the swathe of fabric. A pin.

"Heaven, Azalais, you weren't exaggerating when you called this armor," he muttered some moments later.

He felt her laugh. "What good are you as a knight, Guilhem, if you cannot disarm your opponent?"

Her fingers replaced his, and the fabric loosened almost immediately.

He ran his hands slowly up her smooth arms, his palms tingling, then laid a line of kisses along one bare shoulder. "You are not my opponent, and it is my ambition to be a very bad knight," he murmured against warm, warm skin.

Then he slipped his hands back down to hers. Her hands

lingered upon the lower reaches of her binding, holding it closed, now the pin was unpinned.

"May I, my lady?"

He did not attempt to loosen her hold, no matter how the thought might appeal.

Her fingers moved, her hand turned in his, and Will touched linen—the loose end. She had stuck the pin back in it, but it secured nothing now. It was his, and it was time to turn a man back into a girl.

Will frowned. The unwinding evidently required he create some little distance between his body and hers or the fabric would never be freed. A sad necessity, but at least it meant he could see a little more of her. He stepped away, the end of the linen in hand, and unwound the first layer. There was tension in her, he could see—but what variety of tension? Anticipation? Terror? No, the latter was intolerable. He would banish all trace of fear. So, Will stepped closer and nuzzled and nibbled the sweet angle between her shoulder and neck until she softened against him.

And then it was time for another layer to be unwrapped, another step away.

But every time Will moved close—to pass the linen from one hand to the other in front of her, he deposited a kiss on some part of her torso. And felt the frisson of her reaction as if it were his own.

Then another step back to keep on unwrapping her, never hurrying. No matter what the process was doing to his nether regions. Or that the binding did not appear to be noticeably reduced.

"Christ, Azalais, there's enough linen here to keep a nunnery in undergarments for a year. No, ten."

That earned him a chuckle—for the wrong reasons. "What do you know of nun's undergarments, Guilhem?"

He sank his head briefly on her shoulder. "Damnation, woman, I am not so bad a knight as all that." Then he trailed his tongue tip to the base of her neck. She shivered against him. "Although I might make an exception in your case, my lady nun-to-be."

That gave his conscience an almighty jab. But Sir Will could be stoic—he could ignore jabs and stabs all night so long as he could make her laugh. Although when she nudged her posterior against his groin—as now—he knew stoicism had its limits.

"Speaking of exceptions," she said—and turned abruptly in his arms, effectively unwrapping another layer by her action. "You," she poked him in the chest, "are making an exception of yourself. You still wear your tunic, Guilhem. I do not. I want it off."

And before he had a chance to reply or react, she was tugging his offending garment up. Of course, being taller than she, he had to finish the task himself. He dropped the fabric onto the leaf litter and slowly turned back to her. To meet her gaze as it roamed over his chest, his arms, his shoulders, and set his very skin afire. What in hell did she see? Yet another knightly thug? Or maybe one who wasn't knightly enough.

Then her hands were on him, her palms grazing his skin, the planes of his chest, his abdomen, shaping themselves over his shoulders and down his arms. Will closed his eyes and heard nothing but the thud of his heart and the hush of her hands over bare skin. Pray God she keep her hands well above his waistline. Dip any lower, and he might not be responsible for his actions.

"You can open your eyes now, Guilhem. We are even."

"Not quite, my lady." But he opened his lids in all obedience. He saw how her hair caught the firelight, her curls soft waves of flame, a fiery halo. The same light burnished pale skin still bound about by linen. He plucked up the loose end of linen between finger and thumb. Her hands were still on him, sitting low on his abdomen. Too low. He set his teeth. "Turn around."

She did. There weren't many layers left. Two more passes and the last of the linen dropped from her torso of its own accord.

⟫⟪

HER ARMOR WAS gone. It lay in a pale puddle on the forest floor. Azalais could see it if she glanced down—which she did now, for anything was preferable to simply standing, wondering what Guilhem would do next. And what he saw.

A finger touched her back. Azalais jumped. Not that his touch was unexpected, of course—it was simply *too* expected. The fingertip moved slowly down her back, tracing the slight ridges left by her binding.

"How long since you were last a lady, my lady?"

"Since I last removed the linen, you mean? Bordeaux, I think. Yes…"

His fingers were still moving over her back, raising goose-bumps, anticipation, trepidation. What was he hinting at? Did she smell bad? Was she infested? Surely she would have felt fleas if they were so snug against her skin? O, God, this was a bad idea.

"Shh, my minstrel. Be still." Hands took her shoulders and drew her back against him. *Ah, the touch of his skin upon hers. Solidity, warmth, the thud of his heart. So much sensation.* She wanted to rub herself against him, luxuriate in the feeling of flesh on flesh. She was tempted to turn about, to press her chest to his. But no, that was far too much. He might look at her, find her wanting. He would see a pair of too-small breasts, much squashed after weeks of binding. That delicious hardness she felt whenever she moved her buttocks against him would droop, disappointed, and that would be that.

At least his hands had not crept around to her forefront. They simply rested on her shoulders, his forearms against her upper arms.

"I have an idea, my lady." She felt his breath on her earlobe, his head resting against hers. Oh, she could stay like this all night. Until he added: "Pray do not take it amiss."

She tensed. "What?"

"We have water warmed by the fire. Let me soothe your skin, my lady. Let me wash where the linen has pinched."

She was about to retort when he licked her ear—not like some eager spaniel but delicately, with his tongue tip. Then he took her earlobe into his mouth, and she forgot whatever it was she was going to say.

"May I?" he murmured.

Of course. He could do whatever he wished with her—just so long as he returned to suckling her ear. Then she jolted back to earth.

"Do I smell?" she demanded.

A soft laugh. He nipped her earlobe. Spikes of pleasure danced through her.

"You smell so delicious I could eat you. No, I do not wish to wash you because you smell, my minstrel. Lie down on your stomach. Relax and let me soothe your back."

Azalais frowned. If she lay on her stomach on the ground, then she wouldn't be able to touch him. And she *needed* to touch him, to explore the planes of his chest, run her fingers over the textures of his abdomen—muscle softened by warm skin, wisps of dark hair arrowing down.

"No. I could not bear it." She uttered the words without thought, never considering how he might interpret them.

Until his hands dropped from her shoulders and he stepped away.

She whirled around, stepped quickly to him, and snaked her hands up around his neck. She nearly laughed at the look on his face—startlement, a flare of wild hope—but then other sensations took over. Her naked breasts against his chest, the warmth of him, the hardness, oh the dizzying hardness.

"I could not bear *not* touching you, Guilhem," she said and tugged his mouth down to hers. And drank him.

Moments—eons—later, he lifted his mouth from hers sufficiently to say, "Azalais, this cannot continue. I—" He shook his head slightly.

"You cannot continue because you *want* to continue?" she suggested. "Because you want to use this?" Azalais dipped one hand down between them. Greatly daring, she reached out and she found. Yes—solidity. She wrapped her hand about it. It flexed beneath her fingers as if to communicate directly with her. It did not need words, and Azalais knew what it wanted.

Guilhem groaned. "No—yes—damnit, Azalais. For both our sakes, release me. Christ, did no one ever tell you this is not how nuns behave? Release me, woman, and turn around."

She glanced up into his face and smiled. Not that he could see her do so—his eyes were tightly closed. His expression, or what she could see of it in this light, seemed almost pained. Oh, but his body spoke a different message to his mouth, and it was doing the most peculiar things to her innards. This beautiful man, the knight-minstrel who set fine ladies and tavern wenches a-swooning with his music, wanted *her*. At least his body wanted hers, and so badly she felt his entire being quake. And this item she wrapped her fingers around—its breadth and solidity fairly taking her breath away—what would happen if she freed it of its fabric covering?

And then remembrance descended. Recollection of another man's member freed for action. Thick, detestable. Her maid's cry of anguish.

Azalais's hand had dropped its prize and whipped to her side for safety before she could register its action. Feelings swirled. To cover her confusion before he could see—before he opened his eyes—she obeyed his command. She turned around.

HIS HANDS WERE upon her, soft about her lower ribs. She leaned into him, but only her back against his torso. It was safer that way. His lower quarters might still be clothed—as were hers—but she wasn't sure quite what to do about the terrifying and fascinating solidity contained therein.

"Azalais …" Her name was a caress on his lips. "What am I to do with you—with us?"

He was holding her gently, yet she could feel the tremors course his body still. The restrained want.

"Just touch me, Guilhem," she murmured. *And hold me forever,* she added only to herself. *Your skin on mine, your heartbeat, your breath—I only pray my music can capture this. To keep forever.*

So, he did. His hands began to move. Slowly, incrementally, they moved over her midsection, wandered over her abdomen. His head leaned against hers, dipping down over her right shoulder, but there was no nibbling at her neck, no kisses. He seemed instead to focus solely on the sensation of his hands. So, she did, too. And he trailed slow ecstasy across her skin.

She relaxed against the warm chest behind her and closed her eyes. The world was nothing but sensation—the slight roughness of his fingertips, the breadth of his palms, and the tremor that shook her when he traced along the loose waist of her braies. His fingers lingered just under the waistline a moment, then seemed to reconsider their direction. They moved up her torso instead. Up and up, to brush against the undersides of her breasts.

Azalais sucked in a sharp breath. She did not tense—not exactly, unless you counted the tightness deep in her abdomen. All the same, Guilhem's fingers paused.

"May I?" the warm voice whispered in her ear.

Oh, she knew what he was asking—and why he had paused. And it melted her defenses just a little further. She knew her breasts were not made in the bounteous mold men preferred. Robert had told her so in no uncertain terms. Add to that, the weeks-long binding would have done her breasts no favors. But Guilhem was safely behind her. His fingers might perceive the inadequacy of her proportions, but his eyes would not compound the crime. And besides, her skin was afire with his touch. She *needed* him to continue.

"Touch me, Guilhem," she whispered, and she relaxed

against him just a little more.

His fingers moved again. Slowly, they circled the very outer curve of each breast. Their insignificant dimensions. But no, that dart did not hit home. A tingling tension was building up in her, robbing her of breath, of thought. There were only his fingers, tracing a narrower circumference. And then his palms, cupping her breasts from below so that his thumbs—*O, God in Heaven*— brushed directly over her nipples.

She gasped and arched against him. His simple touch sent a streak of lightning through her very core. Her movement planted her buttocks square against his thighs—and the hardness between. She didn't care. No recollections intruded now. The feel of him was pure intoxication instead. She shifted against his groin, luxuriating in its rearing need—and the tiny groan it elicited from her tormentor.

And his fingers continued to trace her breasts, returning again and again to the tight peaks of her nipples. The tingling that filled her intensified, built unbearably. Her head tipped back against his shoulder, mouth ajar. Just feeling.

Until he claimed her mouth with his, slipped a questing tongue between her teeth, and she completely dissolved. No, she juddered and writhed. The feeling racked her frame. It was a flood of honey, a clenching delirium. And Guilhem held her throughout, for she was fairly sure her legs could not. His mouth never left hers. The hardness between his hips shifted against her as if restless, a barely caged beast. She shuddered against him, a victim of a strange and fierce fever until the shudders subsided, and she sagged, secure in his arms.

What happened after that was distinctly foggy. He must have lowered her to the ground—or had her legs simply given way and she had slumped there of her own accord? Anyway, she found herself curled on the ground, cushioned by leaves and warmed by her cloak—and Guilhem. Her minstrel was wrapped about her, his chest to her back, his upper arm draped about her waist. So warm and safe, such an unaccustomed sensation. Azalais attempted to examine the feeling. Was it to be trusted? But there was no fighting the flood of lassitude. She sank into the arms of sleep. And of her minstrel-knight.

Chapter Seventeen

H E WOKE UP against her. Warm, content, and distinctly hard. Will shuffled back a little, just enough to place a little distance between his hips and her buttocks. But he kept his torso snug against her. It just felt too good not to.

Then recollection of the previous night flooded back, and the distance between his hips and her suddenly wasn't anything like enough. *O God.* He had nearly disgraced himself and come in his braies like a green boy. Or worse, far worse, succumbed to his cock's craving to break his oath. Maybe it would have been better if he had—decorated his braies, that is. At least then the same organ that was clamoring for attention now might be more malleable. Literally.

He tried to slip his arm from around her waist—but his cloak was wrapped tight about them both, binding them together in intimacy far from wise. Delightful beyond belief, but not wise.

What had he done? She had crept under his skin, her and her celestial music. Her determination, her fragility, the way she bantered with him. Or just looked at him, her golden gaze piercing through the barrier of that banter. And so last night he had let himself be convinced. She wanted him to touch her—to give her memories, to fuel her music—fine. But William of Fauconberg most certainly did not wish to cease at mere kisses. That much was being made abundantly clear at this very moment.

No, thinking about the state of his cock was not helping matters in any degree. If she woke to find him thus, and if she encouraged him in any way, he might not be responsible for his actions. So, Will wrenched his attention to regions of his anatomy less mutinous. His heart, for example, and its long-standing affection for straightlaced Brother Ben, one of his oldest friends. Benedict had not judged Will's yearning for minstrelsy. Instead, he had offered him this golden opportunity. And entrusted Will with his sister and the rescue of his father.

And it was no longer that simple. Lying here, wrapped around this complex bundle of womanhood—minstrel, lady, and would-be nun—Will could no longer deny the realization that had been creeping up on him for days. His cock wasn't the only recalcitrant part of his anatomy.

Will squeezed his eyes shut and simply listened to her breathe. His minstrel-lady lay slumbrous and pliable in his arms. Relaxed and trusting. And in the quiet predawn, William of Fauconberg finally faced his own feelings. The awful fact dawned on him with all the brilliance of a southern summer day—he wanted Azalais de Keldy with his whole being. Cock, heart, and soul. Will wanted her music, her mind, everything. To have and to hold. Forever.

And it was impossible.

He was a practically penniless not to mention reluctant knight. Her father would never countenance their marriage. And what of Will's own precious plans of tossing away knighthood for a life of minstrelsy? He most adamantly did not wish to return to the battlefield—the fine art of devastating France—but neither did he have the funds to live the idle life of a wealthy lord. Nor could he subject a lady to a wandering minstrel life. Why, if he so much as attempted it, her family would sever his balls from his body, if not his head from his shoulders.

What an unholy mess.

Seeming to sense his tension, his sleeping minstrel-lady

stirred. Just slightly, but it was enough to brush up against Will. He set his teeth and swallowed a groan. He had to untangle himself and soon.

THEY KNOCKED ON the chateau door. That was, Guilhem did. Azalais had not the slightest desire to enter the castle. Nor could she imagine was it the usual practice to simply amble up and rap upon a chateau's front door, no matter how impressively iron-bound and oaken-thick the thing was. Proper castles had gatehouses and guards bristling in attendance. This unprepossessing example of a fortification was a mere three stories high, a blocky, square-tower affair with a smaller and circular tower peeking up behind it. Nor was it *the* chateau—not Bruniquel on the Aveyron, dungeon to the Lord of Keldy. Nevertheless, here they were upon its doorstep—two scruffy minstrels leading horses that barely warranted the title, especially in their current state of exhaustion.

A small wooden panel shot back high in the door.

"Aye, what is it? What're you about so late in the day?" was demanded in French so thick Azalais could barely piece it together.

"God's greetings, monsieur gatekeeper. You see before you two minstrels, who humbly beg the honor of entertaining your lord tonight. We have pushed our horses to the point of collapse so we might reach your magnificent abode before dark—"

"Well, I reckon you failed there, eh?" the gruff voice overrode Guilhem's speech. The portion of face framed by the grill squinted at the dimness outside, then snapped back to scrutinize what was to be seen of those begging entry. "Looks pretty goddamn dark out there to me. Reckon you're right about your horses, though." The mouth stretched wide, and an odd assortment of teeth gleamed in the low light. "They look fit for dog food." Then the teeth disappeared. "But I ain't no monsieur, minstrel-man, and the real *mon Sieur* of the piece has already got himself a minstrel."

Azalais blinked. If true, then this was the first time they'd encountered another minstrel since they'd left Bordeaux. English-held France had seemed stripped of players. Doubtless most of them had followed the prince south to Spain. But the lands they traveled through now were under French seigneury, she reminded herself.

All the same, she could hardly believe her luck.

So, Alain the Minstrel rose on tiptoes to address the iron grille. She opened her mouth to thank the guard graciously for his time and to assure him that their drooping nags could still carry them some short way further. Fear not, these two wandering minstrels would bed themselves down under some friendly tree. In fact, they quite enjoyed it. But she never got the chance.

Guilhem laid a warning hand on her arm and Azalais startled. It was the first time he'd touched her since that night under the stars, two days before and an eternity ago. The following morning she'd woken cold and alone. Guilhem hadn't even been in sight. And when he'd reappeared through the trees, it was as if the evening before had never happened. He acted much toward her as ever, then and in the two days following—that was, with respectful distance and disrespectful banter. Nevertheless, it was a banter employed to keep her at a distance. Now his touch, even through cloth and for a purpose quite impersonal, was enough to send a bolt of warmth through her.

And delay her reply an instant too long.

"Pray indulge us, good gatekeeper," Guilhem returned smoothly. "Inquire of your noble seigneur whether we might offer him some small supplement to the doubtless fine entertainment he is already afforded. We require but a space on his lordly floor for the night in return, and the smallest morsel of food if he has it to spare."

The brow at the grille creased. Azalais swallowed a smile. She could practically see the fellow parsing Guilhem's words—a miracle in itself, given the paucity of light.

Any inclination to grin evaporated a moment later. The guard's brow had cleared. The slight bob of his head suggested that the shoulders below it had shrugged. "Reckon I could do that, minstrel-men. Seeing as you're so fair-spoken."

At which the wooden shutter snapped shut and Azalais's heart sank.

She swung around. "We don't need to stay here, Guilhem. I don't mind sleeping on the ground. It's not much of a castle anyway. For God's sake, look at it! It's even smaller than Keldy."

"Forgive me, O lady minstrel. I did not realize you have size requirements—in castles, that is."

Azalais's lips twitched. He was trying to distract her. She was not going to be distracted.

"This idea of yours to inquire about my father will only raise suspicion," she retorted, but quietly. It was entirely possible another man lingered behind the grille. Listening. "You stumble in your French at times, Guilhem. You pronounce some words as an Englishman does. What if you are discovered as a result? What if *I* am discovered? We are safer under the trees."

"Set your mind at ease, my minstrel. I do not intend to swagger up to his seigneurship and inquire 'Pray, what do you know of the English lord clapped in irons a few castles upstream? Reckon his ransomer is open to negotiation? Or mayhap there's a secret passage that will allow we two minstrels to free said lord, sans silver?'" murmured her companion. Then he grinned, a flash of white in the gloom. "Have faith in my snakelike subtlety, sweet Alain. Trust that I can worm information from this lord and his retainers without their ever realizing it."

"Hmph. And what about your accent?"

"Has it been a problem so far, O little doubter?"

"We were in English territory until just recently," was the obvious response.

"Even if they hear it, they will not care. Everyone knows

minstrels deal in information as much as in music. If I sound like I've been consorting with the English, my information will only be of greater value."

But I just want you to myself, was what she really wanted to say. *If we enter this castle, I will be forced to sleep on the hall floor within an arm's length of you and yet never so much as touch you. Just like last night.*

But she couldn't say that. It would sound downright desperate. She'd seen plenty of evidence of Guilhem's near-magical effect on women—ladies and bar wenches both. It would be too humiliating to join their ranks.

Or perhaps she already had, and Guilhem knew it.

After all, her knight-minstrel had been bone-headedly determined they would sleep within castle walls tonight. They had urged their horses on till the poor things were wobbling just to arrive at this excuse for a chateau before dark. Azalais would have preferred a bed of moss in the woods over any number of stern stone towers—a bed of leaves with Guilhem beside her, that was. But her companion wasn't having it. Not tonight, or the night before, for that matter.

He had tired of her kisses already. He wanted breasts that could not be concealed beneath any amount of linen.

Last night's accommodation had been a tavern so low and dark the only thing distinguishing it from the other buildings on the lone street was the painting hung outside. If one squinted in just the right way, it might be said to depict a jug of wine. They had played to an audience of ten and then slept on a taproom floor occupied by a good proportion of that audience. Azalais would have preferred to sleep in the forest, but Guilhem wouldn't hear of it. He made some mutter of brigands and his duty to her brother, and she had acquiesced. She wanted to play music, after all. She *had* to. It was practically leaking out of her pores.

For now, she understood why so many troubadours sang of love—or its physical manifestations, at least. It was because they had to. Once they were touched by this feeling, there was no holding it in. It *must* be expressed and what better expression of feeling than in soaring song? So, she filled the dingy little tavern with *canzos* of love and longing. She and Guilhem. And every time she looked up at him, moving as one with his vielle, a warm brightness coursed through her. His eyes lingered on her, full of promise. His mouth curved in a smile just for her. It seemed he felt as she did—overflowing with feelings that could only be expressed in song. And that golden thread of musical connection twined between them, stronger than ever. Oneness. Joined in song.

Until they stopped playing and a strange distance rose up between them.

She had hoped that tonight she would play for an audience of one on a stage of earth beneath the stars. She would crumble that invisible barrier between them somehow, and then her minstrel-knight's lips would find hers, his hands would roam over her tingling skin, and—

But no. Guilhem had insisted on a castle. She would suspect he was deliberately avoiding being alone with her if it weren't for the explanation he gave. It was true—they *did* need information about her father. Freeing the Lord of Keldy was the whole point of this journey.

Wasn't it?

In the meantime, she still hadn't scraped up a counterargument to Guilhem's reasoning, and now it was too late. Bolts were scraping back behind the door, and the cumbrous thing was creaking outward, forcing them to step back or be flattened.

"You're in luck, minstrel-men. Reckon monsieur's tired of the fiddler he's got," was announced. A blocky man-at-arms materialized in the doorway. "Says he fancies some new tunes. That, or he fancies himself a minstrel lad." A gap-toothed grin in Azalais's direction.

Azalais shrank back, but the fellow reached out a sizeable paw and clapped her on the shoulder.

"Nah, fear not, little man. Monsieur only likes girls, far as I've seen. Come on then, drag your dying nags this way. There was a stable around here last time I looked. Unless we save time and just drop the beasts at the kennels?"

It seemed the guard was now disposed to be friendly, after a fashion. Guilhem was already following the man's lead. All that was left to Azalais was to tug her reluctant mount into motion and follow.

So, a pair of sorry mounts were housed, and—having fed and watered the drooping beasts and most adamantly not fed them to the hounds instead—Guilhem and Alain entered what passed for a chateau.

To play for a hard bed and a meager board. Just like last night.

THE RESIDENT MINSTREL really wasn't bad, Will considered. He played the vielle adequately. If he were forced to be honest, Will would admit the man's voice was outstanding—a beautifully controlled falsetto, easily reaching notes higher than anything Azalais achieved, which he alternated with a mellow tenor when the song seemed to call for it. Damn the fellow. He was simply showing off.

To Azalais's willing accompaniment.

Will raised his mug of wine and took another deep draught. Or that was the plan. All he actually got was a mouthful of lees from the bottom. He spluttered at the unexpected solids. His adverse reaction to a lack of wine attracted the attention of a nearby maid. Actually, she'd been lingering nearby quite a lot. Will's cough simply gave her the excuse to sashay over and make a performance of refilling his mug. Then she patted him on the back, too. Really, he couldn't complain about the service.

But he could complain about the company.

Will glowered at the pair occupying the upper corner of the hall, just to one side of the now-empty high table. The resident minstrel—what was the fellow's name? Marcabru or some such troubadour affectation—was crooning love songs to his minstrel-lady's rippling accompaniment. *His* minstrel-lady. All the while, the fellow gazed down at his accompanist, seeming quite taken with Alain's technique. And with Alain, too, for that matter. Curse him.

Will took another, more successful draught of his wine. An excellent brew, he had noted upon his first cupful. Rich, red, and not a trace of vinegar. But now it might be tavern slops for all he tasted it. He took another draught, and the serving maid settled down snug on the bench beside him. Evidently, she understood he would need another refill soon.

Will had already played. Oh, he had played long and hard. He deserved this wine. He and Azalais had entertained his lordship for the duration of his nobleness's appearance in the hall. Will had even managed to slip some casual-seeming questions concerning nearby castles and their occupants into their interview with the seigneur during a well-deserved break in performance.

Bruniquel was touched upon. It was a sizeable fortress, and its lord, a vicomte, actually, was said to be fond of minstrels. Little more was to be extracted without seeming too obvious. Will determined he would strike up conversations with various menials before he left. Surely something more could be got?

Now the lord had withdrawn to his chamber, and his tame minstrel was free to experiment with the intriguing new visitor. With the minstrel Alain, that was. Oh, Marcabru had some gracious words to say to Will after his performance, but it was Alain he was evidently most interested in. And his minstrel-girl? She seemed entirely at ease with the strange Frenchman. No evidence of any fear of discovery. Now just look at them—the dashing southerner warbling his love lyrics as if for Azalais's ears alone, and his minstrel-lady was utterly absorbed, transported. Transcendent in music.

An angel on earth.

A hand touched his thigh. Will nearly slopped his wine—not that there was much left to slop.

"More wine, minstrel?" was purred in his ear.

Will swallowed a groan. He was busy, damnit. He had a minstrel-girl to watch over. He must see she come to no harm. And by God, that Marcabru was looking far too intently at his companion.

But he also had a mug to refill and information to collect. Who knew, maybe this attentive maidservant had once dallied with a guard from Bruniquel. She might know something about odd crevices and corners around their destination. So, he nudged his cup in her direction and did not dislodge the hand from his thigh.

"If you please, demoiselle. But pray tell me of your sweet self. Have you dwelt in this region long?"

If his tongue stumbled over some of the syllables, it really didn't matter. The maid knew what he meant. She snuggled a little closer on the bench, if that were possible, and proceeded to tell him of the mysterious regions he would soon travel through.

It WAS THE perfect opportunity.

Azalais had wanted to try making music with another minstrel, and here one was. Better still, Marcabru reminded her of the Frenchman who had first taught her the lute. She had been a little girl and he the steward of Keldy. Not a soldier precisely. He was a Gascon who had known her mother. He owned a lute, and she had been fascinated, so she became his one true audience. The men-at-arms of Castle Keldy had little time for minstrelsy. Oh, they endured the tinkling racket in the background, but to actually listen to it? They had more important matters to pursue. Like serving maids.

Perhaps because no one else cared for his music, the steward taught his master's daughter the way of the lute. His name had been Mark, oddly similar to this Marcabru. Was that why the two seemed to trade places in her mind? No, there was something more. It was his accent, his age, and the love of music that lit his eyes. Yes, she was glad she had entered this castle after all. Or mostly.

She had wanted to try making music with another to see whether the same sensation arose—that magical sense of connection to another human being she felt in playing with Guilhem. But now she was simply confused.

Marcabru was good. Very good. In fact, accompanying this vocal prodigy was like making music with not one man but two, each in possession of a wildly different voice. Maybe that was the problem. You couldn't feel oneness in the presence of such duality. Besides, had she felt a connection with Guilhem the first time they'd played? Azalais's brow creased. She couldn't remember. She'd been too intensely aware of *him*—the sheer magnetism of the man. Yes, and of his music.

But connection? Maybe that took time to grow.

The thing was, a nagging little voice at the back of her head was insisting that it didn't want a connection with just any musician. It wanted Guilhem and Guilhem alone.

Azalais stumbled in her accompaniment. Her fingers had forgotten what they were about, and her eyes had strayed from the strings. Of course, they found themselves fixed upon her erstwhile companion instead. And now her stumbling fingers were turning into claws, a shape entirely unsuited to lute plucking.

Guilhem had found himself a friend—a very well-endowed and friendly friend. Sweet heaven, if the maid snuggled any closer, she'd be sitting in the minstrel's lap. Nor did Guilhem seem adverse to her company. His head was bent to his new friend's, and he appeared to be murmuring something confidential in her ear. Azalais could just imagine the velvety tones, the

English-tinged French that was even now melting the wench into a puddle where she sat.

"Alain? Is something amiss?"

Azalais wrenched her attention back to the minstrel nearer at hand. She threw a smile in Marcabru's direction. A bit of a feeble attempt, she feared. "My apologies. I am tired. We had a hard day's travel." Which was true enough.

Unfortunately, the man was not a fool.

"Your companion—he worries you?"

"Worries me? Hah." Azalais gave a little snort. "Every tavern, chateau, or village square we stop in, it is the same. I blink, and there is a woman in his lap."

"And?" Marcabru smiled. She couldn't interpret its precise tone. "He is a minstrel, and not a bad looking one at that. He is not a monk. What better fuel to fire one's music than love?"

Mark had counseled her, too, when she was a little girl. But it had been advice of quite a different stamp. He had most certainly not suggested she fire her playing with love. In fact, his advice not infrequently concerned the avoiding of entanglements. Now this Marcabru was watching her and analyzing her expression with far too much acuity.

"You are a fine lutenist, Alain," he continued. "Young, but with much potential. I have enjoyed your unique style. But I must say—you played better with your companion than with me. And I do not think it is simply a matter of familiarity."

There was an odd weight to the man's words. Azalais frowned, and Marcabru reached out to trace a light finger over her brow.

"Too much scowling ages a young man before his time," the troubadour said. "If you would take my advice, minstrel-Alain, I would say—play with your Guilhem. If you dislike the direction of his attention, encourage him to focus upon you."

Well, she wasn't scowling now. Doubtless, she looked horrified or at least astounded. Marcabru responded by laughing aloud. Then he clapped her on the shoulder.

"Oh, don't tell me you never considered it, lad. I understand. I have been there. Traveling creates a bond. Add music, and music such as the two of you make, and the bond…well, perhaps it is more obvious to an onlooker, an onlooker such as I, who understands music and the love that may exist between men."

The minstrel squeezed her shoulder. A friendly squeeze, nothing lascivious about it.

But his meaning was clear. What could she reply?

Then to Azalais's enormous relief, Marcabru bade her good-night and good luck. And departed with a distinctly knowing smile.

Chapter Eighteen

AZALAIS STAYED IN her corner long after Marcabru left. She remained bent over her lute, only half-hearing the notes. She did not look at Guilhem, busy with his bawd, precisely because she did not want him to see her seeing. As if she cared.

But every sense strained in that direction.

Marcabru thought she and Guilhem shared a bond. He had thought it obvious to an outsider. Well, it evidently wasn't obvious to Guilhem. Her erstwhile companion seemed intent on bonding with quite a different partner tonight.

Azalais *wouldn't* look while the damned maid wrapped her arms about Guilhem's neck and pressed her pillowy bosom against his chest. Why, his loins were probably solidifying in that delicious manner right now, mere paces down the hall. Azalais, had felt them do so, and now that low wench would reach out her grasping hand and—

A voice rudely interrupted the flow of her notes. And thoughts.

"There are precious few left to play for, minstrel-Alain. Time to put your lute to bed. Or does it linger up late awaiting its mate's return?"

Azalais's fingers slipped on the strings for the second time that evening. This time they produced an amateurish twang. She clapped her palm over the strings to still their racket. It was enough to set her teeth on edge—if they weren't there already.

"Do not concern yourself over my lute's bed habits, Guilhem," she returned. "It will bed down very well of its own accord tonight. Be assured my lute and I are content without an audience. We will not keep you from your own."

No reply.

She could feel him standing there, staring down at her. Damn him, would he demand she meet his eyes? It was all very well to sound calm, but to look it as well? One glance at him, and he would probably decipher her soul's sad state from her eyes.

And, still, he didn't reply.

"It is all right, Guilhem," she addressed her lute. "Pray don't keep your admirer waiting on my account. I will not hold it against you. A man has his needs."

Needs that some misguided notion of loyalty and honor prevented from expending upon his companion. Or more likely, Alain-Azalais simply did not tempt him enough.

"He does." That deep, velvety voice. "And doubtless your Marcabru has his needs, too. You have found a minstrel to show you the music of love, have you? But does your falsetto-trilling troubadour realize the nature of the ride he's in for? It would be well to warn him, minstrel-man."

Azalais didn't gasp, probably because her teeth were so tightly clenched. But her gaze did fly to her addressor's face.

Guilhem was looking down at her with apparent calmness—apparent except to one who noticed the banked fire in his eyes and the slate-solid line of his jaw.

"So, you wish me to occupy myself with a serving wench and leave you free to play elsewhere?" Her companion's tone had altered. The velvet was stripped away. Guilhem glanced around. "Where is he?"

"What?"

But Guilhem's hand was upon her upper arm, urging her to her feet. That achieved, he still showed no inclination to release her.

"Come. The hall is being cleared. The trestles are put up," he snapped. "We must find ourselves a cozy corner for the night—just you and I. Side by side, Alain. Be assured, I will not let you out of my sight."

She stared up at him. Had he already stepped outside to dally with his serving maid? It was possible. She knew men did not take long about the business when the mood took them. But she had never seen him like this—stripped of lazy charm, his banter swapped for bluntness. A startling notion suggested itself—maybe Guilhem's buxom friend had rejected him.

Azalais smiled. She could not help herself.

Guilhem's expression turned thunderous. "What in Christ's name are you planning? Remember why you are here, little minstrel. Has it slipped your mind you have a father?"

"Has it slipped *your* mind you were meant to gather intelligence, Guilhem?" she replied. "The little 'gathering' I saw you perform did not seem to require much intelligence. Indeed, it seemed to involve other body parts entirely."

Her captor looked momentarily confused. The expression was soon banished. "You will not distract me," he growled. "In fact, you will not so much as attend the privy without my escort tonight, little minstrel. Be warned."

"What has got into you, Guilhem? I—"

And then she paused. Her eyes widened. Really?

Guilhem didn't pause. He towed the now-unresisting Azalais toward where she supposed he had decided they would sleep. His vielle was there, resting atop a bag. Her belongings had been dumped nearby. He had even found two straw-stuffed pallets. They lay side by side on the floor, so close they almost touched. Azalais felt a smile twitch at her lips. He was determined not to let her out of his reach, even in sleep.

"Lie down," he ordered. "They are snuffing the tapers."

"But I *do* need to avail myself of the privy," she said with all sweetness. "And splash some water on my face and limbs. A girl cannot simply fall into bed without some manner of ablution."

He stiffened and glanced around at the word 'girl.' But no one took any notice. So, true to his word—or threat—he did accompany her to the privy and then prowled around the well as she subjected arms and face to a dousing in cold water. She was tempted to splash some at him, only it was likely to turn straight to steam, the mood he was in.

Then it was back to the great hall—deep in gloom now, apart from the glowing coals of the central hearth fires—to their pallets of straw. Side by side.

WILL DRAPED HIS arm over his companion's in the dark. He didn't think he would sleep, but just in case—he needed to remain in contact with her.

The arm beneath his moved. Straw crackled. He waited for her to snake her arm free of his—or try to—but no, instead, her fingers inveigled themselves into his hand. They laced themselves through his own digits. Like a trusting child's.

Will tensed. It was a ruse. She would lull him into relaxing his guard, pretend she was happy to lie here, warm beside him. And all the while she would be waiting for the opportunity to slip away.

For she had found a better minstrel than William of Fauconberg.

Oh, he knew how much music meant to her. He saw it in her face when she played, in the tone of her voice as she sang, and in her eyes when she looked up at that damn Marcabru. It meant more to her than he could ever do. It might even mean more to her than her father's freedom.

But Will was prepared. And by God, he would do whatever it took to hold them both to their sworn task.

He shook his head. The straw rustled, but the thoughts in his skull buzzed like a hive of angry bees. True, he'd partaken freely of his host's excellent wine. Then there was the long day's ride. More to the point, though, there was the increasing proximity of Bruniquel, of a certain minstrel-girl's domination of his every thought, and the imperative to decide his own future. Perhaps all these he could handle. Just. But there was something else as well—something that simply would not bend to logic. A feeling. A building pressure in his soul. It was a force he shied away from but could not subdue or ignore.

"He reminds me of the man who taught me to play. Marcabru, I mean."

She murmured the words beside him. She cast them in a conversational tone.

As if she wasn't slicing at his innards with every syllable she spoke.

"My mother taught me to speak French, but he taught me to sing French. In the *langue d'oc*. And now I am home. This is my home, Guilhem. Not Keldy. I feel truly at home in this land, and it is a wonderful feeling."

Her hand was still twined with his. Will fought to keep his grip gentle and even. His hands were possessed by the near-irresistible desire to form fists. And then drive them into this Marcabru's body. He could not answer her. There was no answer.

"You are considering becoming a minstrel—a wandering troubadour, are you not?" she murmured but did not wait for a reply. It was just as well, really. "Well, I am beginning to consider the same thing, Guilhem. Yes, yes, I know. I am a mere woman. It is not possible. You have barely begun to show me how to defend myself. But what if I attached myself to another minstrel—a man? *Then* it is possible, Guilhem. Then I can become a minstrel, and I can stay here."

It was as if she had calmly opened his skull and read his mind. And then stirred the whole roiling mess around. Will could not think. He could only feel.

No more words.

He rolled onto his side and angled towards her in the dark. His free hand reached, unerring. It tangled in her short hair, then cupped her cheek, and he dipped his mouth to hers. Carefully, at first—he had no intention of headbutting her in the dark. But once he found her lips, he held back no longer.

GUILHEM KISSED HER. Sweet heaven, she would call it a ravaging of the mouth, a siege to the senses, save Azalais was no unwilling victim.

She had hoped…well, she had hoped for something. A reaction. An admission. But this? They lay in a dim hall full of drowsy bodies, and he was kissing her with glorious abandon, a fierce possession that promised the night would not end with kisses alone. He lay half on top of her, one long leg hooked over hers. She writhed against him, opening her mouth to his, responding in kind. Not caring that there were people within a few paces, people who were likely not asleep yet.

At first, his hand cradled her face, holding her lips to his. But then, when it was evident her lips had no inclination to withdraw, it began to roam further afield. It slipped along her shoulder, over her tightly bound bosom, and then found the hem of her tunic. It dragged the fabric up and delved within.

Ah, skin. The fire of his fingers upon her midriff, nails lightly scraping. And still, he kissed her, until she was dizzy with it. Grateful for the supporting straw.

His lips left her mouth. They sought her neck, her jaw, and nibbled her ear. And the fingers on her midriff roamed. They found the rolled waistline of her man's braies. They were no barrier at all. They pushed under.

Azalais gasped. His fingers had brushed the curls at the apex of her thighs. Each hair contacted seemed to stir pinpricks of need shivering through the skin below.

But the fingers did not stop. They dipped lower. Azalais opened her mouth to—well, to gasp or shriek or protest or demand that he most definitely not stop. But the opportunity was denied her. His mouth had found hers again. Just in time, for at that moment, his fingers slipped between the juncture of her legs. Azalais would most certainly have shrieked. It was electrifying. Just one finger. It parted her nether lips and found the slipperiness at her core.

She bucked against him, cried out into his welcoming mouth. Heard him groan in return. Sweet heaven, surely the bodies around them would notice? Not that she was in any state to care. Meanwhile, his finger took its time. It moved leisurely, but it wasn't going anywhere. It slipped over and around the nub between her legs. Ah, it was ecstasy and agony. And that damn finger knew exactly what it was doing. She arched and writhed against it, but the finger did not desist. She barely registered his kissing now. All sensation was centered upon that single knowing finger. And the mad tension built higher and higher until she thought she must simply shatter.

At which point she did. She shrieked into his mouth. She convulsed helplessly against him, over and over. Felt his body hard upon hers, soaking up her shudders. Until she subsided beneath him, spent.

But still wanting.

⇥⟫⟫⟫⟪⟪⟪⇤

SHE WOULD SLEEP now, damnit. She *must* sleep. And now she would dream only of him and not of some overly talented falsetto singer.

Will shifted his body so it wasn't entirely asphyxiating his minstrel-girl—just enough that his hellishly hard cock was not in contact with any part of her, but not so much that she had any chance of slipping away from him in the night.

But it seemed she wasn't asleep yet.

A hand reached out and found his hip. Will froze. The hand wavered there a moment, evidently unsure of where it found itself. Then it began to slip down.

"No." Will uttered the word through gritted teeth.

The hand did not appear to have heard. It was traveling over his tunic, learning his landscape by touch. Any moment now it would—

Will rolled abruptly away. Onto his back. He seized the hand just before it contacted the damned tentpole of his tunic.

"Guilhem, I want…I need…"

The hand struggled within his.

"No, you don't, my minstrel," he said softly. "We have given our good hosts enough of a performance for tonight. Anything more would confuse them no end."

A sudden vision of two silhouettes joined in the dark in a way no two men ever joined assailed him. And he thought his groin could get no harder.

"No one cares. No one's watching," whispered the siren beside him.

Will blasphemed under his breath.

Then, "Your brother cares. And I daresay your father would part my…" He broke off. A mad urge to laugh nearly shook him. Mad indeed. Half drunk and half desperate. And wholly in lust.

"No," he managed to growl again. "Hands off."

"Well, I must say that is hardly fair."

He captured her other hand and held her still. She must listen to him.

"It was you who wanted to experience the fruits of love, O minstrel." Then Will took a deep breath and added, "*I do not. I do not need to.*"

THE FOLLOWING DAY was as close to perfection as was possible to attain on earth. Sunshine sparkled on the River Aveyron, a soft breeze tickled verdant spring leaves, wafting upon it an ecstasy of birdsong, and they passed through a succession of quaint little stone-built hamlets. To top it all, Will rode through the land of song with a beautiful woman by his side.

And silence stretched between them, taut as a bowstring.

But at least he had her with him. She had not left him in favor of the too-talented Marcabru, although he wasn't sure how long that would last. It was always possible she would double-back to Marcabru's arms tonight. Or perhaps she was simply waiting until after they had freed her father.

Well, that was all right, wasn't it? What Azalais de Keldy did after her noble sire was ransomed was none of Will's business. His duty would then be done, his promise fulfilled. William of Fauconberg would be free to pursue a lifetime of music. He could become Guilhem in truth.

It ought to make him happy—deliriously happy. He had decided. At last, Will knew that he would never return to his half-hearted career as a hired sword. He would be a wholehearted minstrel instead. No, he would be a troubadour.

Except the long-sought victory felt hollow.

"Did you find out anything more about Bruniquel or my father last night?"

The words lingered in the air between them for a few heart-beats before they made any sense in Guilhem's head. He hadn't been expecting speech, not after a morning's worth of silence.

"Last night?" he echoed.

He didn't want to think of last night. Of what he had done. Christ, he couldn't remember feeling this awkward since he was a stripling youth caught tugging on his member.

"That was the point of our sojourn in a chateau last night, was it not?" she went on. "Information. I heard you ask the castellan. Did you find out any more beyond that?"

It was a reasonable question and asked in a reasonable tone.

Too reasonable. His lady spoke as if there was nothing between them—as if he were merely her companion and guardian along the road.

As he ought to be.

Will began to shake his head, then stopped. No, that was a bad idea. His brain felt decidedly unmoored in his skull this morning. And it was only in part due to the wine of the night before.

So, he spoke instead. "I asked around a little. No luck."

"A little?" His companion sniffed. "What, did you ask the serving maid when she'd last humped a fellow from Bruniquel? Oh, you're a smooth talker, Sir Minstrel."

Will felt his brows shoot up. He wiped away the expression under cover of a hand through his hair. So much for reasonable, companionly questions. True, it was what one merely fraternal companion of the road might jest to another, but not quite in the same tone. Definitely not the same tone.

Besides, it approached too close to the truth. In all honesty, he'd been too busy eyeing Azalais and her minstrel to bother questioning further afield. And the maid *had* been friendly.

"Perhaps I did," he said and managed to produce a smile to leaven his words. "But rest assured, she got no humping from this Englishman, to employ your delightful turn of phrase."

Azalais laughed. Did it sound a little forced?

"Yes, when I compose my next *canzo*, I'll attempt to phrase matters more poetically. But as for acquiring information on Bruniquel, I believe I had more luck than you, Guilhem."

She gave him a level look. He felt it. Will kept his eyes on the road—or more accurately, track. This path along the Aveyron was narrow and picturesquely overhung with trees.

"Marcabru. He spoke of the lord of Bruniquel's love of music, Guilhem. He informed me that the vicomte is very fond of minstrelsy. He even dabbles a little himself. Marcabru has played before him. He even composed verses in honor of the lord of Bruniquel at his request. He was rewarded well for it."

Christ, the very mention of the man's name had Will's hands clenching. The fellow had evidently made a deep impression on Lady Azalais. So much for hoping to drive the thought of the talented Frenchman from his lady's mind by means of—

No, he refused to think of last night.

"Devil take him," Will muttered instead. "May he rot in deepest hell."

"Who?"

Will just shook his head in reply—and regretted it. He cursed himself as much as anybody. He had lost that little bit more control over himself last night—and in a hall surrounded by sleepers. Or people lying wakeful and listening. He wanted her, and he was losing her. He would lose her soon anyway. It was inevitable. But last night he had demolished a boundary that should never have been crossed. It was nothing to do with her request to experience physical love. It was everything to do with his own desires—and his need to claim her wholly for himself.

He invoked the Devil and his fiery demesne a second time. And felt Azalais looking at him.

"You seem out of sorts this morning," came the neutral comment. "Pray, relieve your mind of its burden, Guilhem. You can tell me."

No, he damn well couldn't.

"You did well to discover your father's captor's musical weakness, Alain," he offered instead.

"I did. And I am not a man, Guilhem. I am not Alain to you. I would have thought last night would have made that abundantly clear. Or were you so drunk it has slipped your mind?"

For a moment, he was tempted to take the easy route out. He would excuse his mood upon a king-sized headache and plead ignorance of all that occurred after the first few cups of wine.

But he hadn't been drunk. Just a little more relaxed than was good for him—or his companion.

"It has not slipped my mind, Lady Azalais." He turned in the saddle to look at her. Their ponies were walking, side by side, along the river path. They hadn't seen a cottage for a while now. There was no one to hear. "I can only beg forgiveness for taking unforgivable advantage of you in such a public place."

He met her eyes. It was so hard to hold her gaze. Her wide amber eyes, defenseless yet too discerning. And so beautiful.

The delicate brows above them lifted. "Forgiveness for the unforgivable? Is it possible, Guilhem?"

Silence hung heavy between them. Will forced himself to keep looking at her, trusting his mount to continue its ambling along the path. Bravery in battle be damned. Facing someone who was entirely the opposite of his enemy required far more courage.

"Did you hear me objecting last night, Will?"

"That is not—"

"It *is* the point, Will. And your only unforgivable offense is in not listening to me. In not taking my wishes as seriously as those of my brother—or my father. Or the wishes you *assume* my brother to hold." A pause, before she added softly, "But even that is not unforgivable if you change your ways."

It was her turn to look away now. As if she had said too much, revealed too much. He didn't know what to reply.

But she hadn't finished scouring his heart yet.

"I meant what I said about becoming a minstrel, Guilhem."

Will's heart sank a little. It hadn't escaped his notice that she'd called him Will before. As if she was speaking directly to him, and not the disguise he wore. Now he was back to Guilhem.

Then the rest of her words sank in.

It was what she had said last night, just before he had gone entirely mad. It was why he'd gone completely mad.

Will reined his horse in so sharply the poor beast's hoofs fairly skidded on the track.

IT WAS ALL the excuse Azalais's mount needed to cease its clopping. A moment after its companion came to a sudden stop, Azalais's pony likewise halted and drooped its shaggy head toward the grass in the middle of the track. And who could blame it? Guilhem had pushed their mounts to their unimpressive limits yesterday, and today they'd made a horribly early start and hadn't stopped for a rest since just after dawn. Anyone would think the man was in a hurry to get rid of her.

She looked back. Her companion's face was the image of embattled emotions—embattled in part because he was busy forcing them back under control.

"I agree entirely." Azalais slithered off her mount's blanketed back. "My backside is in dire need of a rest, and my stomach declares it has been too long since breakfast. Let us recline a while by the river, Guilhem." She pointed through the trees. "You and I need to talk."

She sounded quite firm and decisive. So much so that, after a wary look, Guilhem likewise dismounted and led his steed in the direction of her finger. Into a secluded glade, barely glimpsed from the road, and edged by the chuckling Aveyron.

It was an illusion. She did not feel firm.

Guilhem led the way, his mount's reins in one hand. That was why she noted his free hand curl surreptitiously around his sword hilt. It was certainly not because Azalais was ogling the buttocks moving before her in their tight-fitting tunic and hose.

They didn't bother to tether their mounts. The beasts were all too happy to set about reducing the sward in the little clearing to a tight-mown lawn.

"You are hungry, my lady?" Guilhem was unbuckling a saddlebag.

"Yes, I am hungry, but mostly for talk." She drew a deep breath. "Too much has gone unspoken between us, Guilhem. We will reach Bruniquel in a few days, and I think you have been avoiding me."

Her companion stilled. He had been lifting the leather flap—

hopefully to obtain something edible—and now it seemed he'd been turned to stone. Azalais's stomach clenched. A moment ago, she'd been ravenous. Now she wasn't so sure.

But she had to speak to him, and now. The set of his jaw told her the moment was anything but auspicious, but who knew when she'd have the opportunity again? The right words…what were they? If only she could sing them instead. But no, it was no moment for poetry—it was time for plain speaking. There must be no more misunderstanding between them.

Chapter Nineteen

"THE GREATEST SOPHIST in the world could hardly accuse me of avoiding you, my lady."

Guilhem had settled himself on the grass beside her, but he was well out of arm's reach. He had torn a loaf of bread apart and handed her half before sitting down. Now they passed a flask of wine between them. He had to lean precipitously to transfer it to her grasp, but he moved no closer. Nor did she. It was intimate enough, for now, to place her lips where his had touched a moment before. Wine and bread. It felt like the Last Supper. She just hoped there wasn't a Judas kiss.

"I think you know what I mean, Sir Knight."

Something flashed in his eyes. He eyed the loaf in his hand, as if in silent debate with it. Then spoke. "I will shortly have no claim to that title. I shall be a knight no longer, my lady. I have decided—I intend to renounce my gentle birth. After we free your father, I will become a minstrel in truth."

She stared at him. He still looked at the bread.

"Why are you telling me this?" she whispered.

"I will become an itinerant entertainer, Azalais. I will live hand to mouth. No home, precious little money, and no security. I will become that being despised by all men of worth—a homeless wanderer."

"You are trying to talk me out of *my* decision."

He turned to her then. There was no trace of humor in his eyes, no gallantry, no mockery. Just a pair of dark eyes piercing her soul.

"In part," he said. "You cannot become a minstrel, my lady. Precisely because you *are* a lady and a beautiful, desirable one at that."

"I could remain a man."

"With Marcabru? Do you not think he would see through that in time?"

This was her opening. It was now or never. And Azalais's heart was behaving most erratically beneath its bindings.

She held his eyes.

"No, with you," she said.

⤜⤜⤜⟓⟓⟓

WILL GRAPPLED FOR words—for thought. By God, he struggled beneath a floodtide of mad hope that threatened to sweep all other considerations away. He opened his mouth, unsure of what would emerge.

He never got the chance to find out.

A movement flickered at the edge of his sight. Will glanced around—and his pulse spiked. Figures were emerging from the surrounding trees, five or six figures, and they were limping and lumbering toward them.

With naked weapons in their hands.

"What do we do?" came an urgent hiss beside him.

He had no idea. Saints have mercy, this looked bad. Will's hand flew to his sword-hilt, loosened but a short while ago. There had been something about this clearing that had nagged at him; he wasn't sure what. Now it seemed his hand had been aware of potential danger, but his heart had not. It had been too full of her. His hand tightened on the hilt, undecided. There were too many of them. There was no way he could beat off six armed thugs and protect Azalais at the same time. But what was the alternative?

There was a sharp movement beside him. A flicker of light on steel.

"Sheathe it," he hissed back. "Do not invite violence."

She was scrabbling to her feet, a naked dagger in hand. At the sight, Will practically levitated to a standing position.

"Stay behind me," he snapped in French. The men were well within earshot now. Pray God they had not heard his and Azalais's earlier exchange.

"Behind you? What good will I be there?" she bit back.

He did not answer. The men—if men they really were—had halted in a rough semicircle around them, out of arm's reach but not out of weapon's reach. And Will's was still sheathed. As he prayed Azalais's was as well.

But he could not glance behind to make sure. He must not take his eyes of these ... *beings* for a moment.

"Good day to you, gentlemen." Will spoke calmly in what he hoped was perfect French. "Beautiful day for a picnic by the river, is it not? Have you dined?"

He waved the stub of bread he still held by means of illustration. Just in case all of his listeners lacked their ears.

As the one who stood directly before him evidently did.

God, the man was a horrible sight. The mangled remains of what used to be his ears only enhanced the general air of wreckage. Will heard Azalais gasp.

The fellow to his left cocked a face in which beard fought scar tissue for dominance. "What are you?" he grunted. The language was nominally southern French.

Will felt his brows rise. A fine question from such a creature as this! Although he was fairly sure he knew what *they* were. The assortment of weaponry they held in their fists was a dead giveaway.

Will dipped a small bow toward the speaker. Not so much of a bow that he lost sight of the fellow, though. "I am pleased to present two poor wandering minstrels, my lord. I am Guilhem, and my companion is called Alain."

He enunciated the last noun very clearly indeed. He hoped the bearded brute had also taken careful note of the adjective "poor."

The fellow's eyebrows rose.

If Will's stomach clenched any tighter, his interrupted lunch would make a reappearance. These men were the very wreckage of war. They were the maimed leftovers of battle, too decrepit to fight. But not too decrepit to slit a defenseless man's throat. What they would do to a girl did not bear thinking about.

"Poor, eh?" the man echoed. "You'd be gobsmacked how many merchants and lordlings are poor as mice when us lot make their acquaintance. Perhaps they're humbling themselves to suit present company. P'raps not." Then the fellow grinned. His teeth had not survived any better than his brows. "No matter, they're poor enough when we leave 'em."

Leave them how? Whole and unharmed, Will could only hope. But it wasn't enough simply to hope. He must protect his lady at all costs.

"You want our money? Is that it?"

Azalais had stepped from behind him. It took an iron will not to rip his sword from its sheath this moment and defend her. He knew if blades started getting bandied now, the odds were his minstrel-girl would end up on the wrong end of one. But it was the knowledge that went against his every instinct.

"We do not have much," she was saying. "But what we have we are content to give you. Just leave us our instruments. That is all we need. As minstrels, we can always earn more coin."

It was well put, Will had to admit. It was the path of least resistance—and hopefully of least harm. They were only a few days from Bruniquel. They could make it without money. But arriving without the ransom was another matter. Where in hell had she stowed the silver? He had a shrewd idea it was tucked into her lute's leather case. After all, she never went anywhere without the instrument. She wouldn't offer the key to her father's freedom to a bunch of maimed outlaws. She would hold onto it at all costs, for it was the key to her freedom as well.

The thug who had spoken before narrowed his eyes. His delightful selection of companions muttered amongst one another.

Then the fellow flicked his weapon. But the rust-speckled falchion did not lodge in anyone's soft innards. Thank Christ. It merely gestured.

"Show us this dough of yours, minstrel."

"No! Stay beside me," hissed Will, but Azalais was already moving past him, lute slung across her back as usual. She was moving toward the ponies. The falchion wielder followed close behind.

Will's heart was lodged in his throat. His every sense was honed painfully sharp—they picked up scents of horse dung and rotting teeth, the sight of Azalais's finely made fingers as they fiddled with the saddlebag, and the sound of a guttural voice speaking in English. *In English?*

"Couple of pretty minstrel-men, eh Dickon? What d'ya reckon?" the English voice said.

A snort. "Reckon they should've cut off more than your ears, you goat."

"Take it or leave it, I'm not passing up a nice bit of bum. Don't reckon I'll be the only one, neither. Which one do you want?"

Will's eyes went wide. Some part of his brain registered Azalais handing over a heavy pouch of coin to the hovering ruffian. The man hefted it with a grin, then reached out to tap the leather case on Azalais's back. Will's heart nearly stopped. The oaf evidently wanted it off her back so he could more easily have his foul way with her. The fellow had sheathed his falchion the better to grasp his newfound silver—and Azalais herself. That reaching hand had taken a hold of the lute and was trying to twitch it off Azalais's shoulder.

And Azalais turning to him—Will—and catching his eyes in a

moment to still time itself. Her wide eyes asked him a question. It was just a slight turn of her head, a lift of her brow. It carried an appeal. An apology.

And then she rammed her dagger into the thug's throat.

It was a well-aimed blow. She had a solid backhand grip on the dagger, just as he'd taught her. The results were immediate—and wet. Her target clutched his throat and staggered, and Will judged his minstrel-girl didn't need any more assistance, at least not for the next two heartbeats. He was free to clear the air a little in his own vicinity.

He liberated his sword from its sheath and sliced it across the nearest man's throat in one swift movement. At least, he'd *intended* it to slit the fellow's throat—Azalais was on to a good thing—but the man stumbled back just in time. In the process, he fell backward over a tree root and Will had to content himself with skewering the earless man instead. It was only fair—the fellow was doing his damnedest to decapitate Will with a halberd.

"Stop!" Will bellowed the word in English, and then followed it up in French just to make sure. He'd ripped his blade free of his last victim's chest, and now the bloodied sword tip hovered over the fallen brigand's neck. "One move from any of you and he's gone," he snarled, in case the gesture wasn't clear.

He dared a look around. Three thugs with weapons raised stood in various attitudes of frozen motion. Azalais was by her pony, a bloody knife in her hand. The moment wouldn't last, he knew.

"Alain, get on your horse! Ride! Leave this place—now!" he barked.

His minstrel-girl stared at him, eyes wide. He thought for one long, awful moment she would defy him. But then she grasped her pony's shaggy mane and swung herself onto its back.

She rammed her heels into the poor beast's sides and charged the thing directly at Will.

THE ONE-ARMED THUG was creeping up on Guilhem, a raised war ax in his remaining hand. He had taken advantage of Guilhem's momentary distraction, and he evidently wasn't too fussed about the fate of his fallen companion.

Her minstrel saw her coming. His eyes went wide, and he sprang aside, abandoning his hostage.

The one-armed sneak did *not* see her coming. His focus was all upon Guilhem and the bloody, ax-cleaving murder. Thus, it was that Azalais was able to ram her maddened pony fair into the side of the brigand. What happened next was all confusion, horse squeals, thuds, and shouts. Her pony definitely reared at some point. Azalais was forced to cling limpet-like to its back. She could *not* fall off. That would be disastrous. It would probably crush her lute.

She was almost certain her steed's hooves thudded down on human flesh in the descent, but now was not the time to peer beneath its belly and find out. Then her mount made an odd little clambering leap, freed itself of the mess of men, and pounded for the trees.

She hauled it back just in time, only in part because the animal didn't seem to care whether its rider was swept off by a low-hanging branch. And who could blame it? It had had a hard couple of days. But no, she was not going anywhere without Guilhem.

Or without finding out what had become of him.

Hands shaking, she reined her mount around and stared back into what had been an idyllic woodland glade.

No longer. It was a charnel house.

In the middle of it, Guilhem was fighting off not one but two brigands. *O, sweet Lord.* It was like having cold water thrown over her. Icy runnels practically ran over her flesh. Azalais lifted her heels to tenderize her pony's sides a second time and then paused.

Staring.

This was the man who had just told her he intended to be a knight no longer. Sir William of Fauconberg declared he had no taste for warfare, so he would be Sir William no more. Naturally, she had assumed it was in part because he wasn't very good at it. It seemed of a piece with his larger persona—he was a minstrel man, who raked his hands through his dark and silky hair far too regularly to accustom them to a sword. True, he knew how to handle a dagger better than she, but then the merest pageboy probably did, too. But that there was no need to ride to his rescue a second time was obvious even to Azalais. She would likely just get in the way.

Besides, she just wanted to watch. True, her heart still lodged in her throat every time a weapon whistled toward Guilhem. But she wasn't really afraid for him anymore. Even she could see a master was at work. Guilhem simply stepped aside from every incoming blow or neatly deflected it with a flick of his sword.

He wasn't trying to kill his opponents, she realized. He'd had the opportunity half a dozen times in the few moments she'd been watching—an exposed armpit, a wide-flung hand—but still, he didn't strike the killing blow. Instead, he seemed intent on disabling them. Which was a harder task altogether.

For heaven's sake, Will, those beasts would murder you without a blink. Return the favor, for God's sake!

It was her heart talking, of course. Her foolish, wayward heart. Her conscience was more inclined to approve Guilhem's intent. It applauded when her knight-minstrel slipped behind one brutish opponent to fetch him a resounding *clunk* on the head. With his sword hilt merely, more's the pity. The fellow obligingly dissolved into a pile of dirty clothing on the grass. And now there was but one brute standing—and Guilhem had his sword leveled at his throat.

"I propose you put up your mace, my friend."

That was Guilhem's voice, a little short of breath to be sure, but surprisingly calm. And authoritative.

She was not surprised the fellow promptly responded by lowering his mace.

"Alain?" Guilhem raised his voice but did not turn to look at her. "I am somewhat occupied over here. Oblige me by retrieving our silver from your deceased friend's hand. I fear he cannot spend it where he has gone."

Urgh. Azalais very gently prodded her pony into motion. Together they picked a cautious path around the clearing—to stand over the man whose throat she'd opened with such finality. She slid from her mount's back to land on unsteady legs. Azalais swallowed hard and bent to the motionless body. O, God, it was still warm. And sticky. With finger and thumb, she plucked the pouch of coins from the fellow's fist. It took quite a tug to free it—he seemed determined to take the silver with him to hell.

"Well done," came the blessedly calm voice of her companion. "Now my mount if you please. Lead it to me."

Of course. That made sense. Guilhem currently had his sword to a brigand's throat. But Azalais was having trouble putting together a coherent thought in her head right now. The purse of bloodied silver hanging from her wrist was jingling uncontrollably. And she had to be quite stern with her legs in order to make them advance towards Guilhem, a pony's reins in each hand.

"Thank you, Alain."

Guilhem still hadn't looked at her. Of course, his eyes were fixed upon his opponent. The man was still alive and looked as if he'd like to eviscerate Guilhem with his teeth alone. But Azalais desperately wanted Guilhem to look at *her*, to tell her with his eyes that everything would be all right, that she hadn't really murdered a man.

"Now, if I may borrow your mace for a moment, sir?" The minstrel plucked the monstrosity of spiked metal from the fellow's unresisting hand. Guilhem turned the weapon slowly in his grip, seeming to eye it carefully.

This is no time for weapons appreciation. Have done, Guilhem!

As if she had spoken the words aloud, her minstrel-knight obeyed. He lifted the mace high and brought it down with a firm *thud* upon its owner's head. Using the flattest and bluntest surface available to him.

The last standing brigand fell like an oak.

And Guilhem turned to her at last.

Azalais blinked. She did not know this man. He'd tossed the mace aside, but he still held a sword in his fist. A naked, bloody sword. And his expression matched the menace of his blade. Those dark eyes were sleepy and laughing no longer. They were all-seeing and utterly ruthless. Nor did they soften a mote as they gazed upon her.

She thrust the reins wordlessly at him and stepped back. Quickly.

"On your horse, Alain," she was instructed. "We ride."

Chapter Twenty

A ND, BY HEAVEN, they rode. Some corner of Will's head pitied his poor pony, but he kept that corner firmly in its place. His whole being cried out that they ride, far and fast. He must remove Azalais from that befouled forest grove. He must remove himself from the William who had inhabited it.

"Guilhem!"

The call wafted indistinctly from behind him. He reined back—infinitesimally. Continuing at a canter was probably not a good idea anyway; they were nearing another cluster of houses. Who knew what child or chicken might take it into their heads to wander out before a fast-moving mount? A further tightening of the reins, and his pony needed no more hint. It subsided into a jolting trot almost instantaneously. He permitted it to slow to a puffing walk and waited for his companion to catch up with him.

He did not turn to look at her as she drew alongside.

"Guilhem, no more. We have ridden far enough." His lady spoke somewhat breathlessly, but more—her voice was small. Somehow shut away.

The implication sliced at his heart. Will halted his pony alto-gether, slithered off its lathered back, and held his arms out to Azalais.

Her face was quite white. True, her skin was never exactly olive or even tanned, but now it rivaled chalk. Her very lips were bloodless. And she just stared down at him from atop her pony, wide-eyed and wary.

"Please, my lady. Let me assist you from your mount." He made his tone as soft as he was able as if he were coaxing a half-wild kitten from its hiding place. He held out his arms but did not lay hands upon her. She must come to him.

Without a word, she slipped into his arms.

Will didn't give a damn how it looked to any villager looking their way—two male minstrels entwined on the edge of their respectable hamlet. He just wrapped his arms about his lady and held her tight. She was shaking a little, but she didn't resist his embrace. She just melted against him, saying nothing, doing nothing but shivering. And he dropped kisses on her hair and murmured soft assurances in her ear.

"Shall we stay here for the night, my minstrel—if they will have us?" Will ventured when her shaking had subsided to the merest quiver.

He nearly grinned as he heard his own words: *If they will put up two minstrels who mostly evidently want to inhabit each other's braies.* But the grin withered and died. She would want nothing to do with his braies after today's encounter. Not, of course, that he could permit her even if she did. *Fear not, good villagers. It is but a passing illusion of lust. No iniquity will be practiced in your humble homes tonight.*

Azalais must have felt the tension in his arms, for she stiffened and pulled away. He let her go. Reluctantly.

She looked around.

"There is no tavern."

"Would you really want to play tonight?" he said softly.

A shiver rippled through her frame. She didn't answer.

"I propose we swap coin for the privilege of sleeping under some villager's roof tonight, my lady. A *safe* roof, surrounded by four stout walls and a hamlet's worth of honest peasants. No singing for our supper and no drowsing beneath the trees either. What say you?"

She said nothing, but she did nod. That was enough for the moment. Gently, he lifted her to her mount's sweaty back. She made no demur. Then he led his four-legged transport and hers together into what he sincerely hoped was a safe and celibate haven for the night.

IN THE END, it was a barn. Will was unsurprised to find the good villagers were none too eager to host a brace of minstrels of suspect morals within their hovel walls. Thankfully, they displayed no such scruples over accepting minstrel money. The headman of the hamlet himself had flung open his barn doors to the weary travelers and their steeds. It was, he informed them, the finest hay shed in the whole village, and they were most welcome to avail themselves of it—and a flask of wine and two servings of stew. In return for a small quantity of silver, of course.

Will had stayed in less expensive inns.

But a barn was fine by Will. It was dark and cozy and smelled of hay, and he rather thought Azalais needed dark and cozy right now. They were barred from lighting any fire within the barn walls, for the place was stuffed full of flammables. Instead, their headman host had grumblingly lent them a horn-covered lantern and made it clear he required it back the next day—and don't, for God's sake, burn the place down.

Now they were furnished with two trenchers of stew, enough wine to render them both unconscious if they so desired, and blessed solitude. After a long silence broken only by munching—both horse and human—he finally ventured the question:

"How are you feeling?"

Spoken in a carefully neutral voice. He would not push her in any way. Will recalled the aftereffects of his own first kill all too vividly. The horror. The feeling of having murdered something inside one's own soul.

As if that were not enough, she'd also seen *him* as never before. As a madman with a sword, the battle lust burning through his veins. Seized by the near-unconquerable desire to kill anyone who dared threaten her.

O, God.

He cast the trencher on the hay and sunk his head into his hands. *The memory.* The memory would not leave him alone. By heaven, he disgusted himself.

"I am feeling better now, Guilhem. The food…the wine, I think I needed it." A pause. "Will, look at me. What is the matter?"

Will. The word filtered through the urge to pull his hair out by the handful. She was talking to him.

He took a deep breath, loosed his hair, and looked up.

"Eat your meal, Will." She waved her eating-dagger at his discarded trencher. "It made me feel better. Besides—" She offered a tentative grin. "It cost us enough."

A tiny runnel of warmth coursed through him. His minstrel-girl, mothering him? After all she'd seen today.

He tried a smile in return and reached for his trencher like a good boy.

And as he ate, he could feel her watching him.

What in hell did she see? A thuggish knight no better than her elder brother and his cronies? It was inevitable. His training, his battle experience had taken over. The minstrel Guilhem vanished, and Sir William returned in all his despicable glory.

At which a lump of gristle lodged in his throat. Will coughed, swallowed hard, then coughed again.

And Azalais was kneeling beside him, one hand on his back. Patting.

"When I said, 'eat your meal,' I did not mean inhale it."

More pats. Ah, her touch felt good. He did not want to stop coughing—but eventually, he had to.

"Wine, Guilhem?"

The flask was proffered. Will took it, more for the opportuni-ty to slip his hand over hers on its leather surface. He drank. And wondered when she would rise and return to her own personal heap of hay. Not that he wanted her to, but it was most definitely for the best.

He set his trencher aside. He could eat no more.

"Do you feel safe in here, my lady? Do you think you can sleep?"

There. A hint. *Off to your bed, dear lady. Enough excitement for one day.*

"Yes, Will. I feel safe because you are with me."

He nearly snorted at that. A hard swallow on his wine. Still, she did not move from her position beside him. Her hand rested lightly on his shoulder.

"I did not realize how skilled you are with the sword," she murmured. "After you've taught me the dagger, I think you ought to train me in swordplay. I know I'll never be as good as you, but after today, I feel the need to know my way around a sword."

It was as well he didn't have wine in his mouth at that moment.

"Nuns do not play with swords, my lady. And if your Lord L permits you a dagger in his vicinity, I have grave fears for the state of his throat."

He ought not to have added that last jab. Azalais's eyes widened. Her hand left his shoulder and crept to her own throat. "I regret the necessity of what I did today, Will. But it *was* necessary. They were not going to let us live." A pause. She held his gaze. "But I'm still going to be a minstrel. Like you, I have decided. I am not going to be a nun, and I am *not* going to subject myself to Lord Leonard."

Will squeezed his eyes shut. It was too much—the strange blend of pain, plea, and hope in her eyes. It was his clear duty to crush that hope. For her own good.

"You cannot be a minstrel, Lady Azalais," he said, his eyes tightly closed. "What happened today should be proof enough. You came within a whisker of dying today. Next time you might not be so lucky."

"And *you* came within a whisker of being dishonored, William de Fauconberg. And doubtless, they would have slit your throat afterward, too. You heard them, did you not? They fancied your arse as much as mine. And has it put *you* off your minstrel plans?"

He sighed. A completely unstaged exhalation for once. And opened his eyes.

She had edged round to kneel before him, but her posture was anything but humble and supplicating. And her eyes fairly blazed in the low light.

"No, it hasn't," he said. "Although it has caused me to become more circumspect about entering lonely forest groves."

"And why shouldn't I simply be more circumspect, too, Sir Minstrel? Not to mention more familiar with a sword? There is safety in numbers—two are better than one—and this is the only time in our travels we have had any trouble." Her glorious eyes narrowed then. "But none of that matters to you, does it? You're just making excuses. The reality—the reality you have not the courage to admit to my face—is that you simply want rid of me."

His eyes widened at that. "What?"

"You heard me—my presence constrains you. For some misguided reason, you feel obliged to act honorably around me. You can't bed a woman in every *ville* while I am near, not after Bordeaux."

"Bordeaux?"

"By God, Guilhem, was it that forgettable? *Two* women— don't you remember? You left the taproom with two willing women, and I...well, admittedly I gave you the cold shoulder for days after that. But you haven't touched a woman since you discovered what I am. Even though I said you could."

He shook his head in bemusement. "How long have you viewed me as the fiend of lust incarnate, my lady?"

Then he leaned forward and took her face in his hands. She stiffened.

"Or perhaps I have indeed been possessed by a spirit of lust in the time you have known me, Azalais. Perhaps you have some reason to suspect me after all."

The face between his hands frowned at him. "I've told you—you may do as you please around me, Guilhem. Act the rakish minstrel to your heart's content. Just consider me your minstrel companion. For heaven's sake, if you want to take two women at once, do so! Just so long as you do it out of my sight," she added in afterthought.

He leaned forward and brushed his lips over hers. She softened against him—but a heartbeat later, her lips firmed and drew away.

"A minstrel *companion*, remember," she muttered.

He smoothed a thumb over her stubborn lips. "Don't you want me, your lady?"

"Not if it stops you from accepting me as your companion! Listen, Guilhem. I want this life. I do not have the vocation to be a nun. My heart is given to music, not to God. Entering Wykeham was a last resort. Surely you see that? I didn't think anything else was possible beyond celibacy or marriage. But now I see clearly. Take me with you after we free my father, Guilhem. Let me travel with you as your fellow minstrel."

I can just imagine what your dear papa would think of that.

He didn't say it. There were other, more pressing matters he wished to address. Such as:

"It is true, I have indeed been possessed by a strange spirit of lust for the last few weeks, my lady. You ask if I recall those two ladies of Bordeaux? I do, if only barely. You see, I did accompany those two noblewomen to their lodgings with intentions to...well, I will leave the planned proceedings to your imagination. Suffice to say, they did not proceed very far. I found myself unaccountably stymied by the image of a certain young minstrel whenever—"

He stopped. Even voicing it seemed disrespectful.

"You see? That is exactly what I mean, Guilhem. That is what I'm saying—you don't have to feel constrained by my presence. I am no prude. For God's sake, I've seen where men like to put their members."

"Shh." His hand traveled over her cheekbone to slip into her hair. Golden curls in the lantern light. "That is not what I mean. I did not feel constrained, precisely. No, all that came to mind when I touched those women's bodies was my minstrel companion." Will tried an apologetic smile. "Dastardly of me, wasn't it? I thought you *were* a man then, too. Christ, it confused the hell out of my nether regions, believe me."

He let his hand drop. She would likely shake it off in disgust anyway.

Sure enough, Azalais was frowning at him.

"So, you didn't have your way with them?" A tone of disbelief. "Or with any of the others?"

He chuckled. "You have an interesting opinion of men, my lady. Or is it just me you suspect of wishing to broadcast wild oats through every town in France?"

OF COURSE, IT is you. True, my prior experience with men hasn't helped matters. But you, William de Fauconberg, you are too… Oh, you have everything, charm, looks, and music to make my heart burst. Women fall over themselves to get their hands on you. I have seen it, over and over. I am just one of many.

But she couldn't say that. Instead, what she said was worse.

"You forget, Guilhem, I know what you can do to a woman. You kindly demonstrated your skills at my request. Your lips, your hands, they have had practice, I can tell. Much practice."

He looked at her a moment. A long moment in which she wished to curl into a ball and sink beneath the hay.

"This is a novel way to deal with the aftermath of battle," he said at last. "I applaud you, my lady. You have diverted my mind completely from the affairs of the afternoon."

"And you, Sir Knight, are avoiding the question."

"Which is?"

She took a deep breath.

"Let me be a man—and let me be a minstrel. Take me with you as your partner in music." Then her gaze dropped to the straw. "And treat me as a woman, too, if you wish. Only let me accompany you."

Then his palm was warm against her face, his fingers in her hair.

"Azalais."

She had to look at him. She didn't want to look at him.

"I am not worthy of you. This life you ask for, it is not worthy of you either. You would be discovered. And if I treated you as you suggest—" He lowered his lips to hers, kissed her gently. "Sooner or later there would be consequences."

His eyes, pools of deep darkness, looked into hers. His lips lured her. So close. Oh, she wanted them. But she must speak.

"You mean I would get with child," she bit out. "And then I would be a minstrel-man no more. You would have to leave me."

"Oh, sweet heaven, Azalais—"

And without fully understanding how it came about, she was scooped up, deposited on his lap, and wrapped about by his arms.

For an indefinable period, he kissed her. His mouth was possessed by the magical power to make the whole world disappear, thought vanish, and bones dissolve. And when he finally abandoned her mouth for her neck, ear, shoulder blade, the world did not noticeably reappear.

Until he murmured against her skin, "Azalais, it would be a dream come true if you were to travel with me as my companion in music, and heaven on earth if you were to share my bed at night." Nibble. "O God, have you any idea how much I want you, my songbird?"

A sharper nibble. She snuggled deeper into his lap—and found what she was seeking. The unmistakable evidence of his want.

"Then take what you want, Will."

A heartfelt groan. His mouth left her skin.

"I cannot, my lady. Do you not understand? If it were at all possible, I would wed you and treat you as a gently born lady ought to be treated. I would dress you in silks and supply you with servants and house you in a castle overflowing with tapestries and silver plates. And you and I would play music all the days of our lives."

Chapter Twenty-One

T HE WORDS SWIRLED in her head, lodging nowhere. Making no sense.

"But I cannot," her minstrel went on. "Azalais, I cannot. I am miserably poor, and the one avenue that offers me any wealth I absolutely refuse to take. I will not murder men for money."

Still, he held her. Azalais laid her cheek against the crook of his shoulder. Her head felt unsteady, too full of conflicting signals.

"I did not ask you to marry me, Will. Just to play music with me—and bed me if the fancy so takes you." A little wriggle in his lap to make her point.

His mouth sought hers. The ferocity of the kiss made it clear that her point was taken.

Such a kiss could not continue long without causing spontaneous combustion—or consummation. They parted, albeit reluctantly.

Once she had caught her breath—and some of her thoughts—Azalais took his face between her hands and held his gaze. "I don't want you to be a soldier, Will. I don't want tapestries and silks either. But I do want you. I want Guilhem the Minstrel."

"Your father and your brothers would never permit it. *I* cannot permit it, my love. To expose you daily to such danger as we faced today—"

"Successfully," she interposed. "You forget, I have seen you wield a sword now. I would wager not many men could match your skill."

"But they could outnumber me. And think of the dishonor—not just the loss of your maidenly honor, but of your status. Azalais, you have seen how minstrels are regarded. We are disreputable wanderers, moral lepers. You would be despised. Why, you could wed a shoemaker with less social ruin."

"Do you think I care about social ruin?" she demanded. "What great privilege has being a lady afforded me so far?"

He shook his head slowly between her hands. The stubble of his cheeks prickled her palms, little spikes of pleasure-pain.

"We will ransom your father in a few days, my lady. And that will be the end of matters. He will perhaps be grateful to me for safeguarding you, but that gratitude will not stretch so far as to grant me his daughter and certainly not to the fate you propose."

"And if we fail?" she whispered. "We nearly failed today. Dead minstrels do not free noblemen, nor do penniless ones. Besides, other things may get in the way."

His lips curved at that. Her eyes were immediately drawn to them. Fascinating lips, and what they could do was more fascinating still…

"You tempt me, my lady. As always, you tempt me. So, we abandon your father after coming all this way? We slip away with your dowry—wherever you have secreted it—to live a wildly passionate but inevitably short minstrel life?"

His mouth was smiling, but his eyes did not.

"Of course not! That is not what I mean and you know it. I simply fear freeing my father is no foregone conclusion. And even if we do, he may still wed me to that—that animal. It has been two years since I saw my father, Will. He was never precisely a doting guardian, although he was a sight better than Robert."

She didn't want to think of Robert and his company now. She didn't even want to think about her father. But the turn in topic had prompted another consideration, one she had been meaning to mention. She had never been quite bold enough—or sufficiently brazen.

But now, well. As Will said, they were only a couple of days from Bruniquel. And if this day of mad contrasts did not call for boldness, what did?

So, she leaned toward those fascinating lips and kissed them. Oh, she was no old hand at this game, but she was willing to be tutored. His mouth softened and shifted beneath hers immediately. Opening, inviting her within. A delicious drowning of thought.

But no, she could not drown all thought quite yet. There was something she needed to say. "Will—" She withdrew her lips a finger's breadth from his—and steeled herself. "There is something else I wish you to bear in mind. If after all this my father or Robert still forces me to marry, then I prefer to bear your child, not Lord Leonard's."

WILLIAM DE FAUCONBERG stilled. Oh, part of him leaped to attention, all willingness to obey his lady's command. She was so close, cradled in his arms, nestled in his lap. Practically sitting on that most willing member of his anatomy.

"And if you enter a nunnery?" he forced himself to say. "The sisters are unlikely to believe you blessed by an immaculate conception."

She shook her head. "I will not enter a nunnery. It would be wrong—I realize that now. It was only desperation that made me seek it, Will. I was running from the world."

He did not ask her what she would choose instead. He would not argue with her again, not tonight. She could not become a wandering minstrel, disguised as a boy until that disguise was rudely ripped from her. She would realize it herself, given time. Or her father would impress it upon her in no uncertain terms.

But there was a far more pressing matter demanding, yes,

pressing itself upon his attention right now. The soft pressure of her derriere upon his thighs, the warm, lithe body pressed up against his.

Before he knew what he was doing, he was kissing her again. And if there was thought in his head, it consisted of vague, fleeting images—an imagined Lord L claiming his bride, the imminence of their arrival at Bruniquel, and of his losing Azalais—soon, and forever. He kissed her with a ferocity that had her gasping, winding her arms about him for support, then inveigling her fingers beneath his tunic and exploring his torso with hungry hands.

"Off!" she demanded, tearing her mouth from his for a breathless instant. "Take your tunic off, now!"

He obliged. Still sitting, he fairly tore the linen off. A moment later, Azalais was pushing him back upon the hay. She straddled his thighs now, both of her palms flat against his chest. He let himself sink back, content for the moment just to feast his eyes on her—a golden goddess in the lamplight. A fully-clothed goddess, more's the pity. Meanwhile, her gaze roamed over his body, followed by her hands, then—O God—her mouth. She nibbled at his neck, traced his Adam's apple with her tongue, and then—sweet heaven, what gave her that idea?—her tongue discovered his right nipple.

Will's hips jerked involuntarily. He heard her gasp, then a soft laugh followed. She traced the contours of his second nipple with the care of a miniaturist, then sat up, palms holding him down, and looked at him.

That look. If he was tinder, it would set him smoldering. Her mouth was slightly ajar, lips a little swollen from the attention he'd been giving them. Will attempted to lift himself to his elbows. Those lips demanded more attention. But she pushed him back down.

"No, Will. I have a favor to ask of you."

His heart was pounding in his ears. Her voice was low and sweet, but insistent, too.

"A favor, my lady?" was all he could manage.

"You remember my telling you of my unfortunate encounter with Lord Leonard and his henchman?"

A nod.

"You remember I said the henchman took his member out?" She closed her eyes at that, a little wrinkle marring her brow.

Ah. Of course. That was the primary experience she had of men and their urges—the vile fellow who saw fit to tug himself off before his lady. Will's chest deflated.

"Well, my favor is this, Sir William—I wish to counter one memory with another. I wish you to take your hose and braies off."

Will no longer felt deflated. He didn't know how he felt. His boyish lady, victim of previous men's lustful displays, wanted *him* on display? Part of him quaked at the thought. He cherished no particular illusions concerning his nether regions. True, William de Fauconberg was passing vain about his outward appearance, but in his undressed state? Women hadn't usually required him to present his naked self as an *objet d'art*. Besides, he had no idea of the dimensions or artistic merits of said henchman's nether regions. What if she were disappointed?

Evidently, his thoughts had occupied too much time, for Azalais dipped down against his bare chest and brushed her lips against his.

"Please, Will. I do not want that to be my sole memory of a man."

His chest tingled to her soft weight. He looked into her eyes, deep amber in the low light, their pupils wide and dark, and said, "I cannot promise you an object of surpassing beauty, my lady, but if it is your wish…"

His hands slipped down to encompass her waist. He lifted her from his thighs and set her on the hay beside him and cast her a half-smile.

"If you would give me a moment, my lady? I suggest you close your eyes until all is arrayed for your inspection."

His heart was behaving most erratically now. Like an obedient child, Azalais had settled herself cross-legged on the hay. Her lovely eyes were closed, but her lips curved. There was a flush on her cheeks. She was waiting.

Will only prayed this would not traumatize her afresh. The sight of another hungry cock would likely have her rethinking her nunnery plans post haste.

But it was her wish and her command. What could an obedient knight-minstrel do?

Will's fingers fumbled on the ties attaching his hose to his braies. True, the light was low, but that was not the reason his fingers suddenly felt doubled in size. He shucked his boots off, and his hose quickly followed. Now there were only his braies left—they were not so easily removed from a sitting position. Especially in their current well-filled state.

But Will would not stand. That would be to echo her previous experience—a thug standing over a helpless maid, dominating her by means of his maleness. Instead, Will was determined to lie prone. She could stand over him if she wished. An icy trickle threaded his shoulder blades. The thought of it—his lady standing over him, judging him, taking in all his exposed maleness, and finding it wanting.

He shook off the feeling by means of movement, loosened his braies belt, lifted his buttocks, and eased the linen over the couched lance of his nether regions. The braies were flung aside, and Will stared down at what was revealed.

He saw it every day, but he never really looked at it. What would *she* see?

Oh, he was certainly erect. Despite his heart's seesaw of emotions, his nether regions were in no doubt they wanted to be admired. They strained for attention.

Will shook his head and turned away. He looked at Azalais; her lids were still sealed. *Enough delay. Thy will be done, my lady.* Will drew a deep breath and lay down. He arrayed himself flat on his back, legs slightly apart, palms up. And felt quite horribly vulnerable.

When he spoke, his words emerged distinctly rough-edged. "Azalais, you may open your eyes now."

HE WAS TEMPTED to close his own. He wasn't sure he could bear to watch as she surveyed every last portion of his exposed self.

But that was the coward's route. Sir William may not wish to be a knight, but that did not permit him to turn craven. It had to be admitted, though, that his jaw was fit to crack walnuts.

She did not stand. She simply remained sitting cross-legged—and looked at him. She blinked. Her lips compressed. Then her head tilted ever so slightly to one side.

God in Heaven, say something! Do something!

He could not parse the expressions on her face, the flicker of emotion. Her brows dipped, but then immediately uncreased—only to rise. Was he truly so paradoxical a sight?

"Azalais—"

So much for his minstrel tones—a frog wouldn't envy his voice at this moment. She started at the syllables, as well she might.

But she didn't speak. Instead, she moved from her sitting position to kneel upright, so close to his buttocks that he felt the straw shift under them. Again, her head tilted to one side—but this time her arm moved as well.

She extended her right hand. It descended to rest on his chest. His turn to startle. Her eyes widened. Damn it, his cursed nether regions had likely bobbed her a friendly greeting.

"You are nicely shaped, Will," she said, her gaze roaming over him, taking him all in. Then the hand on his chest began to move, too. It explored his torso at a snail's pace, running curious fingers through the sprinkling of hair, circling his nipples. He almost smiled at that particular examination—was she comparing them in memory to her own? He would lay oath they were surrounded by less hair.

But he didn't smile, for her hand had begun to dip lower. It abandoned his chest and now wandered over the realms of his stomach.

"I like these ridges," she murmured. Her fingers spread wide, trailing over his abdomen, learning his contours. Darting rivulets of sensation spread over his skin. Rivulets that arrowed ever down.

He wanted to close his eyes. He just wanted to feel. But William of Fauconberg could not. He kept his gaze on the intent visage bending over him, watching her lips part, her tongue dart out to moisten those lips, and listening to her shallow breaths.

Then her fingers brushed hair—and it wasn't the hair on his chest.

Will swallowed a groan. He must not startle her. But the sensations—dear God.

But that was nothing.

For a moment later, she touched him—really touched him. His lady reached out and ran a single finger slowly along his shaft—and Will had to anchor his hips to the barn floor and grasp handfuls of hay to hold himself in. In the midst of it all, the groan simply could not be stifled.

The finger was quickly withdrawn.

"Did I hurt you?"

Will registered a worried look upon the sweet face bending over him. He chuckled. The sound seemed to come from far away. "Anything but, my lady. Pray, do not concern yourself with my comfort. Continue your examination, by all means."

Her lips curved.

"If it pleases you, Sir Knight." And the finger extended again.

A shiver of anticipation rippled over him. "Oh, it pleases me, sweet lady."

The finger paused.

"Are you cold, Will?"

"Cold is the furthest thing from my mind at this moment, my lady. But if you wish it, I would not refuse a little extra body warmth. There is nothing like the bare skin of another to warm one's flesh, I find. Purely in practical, campaigning terms, of course."

A little smile in return. The finger withdrew. It busied itself with the rest of her hand in grasping her tunic hem and raising the rough fabric up and over her golden head.

Which of course left the binding beneath. Layers of the stuff, wrapped around and around the pale skin of her torso.

She evidently caught his expression, for she deftly unpinned the binding's end and let the linen droop free. Will smiled. She was not revealed yet, but the potential was there.

Then she leaned over him, and her hand stretched out again. But only to rest, palm down, on his abdomen. He caught the end of her linen binding and tugged a layer or two free.

She didn't seem to notice. She was staring at his erect and restless shaft.

Oh no. Past memories had returned to haunt her. She wasn't seeing him, but a potential rapist, his weapon rearing rudely from his braies.

Her next words confirmed his fears. "Lord Leonard's man took his member in his hand," she said, her eyes never leaving the member rearing so ready before her. "He wrapped his fist about it."

A pause, and Will began to wonder whether this was the end. His shaft began to droop. It was no longer wanted or needed, it seemed.

"May I put my fist around yours, Will?"

By God, yes! his cock declared, coming to attention instantly. The rest of Will was not so sure. To copy her previous experience too closely seemed hazardous—not least for his own member. Heaven knows, she was due a little revenge, but Will did not fancy being the means.

But what could he say? Perhaps it was what she needed—to take control of another man's shaft. But he would not put his member on the sacrificial altar for nothing. No, the moment was ripe for a bargain.

"You may, my lady—" Her hand began to move. "If—" It hesitated. He spoke on, "in turn, you agree to relieve your skin of your bindings."

She looked at him. She inclined her head slowly. Then with her left hand, which had until now remained tame by her side, she tugged at the linen that bounded her. She never glanced down at what she was doing. Instead, her eyes were narrowed upon his ever-hopeful member.

Her right hand extended—again—his cock could not help but bob it a greeting. And finally, this time the hand reached its destination. Not a single finger this time, but all four fingers touched the unbearable hardness of his shaft. Will clenched his teeth. The fingers did not stop. They curved around his thickness, flexing against it, to wrap him in a firm, warm grip. His hips strained. He pressed his heels into the floor.

"It is very solid," she said and gave an experimental squeeze.

A strangled groan in response.

Her gaze flicked quickly to his face, eyebrows alarmed.

Then they relaxed. "You like it, don't you?" And her grip strengthened again.

"I do," he managed, all senses honed upon those questing fingers, the slight shifts in tension, the thumb that rubbed gently just below his shaft's head.

"It's smoother than I thought," she observed. Then slipped her hand along his length, as if to confirm her findings.

Will anchored his buttocks to the floor and tried not to react.

"Your binding—" he said in a strangled tone. Anything to distract from the mounting pressure.

She gave him an apologetic half-smile. "Oh, I forgot." And her left hand fiddled with the constraining linen. It fell in slow, white waves. She seemed to pay it no mind, despite her previous concerns. No—Will smiled, trying not to reveal gritted teeth— her attention was all focused elsewhere.

Upon him.

The last layer fell from her, and his lips parted, clenched teeth forgotten. His minstrel-girl was truly a vision in the lamplight.

Two perfect breasts, daintily made, pink nipples yearning for his touch.

Azalais must have noticed his expression—or more likely some livening in the region of his groin—for her fingers tightened and stilled.

Will's chin tipped back; he permitted himself a small groan. "Ah, my songstress, I cannot bear it much longer. Have you felt your fill? Have I supplied enough for a replacement memory yet?"

Her lips curved in a secret smile, and she bent, still holding him firm. She leaned down over him until her lips touched his, and her nipples brushed his chest. *O sweet heaven.* His lips opened to hers, and his hands could remain passive no longer. They discarded their hay and lifted to pull her to him.

Her fingers abandoned his cock, but he didn't care. In fact, it was probably for the best, given his state of arousal. Instead, he had her breasts pressed against him, the entire expanse of her body warm and silken against his own skin, and her mouth open against his. It was an erotic dream. No, he had never managed dreams like this. It was beyond a dream. This was his minstrel-girl, his beautiful companion in music, trusting him, giving herself to him, despite her previous experience.

She withdrew her mouth from his just enough to murmur, "No, I have not felt my fill yet, Will."

Her right hand slipped down his body—and found what it was seeking. Her fingertips traced the smooth head of his shaft. Will's hips jolted up. He swallowed an oath—and nearly choked on it.

"I want this," she whispered. "Will you give it to me?"

AZALAIS DE KELDY, minstrel-man and virtuous lady, felt insanely brazen. But he *had* asked. And it was now or never, every instinct told her. There were only days left before they reached Bruniquel and everything changed. She knew he was tempted, sorely tempted. Just look at his reaction when she did this—

She dipped to kiss him again. At the same time, she drew a gentle thumb over the furnace-hot head of his manhood—and felt his frame shudder beneath hers with barely contained need.

If he said, *No, Azalais. My oath forbids me. My honor will not allow it,* she did not know what she would do.

Dissolve entirely, probably. Or implode. Certainly, she could never look him in the eyes again.

But he was still kissing her. He hadn't thrown her off him in affront. A giggle nearly escaped her—Sir William was in no good position to be affronted when his own front was so evidently unfit to be stowed in his braies.

His hands were traveling slowly down her back, holding her to him but not in an insistent way. More like a slow stroke of a cat. They dipped down to her waist, and then met an obstruction in their journey.

Azalais's breath caught. His fingers were upon her braies belt, the rolled fabric that held the linen underwear up. They tugged a little, loosening the fabric roll, stretching it so he could ease the whole garment slowly down—down over her hips and buttocks, taking the attached leg hose with it.

Cool night air whispered over her bared skin. Her bared derriere, to be precise. She sincerely hoped no peasant host saw fit to check on his guests before he retired for the night. He would receive a vision he would never forget. Will's hands had stalled just above her knees. He could roll her hose down no further from his prone position. She would have to help him. But that would mean sitting up and exposing herself in her entirety to his hungry gaze.

No, there was another means. And so Azalais began to wriggle, shuffling her legs against each other, thus inching her hose and braies down.

A moment later, Will's hands grasped her buttocks—quite firmly, stilling her. Not that she objected to being held hard against the delicious textures of his body—the tickle of hair, both on his chest and elsewhere, the firm ridges of his abdomen, and, of course, the even-firmer part of his anatomy that reared a little below.

"Stop," he said in a strangled tone.

"But they're nearly off," she said. "My hose, I mean."

"That wasn't all that nearly went off," he muttered.

But then his hands softened on her behind. They began to explore, to shape her to him, to stroke and knead. Ah, that and the pressure of his manhood from beneath—it was almost enough to...well, it recalled the shuddering ecstasy of the previous night.

"Let me relieve you of your hose instead, my lady," he murmured a moment or two later.

Azalais tensed. Just slightly, it was true, but her minstrel, lying nearly full length beneath her, couldn't help but notice.

"My love?" he whispered, his hands lying quite still upon her naked rear. "You can change your mind, you know. It is not too late." He chuckled ruefully. "And in so doing, you can hold me to my oath in its strictest sense. Perhaps you will be doing us both a favor."

"No!"

Azalais struggled to rise. Will caught her purpose, for his hands instantly relinquished their possession of her rear. She rolled off him to sit on the prickling hay and seized the hose and braies that tangled her legs.

He, too, rose to a sitting position. Watching her, no doubt. Azalais did not look at him. Instead, she tugged furiously at the fabric. He saw what she was about, for he reached down and gently untangled one of her laces.

Then he turned away. William of Fauconberg rose to his knees and picked up his cloak.

Azalais froze, hands about her ankles, the rest of her quite naked. He had had enough. She had done something wrong. Perhaps she had handled him too roughly. Or he simply wasn't interested anymore.

Chapter Twenty-Two

W ILL KNEW SHE felt awkward revealing herself, so he turned away. He'd never been particularly worried about getting naked in company himself. Will's experience was of boys boarding together in a cathedral school, and later of soldiers together on campaign, camping rough. Neither situation was conducive to modesty. And with women, he was usually too busy attending to their pleasure to worry about what they thought of his anatomy.

Until tonight. Until she had demanded to see his maleness to counter the memory of another. Now William de Fauconberg knew what it was to feel exposed.

And his lady—who had spent so long disguised as a man and whose femininity had only ever been a source of trouble—must feel it to a far greater degree.

So, he turned away from the figure and busied himself with spreading his cloak upon the prickling hay.

Besides, his damned member needed a moment. That wriggling maneuver she had performed on top of him had nearly been his undoing. Had she any idea how good she felt against him, writhing against his all-too-ready shaft?

That aside, honor demanded he give her time to reflect, even now. She must have time to consider whether she really wanted to take this irreversible step.

He was still kneeling over the cloak, smoothing its last wrinkles, when a hand touched his shoulder.

He startled, but he didn't look around.

"Have you had enough, Will? I understand. I will not demand something you are unwilling to give. I know what that is like."

Her voice was hesitant, still a little husky but evidently unsure. He could not bear it. Will turned, rising to his feet, and found himself chest to naked chest with her. His minstrel-girl. Her little pointed chin tangled up as she searched his face, her eyes wide and vulnerable. And he simply couldn't bear it.

Will bent and scooped her into his arms.

She gasped, and her eyes changed expression. They were no longer vulnerable. She looped her naked arms around his neck and drew his mouth to hers.

Ah, that was better. Will lost himself in kissing her for uncounted heartbeats, her body warm and pliant in his arms. For the moment, she felt entirely his.

But it was an awkward affair, holding her while kissing her. Not that he was complaining, but he wanted greater access to her soft skin, her gentle curves. He wanted to truly see her. So, Will bent, knelt, and lowered his lady to the carefully laid cloak and arrayed her upon it.

She clung to him a moment.

Until he nuzzled her ear and whispered, "I definitely haven't had enough, my lady. I will never have enough of you." And she sank back on the hay to look at him, just begging to be kissed.

Will smiled then, and he knew his smile to be wicked. She wanted to be kissed? Why, it would be his pleasure.

OH, HE WAS a beautiful sight, her minstrel kneeling there beside her on the hay. The lantern cast mysterious lights and shadows over his body—a landscape of delicious contours. Smooth muscles, nicely defined, a dusting of dark hair, and then the shaft of his manhood, commanding attention. *Demanding* her attention. A flicker of memory returned then—of Lord Leonard and his man, of poor Meg on the ground. But it was a distant flicker, easily banished. It was a whole ocean away from her current situation. Will wanted her, but he would only take her if she gave herself with all her heart. He would not use his maleness for domination and conquest.

And his smile as he took her in made her melt into the cloak and yet tense deep inside, all at the same time.

Then he dipped down. She thought he would kiss her, but no—his dark hair brushed her collarbone. An instant later she nearly screamed. She managed to choke it back, to reduce it to a mere squeak. His tongue had found her breast. It grazed over a nipple, warm and a little rough. She arched against him and heard him chuckle.

He paid his respects to the remaining breast then, and it never occurred to Azalais to feel self-conscious about their lack of size. Beneath his loving tongue, they felt perfect.

Then his lips were traveling down. His hair stroked her skin in their wake, and his hands were about her waist, then smoothing over her hips. He circled her navel with his tongue. Azalais squirmed, part in pleasure, but also part in doubt at the direction he was taking.

His tongue trailed down. Azalais tensed. His hands slid over her hip bones and then down to her thighs. His fingers trailed over the tingling surface of her upper legs to where they met in the middle. Then those fingers eased her legs apart.

She let him, but she wasn't entirely sure she should. She was in no doubt of where men desired to explore when it came to women's bodies. The serving maid in the stable came to mind. Azalais banished that image. Nevertheless, it was instructive, for she recalled the man-at-arms had shoved his groin between the girl's legs, not his head. And Will had gently parted her legs and was even now lowering his head between them. Surely this was not what men desired to do to women?

Then his fingers parted her folds, and she felt a breath upon her exposed core. She tried not to squirm, acutely aware of the face between her legs. Thank heavens for the dim light.

And then she thought no more, for his tongue touched her. It brushed over her sex and this time she did shriek.

Will had to hold her down. His hands splayed over her thighs, and he lapped at her core. Azalais writhed. The feeling was unbelievable, and it continued to build. Yet, Will did not cease from his attentions. Finally, she had no choice but to grasp him by the hair and wrench his head up.

"No more," she gasped. "Will, I want you. Now!"

And she wriggled down him and wrapped her legs about his thighs, urging him to her.

Will's eyes were wild and dark. He closed them momentarily and looked almost pained. And even now, doubt wormed its way into Azalais's mind.

Then he sank down against her, his body overlying hers, only saved from squashing her by the elbows that held him slightly aloft. He opened his eyes and look deep into hers.

"Truly?" he said. "Are you sure, Azalais?"

"Oh, for heaven's sake, yes!" And her hands found his buttocks, reveled a moment in their firmness and shape, and then grasped them and pulled them down.

The smooth head of his shaft nudged at her entrance. For an instant, she frowned, recalling his dimensions and wondering for the first time about simple mechanics. But then it nudged a little more, and her head tipped back, utterly taken with the sensation.

Will's lips captured hers. He tasted of her, ever so slightly. It sent a jab of recollection of his earlier activity—the way it made her feel—and she groaned into his mouth. His tongue-tip touched hers, lips molded against hers, and his hips slid forward.

He entered her. A sensation of incredible fullness, of solidity, a spasm of pain, and then utter rightness followed. Their mouths paused against each other, and Azalais felt nothing but the fullness of him inside her. The wholeness, the breathtaking satiation. Ah, this was what she had been waiting for.

And then he began to move, rocking gently back and forth. And she had thought the earlier sensation was the pinnacle of bliss. She wrapped her legs about him and echoed his movements with her own hips. *O dear God, how was it possible to bear this feeling?* The ratcheting, nerve-straining tension? The sweet fullness, his possession of her, the warmth and care with which he treated her, urging her to greater and greater heights.

He ceased to kiss her then. His head lifted so his gaze met hers—and Azalais nearly melted beneath the blaze of passion and tenderness in his eyes. He said nothing but continued to gaze at her, and his hips began to rock with greater urgency.

She gasped. "Will. Will, I can take no more, ahh!"

She convulsed. Azalais cried out, uncaring that it might bring villagers running. And she managed to open her eyes just in time to see her minstrel's face transform, an expression equal parts agony and wonder taking possession of his face. And his hips drove forwards, once, twice, with shuddering finality. And he sank down against her, burying his head in her neck, and groaned a long, soft groan.

He lay against her, wonderfully heavy, his frame soaking up the convulsions that still shook her, slowly subsiding.

Then he tugged the side of the cloak over them and wrapped his arms about her, saying nothing. Not that Azalais needed words. She just needed *him*—and she had him, at least for now. So Azalais de Keldy snuggled against her minstrel, luxuriating in the expanse of warm skin against hers, and slipped into blissful sleep.

THEY WERE COMPOSING a song. Will wasn't sure whether it counted as a *canzo*—oh, it was certainly a love song, but it also told a story and, besides, it contained far more stanzas than a *canzo* ought.

It was his minstrel-girl's idea. They had begun it the previous night. More accurately, they had composed it during the rare intervals that their mouths and hands had been free to make music. Both the previous night and this one had been spent in the woods—very carefully scouted woods, Will had made sure. No sneaking brigand was to be allowed within a hundred leagues of his lady.

There was still a danger, of course, no matter how carefully he eyed hoofprints and passersby. But Azalais wanted woods and she wanted him. And, by God, he wanted her. Will's member stirred at the mere thought, but it was a half-hearted stir. A man had his limits, even under the circumstances.

The circumstances were that they would reach the Chateau de Bruniquel tomorrow.

"Are you content with the tune, Will?" Azalais was looking at him, her lute lying across her lap. "I think a vielle accompaniment suits it better, don't you?"

For answer, he knelt down beside her, took her face in his hands, and brought his lips to hers. It wasn't the most well-planned kiss—the lute lay between them, smooth and hard, and it was damnably awkward to kiss from a kneeling position. But Will did his best. God in heaven, he would never have enough of her lips—soft and passionately responsive, the instruments of divine music as well as very earthly bliss.

His fingers were in her hair, his cock was doing its best to rise to the occasion, and her hands were anchored about his neck. Who knows where events would have led if Will hadn't bumped his nether regions up against the damn lute with sufficient force to make him gasp. His groin simply wasn't up to such confrontation right now.

He sank back on his haunches and gave her beloved lute a narrow look.

She laughed, a little breathlessly. "Well?"

"Well, what?" he grumbled. "What are you doing with that instrument in your lap anyway? A man could do himself an injury on it." He patted at the offended part of his anatomy and produced a wildly exaggerated wince. "Dear God, I think it needs tending to immediately. From the goodness of your heart, dear lady, put your lute aside and help a man in pain."

She did. She laid her lute down on her cloak, gently prodded Will to a prostrate position, and then busied herself with divesting him of his braies by the flickering light of the fire.

"Hmm." She cocked her head to one side, considering the problem laid out before her. Then she ran an experimental finger down his length. "Ah," she said, her lips curving. "There is life in it yet, Sir Knight. Fear not, it is not broken—only hard-used. But let me see what I can do."

Will lay back and simply watched the expressions flicker over her face like firelight, absorption, fascination, and yes, a spirit of daring exploration. She was learning the landscape of his body, discovering just how much power she had over him.

Miraculously, he felt himself thickening and firming beneath her questing fingers. How long was it since they had last been tangled in ecstasy on the forest floor? Before or after their evening meal? And now what in hell was she doing? Her golden head was dipping down, down. Will tensed. And nearly levitated from his cloak when she touched him. Her cheek. She had rubbed her cheek against his growing solidity. Then she glanced at him, questioningly, and stroked her other cheek along the length of his shaft.

"I wanted to feel it," she said. "Not just with my fingers."

Will was tempted to make a crude comment at that point, but he was mercifully spared by her mouth. For she kissed him. First on his shaft, and then on his head. A simple open-mouthed kiss. He clenched his buttocks hard and tried to control his hips. It was not a good idea to smack her in the face.

She leaned back and looked at him, an undeniable smile on her lovely face now. "There, I think you are better now, Will.

Don't you think?"

"No," he groaned, and began to elbow himself up, determined to do something about this state of affairs.

But she wouldn't have it. She put a hand on his chest and pushed him back down. "You are wounded, Will. Just lie there and let me minister to you."

Before he could reply, his minstrel-girl had flung her arms up and was wriggling out of her tunic. Will sucked in a breath. She wore absolutely nothing beneath the discarded linen—no bindings, no braies. Ah, that was more like it. Again, he began to lift himself on his elbows. Again, she pushed him down.

"Stay there," she ordered. And in the next moment, Will found himself more than willing to remain prone on his back.

For his lady slipped a silky leg over him to kneel with one leg on either side of Will's hips. Will knew his eyes widened, for his minstrel-girl paused, a flash of worry crossing her intent features.

"Do you mind, Will?"

"Oh, not in the least, my lady. Pray, do with me what you will," he managed.

The worry vanished, to be replaced with a small, mischievous smile. And then carefully she lowered herself, down by minute increments, until Will watched her face transform as she sank down upon his shaft.

"Oh, dear heaven," he groaned, and could not help the answering jolt of his hips.

She rode him. She took control. Her hands gripping his chest, the sweet power of taking him writ plain across her face. She had learned a lot in the last two days. Now she knew her power over him, and by heaven, she exercised it. And it was bliss.

He didn't last long. He should have done. After all, this was most definitely not their first intimate encounter of the day. They had begun just as the first sleepy birds were stirring to greet the dawn. Will had stirred with a vengeance. Then there was their luncheon break beside the Aveyron, not to mention their post-dinner engagement.

Now she snuggled down on top of him, her legs still draped on either side of his thighs, and sighed.

"I think churchmen would have harsh words to say to me about that maneuver," she murmured by way of conversation in his ear. "But I'm not sure I care."

Will began to laugh. "That maneuver only, my love?" He stroked her hair.

Then his laugher died. The church would have nothing but harsh words for the both of them. Particularly for a knight who deprived a noble maiden of her virtue and did not intend to marry her.

Azalais did not seem to notice his change in mood, and Will definitely did not want her to move from her delicious sprawl on top of him. That was another thing—she had never once mentioned marriage. She'd evidently discarded the notion as an impossibility. Sir William de Fauconberg was too poor a knight to consider marrying, and Guilhem the Minstrel was nobody's idea of a good catch. Was he truly just a passing experience for Azalais de Keldy? A light bit of lustful research? Or at the most, a source of potential pregnancy?

He wrapped his arms around her and listened to her breathing. It wasn't that he minded being the object of her passing attentions. It was just the very thought of them nearing an end. It left a gaping hole. Emptiness. They would reach Bruniquel tomorrow afternoon and, with any luck, they would free her father the same day. The end. Oh, perhaps John de Keldy would ask Will to escort them safely back to Bordeaux—he might not lose Azalais immediately—but there would be no more sweet dalliance and probably no more music. And upon reaching Bordeaux, there would be no more Azalais at all. Not for Will.

Will closed his eyes and tried not to tighten his grip upon his drowsy lady. *You have her now. Make the most of it. Nothing lasts forever.*

Was there any alternative? Was there any possible future for them?

The song. It was very nearly finished. It put them into words and set them to melody. It described a poor knight who loved music and a girl-minstrel dressed as a man, and their travels through France. That was all the future they had together. Together, they had immortalized themselves in song. Wherever Will went, however long he lived, he would carry that song with him as a reminder that he had loved and that he had found his soul's partner in music. He would sing it as a wandering minstrel, and his audience would never know why he sang it with such longing.

The form draped on top of him stirred. Will loosened his arms and let her lift her head to gaze down into his face. She kissed him, then gave him a quizzical look.

"I declare I must have squashed you. My apologies, Sir Knight. There is definitely something squashed about your expression."

Sir Knight. He was no knight—he would be a minstrel, and he would lose her.

Will mustered up a smile for the sylph who lay atop him.

"Not in the least, my lady. Pray continue just as you are."

"You know, I think I might." A tentative smile. "Just think, this is how we might find ourselves every evening should you agree to take me on as your fellow minstrel."

Oh, the Evil One himself could tempt him no better. The idea was pure heaven, and it could never be.

"Azalais, we will discuss this after we have ransomed your father."

It was not the first time he had said that in the last two days. She had been quite persistent on the subject of accepting her as his minstrel companion. His answer had always been the same. Her father was the guardian of his daughter's destiny. And Will knew John de Keldy would never give his lovely daughter to a penniless knight or worse, a minstrel. Worse still, the lord of Keldy would be right.

Her expression had changed. It was no longer drowsy and

content.

She sat up. Damnit. Still, it was a lovely view. The fire had sunk to glowing coals and the red light played over small, perfectly shaped breasts, an elegant neck, and the face of a fairy queen.

"There is something I need to do tonight, Will. It is important. It was why I asked if you are content with the melody of our song as it stands."

He frowned.

"Yes," he ventured. Then he smiled. "Do you intend to use me as a stool upon which to perform music, O minstrel-girl? Do I prove more comfortable than a log?"

She wriggled slightly, her lips curving. "Now there's an idea. But no."

And she dismounted. She swung her leg over him and slipped off. Will lay bereft. He watched as she reached for her tunic, shrugged it on over her head, and then turned to her lute.

Chill air caressed his skin, and he too sat up, dragging his cloak about him.

"What are you doing?"

She angled herself toward the light of the dying fire and began to fiddle with the lute strings. Will frowned and leaned closer. She was loosening the pegs at the head of the lute, unwinding them completely. First one, then another, until finally, all the strings were resting slack against the lute's neck.

"I am removing the strings," his minstrel-girl answered, and did so.

"That's going to be hellish to restring and tune-up," Will said.

But it was too late for such warnings. She was already threading the strings out and draping them carefully over the lute's protective case.

"Yes," she sighed. "But it has to be done."

Will couldn't see why. None of her strings were broken. They weren't even frayed. Besides, one frayed string was no reason to divest an instrument of all of its catgut.

Then she cradled the denuded instrument in her lap and inserted the tips of her fingers into the sound hole. Will felt his brows fly up. A lute's sound hole was usually covered over by a rose—an intricate wooden screen carved to imitate a roseate church window. Its delicate lattice let the sound through, but very little else. Now Azalais had her elegant fingers in that lattice and was wiggling it a little, but very, very carefully.

He hoped she knew what she was doing.

"You'll need that lute for tomorrow night," he murmured. "Don't demolish it entirely."

"Ah, got it," was all the reply he got.

Will peered. The light was not good. He ought to stir the fire—but not right now. And then his mouth opened. The rose had turned in her hand and she was lifting it off. He had assumed the latticework was one with the lute, but apparently not.

She looked up at him then, a circular lattice of wood still perched upon her fingers. "No need to look so surprised, my lover. I thought you would have guessed my secret by now."

"*More* secrets?" Will arranged his face into a horrified expression. "Oh, don't tell me. First, you were a man, then you became a girl, and—O, God—you're really a man! Yes, you cut your manhood off and stowed it in your lute for safekeeping. Now you want to sew it back on."

She laughed, a throaty, altogether too-knowing laugh. "Really, my love? After all of our recent activities? Would you still love me if I was a man?"

Then the laughter drained from her face.

Ah, he knew what it was that chased away the merriment, and he would not have it. Will rose to his knees and took her fairy face between his hands. He touched his lips to hers softly, like a blessing, and said, "I would love you if you were a man or a bastard or the queen of France herself. Never doubt it, Azalais."

She kissed him back, and it was awkward with the lute yet again between them. But it was also heavenly. *And unfortunately symbolic,* thought Will. *There will always be something between us, holding us apart.*

He sank down beside her and ran a finger over the polished grain of her lute. "Well then, if it is not your severed man parts hidden within, my love, I believe I can venture a guess at what is." But his brows still creased. "Although it still strikes me as far-fetched."

She smiled at him. "That was the idea. No one would suspect a lute. Maybe the case, but not the instrument itself."

And she laid the rose alongside the discarded strings and picked up a slim metal file that had materialized alongside.

"Now for the tricky part," she said, and slowly inveigled her right hand, file and all, into the sound hole of the lute.

Will said nothing. He could see how delicate an operation it was. She didn't need him distracting her. A larger hand than hers would never have fit inside the lute's body, but even Azalais's slender digits seemed to be having trouble. Slight sounds of knocking and jabbing followed. Finally, after long heartbeats, his minstrel-girl's wrist was easing back out of the lute. Will drew in a breath and waited.

"There," Azalais said and unrolled a short length of silk upon the leaf litter before her. Will exhaled.

Before him, glittering in the light of the dying fire, lay Azalais's dowry. It was truly a lord's ransom. He hadn't believed it possible, that so much wealth could be contained in so small a space. He had wondered where she hid the ransom and had guessed that she had silver or even gold secreted about her person or baggage or in the lute's case. But he had never guessed it was within the lute itself. After all, such a quantity of precious metal would deaden the sound and make the lute positively leaden in weight. Neither were true, he knew, for he had handled her lute upon occasion. It didn't rattle, and it didn't feel suspiciously heavy.

But now all was explained.

Two necklaces lay entangled on the silk. Nor were they ordinary necklaces. Will had never seen their like, even on the snowy throats of the most loftily born ladies he had dallied with. Will bent closer to discern a jumble of intricate gold chain and filigree, interspersed with gemstones. Large gemstones. Not enamel, but genuine polished jewels. Her dowry didn't need to be heavy if it consisted of… His brows flew up.

"Is that a ruby?" He pointed to a gem the size of a pebble. A small pebble, admittedly, but as smooth and polished as river-washed glass.

Azalais shrugged. "So, I am told. As are the smaller surrounding stones. The other necklace is said to be more valuable though. It has sapphires. They have protective properties, you know."

"You'd better keep hold of it then," Will managed. "Does it work against brigands?"

She gave him a small smile. "It has so far."

Hmph. He'd walked into that one. He wasn't thinking straight. He was dazzled by the sight of all that glittering wealth.

"How did you come by it? Them. The necklaces, I mean."

"They are mine," she said sharply. "My dowry. They were my mother's before me."

He raised his hands. "Forgive me, my lady. I meant no accusation. It's just, they are quite magnificent."

"Too magnificent for me, you mean."

He shook his head. But this time he paused before he opened his mouth—just to make sure his foot was nowhere near it. "Not in the least. In fact, I am struck by a strong desire to see them on you." He leaned forward and traced a lazy finger along her collar bone. "To see you, my minstrel-girl, clothed in nothing but gold and jewels."

She shocked him then.

"I will wear one if you will wear the other, Sir William of Fauconberg. To Bruniquel—and beyond, if need be."

"What?"

"For safekeeping. They are no longer hidden in my lute, and the chateau contains many dangers." She lifted a brow. "The Vicomte of Bruniquel not least among them. Keep it safe, Will.

And if anything happens to me, keep the necklace in payment for all the help you have given me."

If ever he was tempted to splutter and pontificate in his life, it was now. Will swallowed the urge, and simply said, "I will keep the sapphires safe for you, my love. But as for payment, let me relieve you off this ill-befitting garment…" he fingered her rough tunic, "…and clothe you as you should be clothed." He scooped up the rubies and cast her a wicked smile. "All the payment I require I shall exact from your sweet self alone."

Chapter Twenty-Three

I T WAS HER father.

Azalais's heart nearly stuttered to a standstill. Her feet certainly did. After a moment, a hand descended on her shoulder. It gave a brief squeeze, and then urged her on.

"The vicomte awaits, Alain. Look, he is watching us."

Indeed, the dark-haired figure seated at the midpoint of the high table could be no other than Rafèu, Vicomte Bruniquel. And his gaze *was* angled in their direction. The wandering minstrels Guilhem and Alain had begged leave to play before his vicomteness, and—true to Marcabru's prediction—the vicomte had reacted favorably. They were summoned to entertain the lord of the chateau as he relaxed with a few friends over supper. The situation was perfect—Rafèu of Bruniquel was cooperating with their plan most obligingly.

She just hadn't expected that Lord John of Keldy would be among those friends.

Azalais's feet obeyed Guilhem's command. They continued their walk up the great hall of Bruniquel. Her eyes even paid some attention to where those feet were placed—the last thing she wanted to do was trip and smash her lute moments before her most important performance. But her mind was a maelstrom.

Her father. He couldn't see her—he mustn't recognize her, at least not yet. The explosion, the expostulations. It would spoil everything. She must keep her back to him if at all possible, angle her head down, gaze averted.

But she wanted to look at him. Was he well? Did he look well-treated? She had never expected to find her father at his captor's table—admittedly Lord John wasn't seated at the high table, but he wasn't far from it. Maybe he didn't need rescuing after all? Or perhaps she'd been mistaken. Maybe it was a man who just *looked* like John of Keldy at first glance.

Now they were before the high table. She could see the em-broidered linen and sparkling silverware before her lowered eyes.

"Bow, Alain," came the barely audible whisper beside her.

So, she did, dipping into a deep bow after Guilhem.

Then there were the usual courtesies—thankfully dealt with by her companion—following which Rafèu de Bruniquel made some desultory inquiry about the state of the lands they had traveled through. Naturally enough, Guilhem mentioned their brush with a half dozen brigands—

"Ah, lordless men," Rafèu de Bruniquel responded. "The flotsam of this execrable war with the English." And the vicomte raised a black brow in the possible Lord John's direction.

Azalais had lifted her head sufficiently to observe the vicomte, but at this, her head dipped again. It *must* be her father.

"You say they were maimed, ugly as toads? They bore weap-ons? And you fought them? *Par Dieu*—" Their host slapped a palm on the table hard enough to make the silverware jump. "That would make a fine song, minstrel. *The Troubadours and the Troublemakers*. No, *zut*—there must be a better title than that."

Will made some demur that there was little to tell, but the vicomte would not have it.

"It is your job as a minstrel, man! You cast the mundane into sublime song. Ah, I can practically hear it now…" Vicomte Rafèu smiled a little dreamily and extended his hands as if to grasp the melody as it floated by.

And Azalais squared her shoulders. This was her moment.

"My lord, if I may?" She addressed the Lord of Bruniquel, her father's captor, and the man who held the key to her future—quite literally.

The dark head inclined, and Azalais observed its owner for the first time in any detail. He was younger than she'd assumed he'd be, probably not much older than William. His hair was midnight black with no trace of silver, and it fell to his shoulders as straight and sleek as a waterfall. His eyes were as dark as his hair, his nose aquiline, and his lips were quite sinfully sensual. Azalais blinked. This was the man who had captured her warrior-father? Why, on looks alone, she'd have assumed the fellow would find a practice round of daggers even against her taxing.

But she'd looked and assumed too long. "We have indeed composed such a song, my lord," she said quickly. At which Will trod on her foot. "That is," Azalais amended, "it touches upon our encounter with the maimed men, but it is not in itself a bloodthirsty song. On the contrary, it is more of a *canzo*—a love song. It is but a humble creation and recently born. But if it would please your lord …"

Indeed, it *would* please him. It would please him mightily. Minstrels Guilhem and Alain were duly invited to array themselves before Rafèu and friends and fill the hall with song. And, for a grand finale, they would perform their newborn composition.

IT MIGHT PLEASE Vicomte Rafèu, but it most certainly did not please Guilhem the Minstrel or William of Fauconberg. What in heaven's name was Azalais thinking? No, more probably, his love wasn't thinking. She had simply panicked.

Will wasn't blind. In fact, he had developed a sixth sense where his lady was concerned. He could practically feel her mood, even when he wasn't looking at her. One moment she was walking down the great hall, light-footed and graceful as ever, and the next she had frozen in place. All Will had needed to do was to follow the direction of her gaze and register a few pertinent features of the man it had fallen upon.

Her father. It must be. He didn't look particularly like Azalais—praise the Lord. But he could discern a certain resemblance to Ben. Something in the man's smile and the deep-set of his eyes.

At least it hadn't been the sight of his vicomteship that had affected such petrification. Will had to admit himself a little startled by the French lord's stark bird-of-prey beauty. And if Will—who, as was well-established, had no interest in men—felt the impact of this Rafèu's sensuality, then doubtless his minstrel-girl did, too. Will had tensed against the oncoming wave of jealousy, but it had never arrived. She simply showed no interest in the Vicomte of Bruniquel.

No, she had seen her father, and she had ceased to think straight. It was only natural. She hadn't seen her *pater* in two years—and there he was, in the flesh, and but a few yards away. Azalais wasn't close to her father, Will had gathered. Nor did she know if Lord John would support or reject Robert's marriage plans for her. But to flaunt the tale of his daughter gadding through France dressed as a man and a minstrel before him was to leap off a cliff and hope there was deep water below. And Azalais couldn't swim.

But now minstrels Guilhem and Alain must play. That was what they were here for—to charm Rafèu de Bruniquel into a sufficiently mellow mood that he would accept an unorthodox ransom in return for his captive's freedom. Had the vicomte not been a music lover, then other means would have been tried. But they were committed now.

Will laid his vielle down and filled his lungs in readiness. It was time to sing. And perhaps if he sang well enough—and the vicomte drank enough—their host would forget all about Azalais's mad suggestion.

THE HALL HAD grown quieter, the night had advanced, and still, they played. Vicomte Rafèu was hungry for music, he declared—famished as a hermit in Lent. He even took a turn on the lute himself—his own, not Azalais's—so giving his performers a welcome chance to wet their throats and rest their hands. And all the while, Azalais angled her back to the man at the adjacent trestle—the man she knew was her father now, beyond a doubt.

For there had been conversation between the Lord of Bruniquel and his captive as Rafèu took up his lute. It ran like this:

"Your late wife played the lute, too, did she not, Keldy? I heard her play once, I think. A sweet voice."

"She did, my lord." A shiver passed over Azalais. It was her father's own voice, speaking in English-edged French, and his tone was soft with memory. "Indeed, she did. But when did you hear her play?"

"You forget, she was from these parts. Ah, she was a lovely woman—an artist with the lute. Why, if you hadn't wed her, I might have married her myself."

"You must have been all of ten years old, my lord," came the dry reply. "Were you such an ardent lover before you passed your first decade?"

"I was eight, Keldy, a prodigy at eight. Ah, but my heart has ever been attuned to exquisite beauty—and song."

And then the Lord of Bruniquel had tuned up his lute and sung a *canzo* or two. William had complimented their host with a smile and some well-chosen words, and then he and Azalais had resumed. And now the vicomte was mellow with wine and song, and the night was drawing to a close. And still, they hadn't played their composition.

Will didn't want to.

"When shall we broach the topic of the ransom, Alain?" he had murmured in her ear between *canzos*.

"After we have sung our song," she replied.

"No," he whispered urgently, but before he could say more, she bent to her lute and rippled out the opening notes of a *pastorela*.

They sang on.

And now the Lord of Bruniquel clapped his hands together. Twice. It was a signal, and those remaining in the hall all quietened and turned to him.

Azalais's heart plummeted. The vicomte was going to draw proceedings to a close and withdraw to bed. He had forgotten his request to hear their song, and they may have left it too late to address the matter of ransom. Rafèu de Bruniquel was tired. He would hear no more tonight.

"It is time, my friends, to draw this night to a close. We have drunk well—" A lift of his goblet. "We have dined well, and *par Dieu*, we have feasted on music. But even Bacchus himself has his limits. It is time."

Beside her, Will breathed out. She could practically feel the tension draining from him. Not so Azalais. She rose to her feet.

"Not so fast, my young troubadour." Vicomte Rafèu waved an elegant hand at her. "I am not finished with you yet. You promised me a song."

"My lord—" Will rose to stand beside her. "It is abundantly clear you have a fine ear for music. We have no wish to pain your sensibilities with a half-finished composition."

"No, *par Dieu*, I will not be denied! You have sung me old songs all evening, man. True, you have sung them well, but now I desire a new song—give me what I was promised. Sing to me of earless brigands, or I shall toss you out of Bruniquel forthwith!"

WILL SETTLED HIS vielle on his shoulder and picked up his bow. Absently, he noted his bow was vibrating slightly. The same went for the fingers resting on his vielle's neck. Ah, nothing like an unintended vibrato. Not that the Vicomte would be focusing on the vielle. It would be the words the man would listen to. The all-too-revealing verses.

At the last possible moment, Will murmured in his minstrel-girl's ear. "We omit the last two stanzas, Alain."

He could only hope she obeyed. He was not the singer. They had agreed the vielle provided the best accompaniment to their composition, and he could not sing with a vielle jolting against his jaw. His bow's mournful tone complemented the scope of the song—more of an epic than a *canzo*—and its underlying theme of hopeless love. Pray God, the Vicomte had drunk enough wine that that particular theme remained well submerged. And as for Azalais's father, if they ever managed to ransom the fellow, he was as likely to geld Will as thank him.

Reluctantly, and with rather more vibrato than intended, his bow caressed the vielle strings and the first notes of their melody floated into the great hall.

Then Azalais's words mingled with his bow strokes and the ordeal began.

The beginning seemed innocent enough—two minstrels wandering through southern France in the spring. The opening verses described the beauties of the season and sketched small incidents along their minstrel path. But slowly, as the song progressed, it dawned on Will that he had been mistaken. It wasn't just the last two stanzas that incriminated him. No, the whole damn composition was laced with longing. It was the central thread that wove the tale together. If Vicomte Rafèu missed the underlying meaning of this tale, he would have to be far drunker than he looked. He'd need to be near insensible. And as for Lord Keldy—Will could not even look in his direction.

Guilhem the Minstrel set his lips and played on. So long as the last two stanzas remained unsung, he told himself, their audience would merely believe this was a song of unrequited love between two men. A little risqué, perhaps, but everyone knew of the questionable morality of minstrels.

Will relaxed a little when they had reached the encounter with the desired earless brigands. He increased the speed of his accompaniment a fraction, adding verve to the martial scene. *Focus on this, your vicomteness. You don't care about forbidden love. You just want a bit of bloodletting.*

He even managed to steer Azalais into a dramatic rise in volume and then a slowing in tempo toward the end of their martial stanza. *Let the pounding of the ponies off the field of victory end this epic,* his intonation implied. It was the ending their host had wanted, and Will could see Rafèu leaning forward over his silverware, utterly engrossed by their song.

Behold, the Lord of Bruniquel was charmed, just as they'd planned. It was only a pity the discussion of ransom would now have to wait until morning. It was far too risky to reveal their purpose now with the song fresh in their listeners' minds. Who knew what strange conclusions might be leapt to?

So, Guilhem the Minstrel bowed his ending notes with aplomb and permitted the final mournful tone to linger in the air. *The end,* it said. And Will dipped his head and lowered his bow. *Finis.* No more.

THERE WAS A moment's pause.

Then Azalais sang on.

Will's right hand closed upon the vielle bow with such force he heard the wood creak. Indeed, it was the only sound in the hall save for his lady's silverly voice—a voice that was far too clear and carrying.

What could he do? If he spoke, even at a whisper, they'd all hear him. If he reached out a foot and nudged her, they could hardly miss it.

She was beginning the penultimate stanza—the one in which the younger minstrel is overcome by how close he came to losing his own life—and his beloved companion's—and reveals himself to his fellow minstrel to be a woman.

Think, man! Do something, for God's sake!

It came to him an instant before she began the incriminating third line. Just in time. Will dragged in a quick breath and commenced singing, too. Just as Azalais sometimes did, he let his notes thread through hers in a countermelody, dipping and winding. Only this time, Will did his damnedest to counter her words. He threw in phrases plucked from other *canzos* to cover any mention of *amor* or *domna*—lady. He drew upon his richest and strongest tones. He made sweeping gestures to catch his listeners' eyes, distracting them, he could only hope.

And by God he did it. When they reached the end of the final stanza, Rafèu de Bruniquel was looking bemused and befuddled. Perhaps it wasn't the most polished of endings, but Will had warned that the song might grate on sensitive ears.

And beside him, Azalais was furious. Will couldn't say how he knew it; he wasn't looking at her, and she made no sound or discernible movement, but it was like the pressure that builds before a particularly ferocious storm.

⇶⇶⇇⇇

THE VICOMTE OF Bruniquel was frowning at her. He had looked at Guilhem, and then back at her. Azalais dared a glance toward her father, and she almost smiled. He wore such a similar expression to his captor that the men might have been brothers.

But she didn't smile. There was too much at stake.

Rafèu de Bruniquel opened his mouth. He pointed at Alain the Minstrel. "Sing it again," he said. "Just the last two stanzas. And you—" A jab toward Guilhem. "Be silent. I couldn't hear for all your caterwauling."

Azalais bowed her assent. She left her lute lying on the stool behind her and simply stood before the vicomte's high table in her plain tunic and hose. But this time, she did not keep her back to her father. She angled herself toward him while still facing the lord of the chateau. And just before she began her stanzas again, she slipped a finger beneath her tunic as if to scratch an itch—and wiggled her binding free. She took a deep breath preparatory to singing and felt the linen begin to unravel.

She sang the penultimate verse slowly and clearly, facing the vicomte but every inch of her aware of her companion's gaze. When she came to the last stanza, she turned to look at him— William of Fauconberg, knight and minstrel, her companion and her lover. He stood quite still, dark hair drooping over his brow, his eyes no longer sleepy but piercing straight into her soul. And she addressed the words to him, just as the minstrel does in the verses:

> *I was a maid in minstrel's clothing,*
> *A woman's heart beats beneath my lute.*
> *You have sung your way into my soul,*
> *And there is room in it for no other.*
> *But now you and I must be sundered forever,*
> *A lady and a minstrel may never wed.*

The last line sung, Azalais paused a moment and simply looked at Will. As if for the last time, saying everything she couldn't say in words and song with her eyes alone.

Then she turned to her father and sang again. She sang the semi-stanza that she had never rehearsed before Will:

> *My duty to my father commands me,*
> *Far have I traveled, and much danger I have faced,*
> *Clad in boy's clothes for this purpose:*
> *Risking modesty and safety for his freedom,*
> *Let his captor hear my plea!*

At which she turned toward Rafèu de Bruniquel, sank to one knee, bowed her head, and took the ruby necklace from around her neck. She draped it across her open palms, and held it outstretched for first the vicomte and then her father to see.

"It is just as I said, my lord vicomte: 'Far have I traveled, and much danger I have faced' to offer this to you. This is my mother's necklace, passed to me for a dowry after her death. I have no lands nor wealth, but I do have this, and I believe it to be valuable. I beg you to accept it in exchange for my father's freedom."

※

Chapter Twenty-Four

S IR WILLIAM OF Fauconberg stood silent as his host had
commanded him, save for the surely audible thundering of
his heart. His lady minstrel knelt before the high table, hands
stretched in supplication, the candlelight turning the curls of her
too-short hair to pure gold. More valuable than anything she held
in her hands.

And no one said anything.

"Wait! Look at me, minstrel!" It was an English-accented
voice, and it quickly added, "If it pleases you, my Lord Rafèu.
This youth makes wild claims. I wish to look at him more closely
and the item he holds in his hands."

"Certainly, Lord Keldy. Examine this man—or maid—by all
means. I am most curious." Then the vicomte grinned wide. *"Par
Dieu,* this minstrel entertainment outdoes all others. It is better
than a play. Must we ask the minstrel to lift his tunic, too?"

The growl in Will's throat was echoed more audibly by Lord
Keldy's. "I do not believe that will be necessary, my lord," the
captive managed. He turned to the still-kneeling Azalais. "Come
here, minstrel man, woman, or whatever you are."

The man's tone, while still gruff, had softened, and Will saw
the deep-set eyes travel over Azalais's face, hair, and frame. It had
been two years since John of Keldy had last seen his daughter.
Besides, the father had never beheld his child garbed as a man, a

270

minstrel-outcast.

Azalais rose and walked slowly toward her father. Her hands were quivering, her gait unsteady, and Will quivered himself with the effort of remaining still. To leap to her side would most definitely not help matters at this juncture. She had to face her father alone. This was her moment, and her future hung in the balance.

Then he noticed the strip of linen unraveling from beneath her tunic. It was as if his minstrel-girl was coming apart before his very eyes. Even as he watched, the fabric descended, until the whole thing fell and lay like errant snow upon the rushes.

She stood before her disbelieving father and held out her hands for his inspection.

"My mother's necklace, my lord. Do you recognize it?"

John de Keldy didn't even glance at the jewelry. He was searching his daughter's face.

"Azalais, what did you do to your hair?"

"The nuns cut it, Father. At Wykeham. I asked them to. I took refuge in Ben's nunnery."

Whereon followed a quick succession of questions from the bemused father, specifically pertaining to why his daughter needed refuge and what in hell was Robert up to.

"He would not ransom you, father—and Benedict couldn't. So, I had to. Hence my disguise."

Lord Keldy exercised some choice language, thankfully in English, but his host-captor evidently caught their gist. Will observed the vicomte was smiling in unconcealed pleasure, leaning on his elbow toward his captive, the better to catch every word. It was a nudge to Will—he remembered he was meant to look flabbergasted. His "male" companion had fooled him through France, and the appropriate expression was thunder-struck. Sir William did his best. In truth, it was no difficult task.

"I take it you recognize this 'minstrel,' Keldy," the vicomte broke in at last. "It seems the mystery of your missing ransom is revealed. No surprises there, eh? Your eldest needs a whipping.

Too tight-fisted to pay the ransom, so his sister must traipse across France dressed as a man in his place? The danger! Set upon by brigands! By heaven, that's a story. No, it's a *song*. Show me your rubies again, mademoiselle minstrel. Dazzle my poor eyes."

Azalais glanced at her father, who gave a nod, and the rubies were displayed before the vcomte a second time. Will surreptitiously checked that its twin was still secreted safe beneath his own tunic. Had she planned this? Christ, was she hoping to pay a ransom at a bargain rate?

"Do you warrant they're the real thing, Keldy?" Rafèu was saying. "Do you recognize your lady wife's jewels? They don't look like glass and gilt to me, but God knows I'm no judge of gewgaws. I'll get my steward onto it in the morning, summon a goldsmith—but I know your word is good, even if your son's isn't."

"They're the real thing, my lord. And this *is* my daughter, Azalais, a truer child than ever Robert will be. They are hers to give. Her dowry, as they were her mother's."

Will heard the gruff pride in the man's voice, and it did odd things to his insides. This man loved his daughter. He valued her. So, he bloody well ought to, given all Azalais had gone through. But his reaction had never been certain. He might have been outraged at his daughter's unmaidenly antics. Certainly, he might still be outraged at her "protector." What was more, a man who valued his daughter would never, ever throw her away on a mere minstrel. Or even a penniless knight.

But there was hope yet. Perhaps Rafèu de Bruniquel would refuse to accept the paltry fee of a necklace, rubies or no, in return for his lordly captive. Ransomed nobles were where the true money lay in this war between France and England. If the vicomte thought he might demand more, Azalais's father would remain a captive, and Azalais herself could…

But could Will really do that to her? Subject his love to the degradation and dangers of minstrelsy?

AZALAIS FELT NAKED before these men. Her breasts were freed beneath her tunic, the shape of her legs evident for all to see under her hose, and her future lay in their hands. She, Azalais de Keldy, had given it to them.

The Vicomte of Bruniquel was weighing the gold and rubies in one long-fingered hand. But he wasn't looking at them—he was looking at her. Every now and again, his eyes would travel to Will, standing stock-still and shocked beside his vielle. There was a smile at the corner of the vicomte's mouth as he looked from one to the other, and Azalais did not like it at all.

At last, the French lord spoke. "You have woven quite a romance—two minstrels traveling alone through France. It was a hardy thing to do, foolhardy I dare say. But you seem to know your way around a sword, Minstrel Guilhem—if that is indeed your name."

Azalais's breath caught. It was Will's turn to speak. He, too, would decide her future.

"It is in a manner, my lord vicomte. My name is Guilhem in France, and William in England. The same name, a different accent." He bowed then, and Azalais could not help but admire the grace with which he did it. It was no rustic's bob, but a courtier's practiced flourish. "Sir William de Fauconberg, at your musical service, my lord."

"Ah, it *is* a romance, then, Keldy. A romance worthy of legend." The vicomte shot a knowing grin at his captive guest. "You are a knight then, Sir William? An English knight. And doubtless, you have pursued your calling at my country's expense?"

Rafèu de Bruniquel still weighed the rubies in his hand, but he seemed far more interested in ferreting out a possible romance. But a romance in the sense of a courtly tale or something more compromising? Either way, her father was going to explode.

"I have fought in France, I admit it, my lord. But I have sworn to do so no more. I have had enough of war. The only weapon I shall wield hereon is my vielle."

The vicomte humphed his derision in a manner most French. "You wielded a sharper weapon than that only a handful of days ago. Or did you wallop your vile attackers with a vielle, Sir Guilhem?"

"I had to protect my gentle charge, my lord. Would you have me abandon a noble lady to the mercies of earless thugs?"

The smile on the vicomte's face widened. "So, you *knew* your minstrel-man was a woman? For how long, eh? And what lengths did you go to confirm her feminine identity, I wonder?"

Her father *was* going to explode. Azalais couldn't even look at him.

There was an abrupt scrape of a bench and a thump on the trestles in his direction. "Enough, my lord," growled John de Keldy. And Azalais got the distinct impression that had the speaker been anyone other than the captor he had sworn to submit to, her father would have challenged him to a duel there and then.

"You heard the song, Keldy." The Lord of Bruniquel held up his hand to ward off the imminent eruption. "Hear me out, man. You're the captive, remember? Shall I toss you in a dungeon? Sit down and listen. I have decided."

Azalais found her hands were twisting together. Keep this up, and she might cause her fingers lasting damage. But her father had subsided—grudgingly—and the Lord of Bruniquel was speaking again. She forced herself to look up at this man who weighed her rubies and her future in his hand.

"I will have my romance, and I will have my rubies, too," Rafèu declared. "I *will* free you, Keldy, but I will exact a price. Two years you've eaten at my table while we've waited for your son *sans honneur* to scrape together his silver. A man has his limits."

She had given him the power over her future by singing the

truth. It was her choice, her gamble. She had hoped this charade would charm the French lord, that their song would tickle his troubadour sensibilities—and it had. But he had seen too much, and now Rafèu de Bruniquel was helpfully pointing out what he'd seen to her father, and Azalais would reap the consequences. She might count herself lucky if her father simply confined her to a nunnery.

"You must finish the song," the Vicomte announced, his dark eyes flicking from Azalais to Will. "You will write me more verses, the two of you. And I want myself in it. I'm your happily ever after, by heaven, so put me in! I'll take these rubies in memory of your lovely *maman*—and as compensation for enduring your father for so long." Bruniquel grinned at his long-suffering guest. "But I have a third condition, too, Keldy, so listen well. Don't give the poor girl to this man of Robert's choice. Her music would be wasted on him. By God, it would be blasphemy!"

"I don't hold he'd take her now, anyway," her father muttered and opened his mouth to say more, but Sir William the Statue moved.

"A moment, my lords." Will stepped up beside Azalais, but he did not touch her. "With respect, my Lord of Bruniquel, you have received a lordly payment already. I will do as you ask. I will immortalize you in song. I will ensure that your name lives forever as the magnanimous and praiseworthy vicomte who put all to rights—but this lady is not part of the bargain. Let her decide her own future."

Azalais felt the words as a physical force. She swayed. Her hand brushed against Will's, and a tingle of warmth—or was it courage?—suffused her.

Rafèu de Bruniquel's brows rose. He cocked one of them at his captive. "Well, Keldy? She's acted the man for weeks, now. Is she man enough to decide her own future?"

"I doubt anyone would believe she's a maiden now, anyway," her father grumbled, but at least he didn't look like he wanted to part the vicomte's head from his shoulders anymore.

"So, am I a man? An honorary man? Will you let me choose what becomes of me?" Azalais said. She just hoped she wasn't required to sing anymore tonight. Her voice seemed reduced to a croak.

She looked from the vicomte to her father, and then finally to Will. Her lover's expression was a studied blank. The tension was plain in his jaw and his lips—she wanted to kiss him there and then, to soften their hard line.

None of the men replied. She could only hope that constituted an assent.

"Well then, I choose my future," Azalais made herself say. "I will help complete your verses, my lord vicomte, for Sir William did not compose our song alone. And—" She turned to face Will. "I declare I choose you, William of Fauconberg or Guilhem the Minstrel. Now and forever, whichever and whoever you choose to be."

She did kiss him then. She slipped her arms around his neck and tiptoed to lay her lips against his. For a moment, he remained perfectly still. Azalais waited for him to respond or push her away. Then his lips shaped themselves to hers, softening and giving. And his arms pulled her to him as if this time he would truly never let her go.

⟫⟪

THEY RODE IN a waking dream back toward Bordeaux—his minstrel-lady, her father, a small guard provided by the Vicomte of Bruniquel, and Sir William de Fauconberg. At least, it must be a dream, because Will still hadn't managed to convince himself it could be true.

Azalais's father did not want to kill him. He didn't even want to part his balls from his body and feed his member to the crows. All the same, it was awkward, traveling with the father of the woman he had seduced, who had seduced him, and with whom he would dearly like to repeat the experience. Except Lord Keldy's constant presence was a distinct damper to that possibility. Or indeed any possibility of baring his heart to his lady.

Which was why the two of them were forced to sneak out of their current elegant accommodation in Agen to conduct a little straight-talking—alone, and in the dead of night.

Of course, some preliminary kissing was a necessary prerequisite to their discussion. Will currently had Azalais pressed between a solid plastered wall and his own increasing solidity. It had been her fault, of course. She had tugged him into this alley and then run her hands up over his chest, over his shoulders, and finally employed his neck to pull his mouth down to hers. Now it was time for Will to take the initiative. He was beginning to wonder just how solid the wall they leaned against was. It wouldn't do to set it crumbling by means of excess pressure. And one of Azalais's legs was already winding itself around his thigh. Pulling him to her.

His lips left hers to trail a line of kisses along her jaw, to nip her earlobe ever so gently, and then whisper in her ear:

"My love, I fear for the fate of the wall—and the people inside it. Your father sleeps now, but if it should crumble...?"

She laughed softly, breathlessly, and tilted her head to grant him greater access to her ear. Then she murmured, "*Am* I your love still? You will not slip away one dawn to flee me and my father, to pursue your minstrel life?"

That worked like a splash of cold water. Will drew back slightly, just enough to look into her eyes, mysterious in the moonlight. "Do you doubt me, my love?"

"I chose you, Will. I did not give *you* any choice. And now my father expects you to remain a knight and..."

"To remain a knight and to wed you, my lady?" He stroked back an errant golden curl. "And you think I will flee instead? I will run away from a substantial dowry and the most beautiful, bold, and brave minstrel-lady in all Christendom? What sort of madman do you think I am?"

"A trapped madman," she whispered. "A man who wishes to be a minstrel."

"And you, Azalais? You wished to be a minstrel, too. Shouldn't I be worried you will run from me? No, I have a better solution, my love." And he laid his lips to hers in a soft, lingering embrace.

After a moment, he pulled back a fraction, enough to hold her gaze and say, "You *are* my love, Lady Azalais. I choose you above any minstrelsy. You inspire me, you lift my music to greater heights, and," he grinned, "by God, you lift other aspects of me to great heights, too."

Then he sobered. "But there is something else I've been meaning to mention."

He saw her eyes widen. A flicker of anxiety. Sweet heaven, how could she think he would prefer anything else in the world to her? He dipped down to kiss the worry away.

Then steeled himself to speak again.

"I've been thinking, Azalais. If you marry me, perhaps you and I could dwell at Fauconberg over the winter months. You know, do our lord-and-lady-of-the-manor duty, play a little music, make love once in a while—" That got him a smile. He hurried on. "And then, come the spring, we could turn into minstrels. We could wander for a season—you and I. So long as the land we travel through is safe."

She was gazing up at him, mouth slightly open, and looking so thoroughly kissable in the moonlight that he had to bite his lip. This was what he wanted to say. This, and one other thing. But she must be allowed to answer.

Her lips widened. "What, and expose you to the lustful gaze of every tavern maid and noblewoman from Bordeaux to Bergen?" She ran a finger over his cheekbone. "You forget how delicious you are to women's eyes, my lord. They will eat you alive."

"Let them look." He ran his fingers through his hair with an exaggerated flip. "You, my fairy queen, are all my eyes desire to feast upon."

"And perhaps your tongue, too?"

"Indeed, you may consider that a promise. One I will fulfill just as soon as… Ah, that brings me to another matter." And Will sank to one knee in the suspiciously damp dirt beside the wall. He looked up into her bemused but lovely face.

"My lady-minstrel, I can bring you little beyond one small manor and my eternal devotion—"

"And your music," she inserted. "And any small physical services you see fit to render me. And I will require them rendered on a regular basis, you may be sure."

The damp was seeping through his hose. A mosquito nibbled his ankle.

"My lady, will you do me the honor of becoming my wife?"

She looked down at him and her smile outshone the moon.

About the Author

Cara Hogarth writes historical romances set in a medieval past full of castles, knights, and damsels who definitely don't need rescuing. Her stories sparkle with passion, adventure, and a touch of humour. Cara studied medieval history at university before realising she much preferred writing fiction to research papers. Now she puts her historical training to good use by underpinning her romances with plenty of research. Her stories are usually set in fourteenth-century England and France.

Cara was born in Salisbury, England. She grew up on a sheep farm, but has since worked as a cake cook, in a fun fair, in a library, and as an academic tutor and editor. She now lives in the wilds of Western Australia with a book-eating ragdoll cat.

Website: www.carahogarth.net
email: cara@carahogarth.net
Facebook: facebook.com/carahogarth

www.ingramcontent.com/pod-product-compliance
Lightning Source LLC
Chambersburg PA
CBHW071222210726
48293CB00002B/543